A LIFE

a novel

WITHOUT

FLOWERS

Cover design by Okay Creations
Book layout by Lori Colbeck

ISBN-13: 978-1-950348-43-5

A LIFE WITHOUT FLOWERS

a novel

MARCI BOLDEN

PINK SAND
PRESS

For Ty.
You are loved forever and always.

ONE

THOUGH THE LATE August sun warmed Carol Denman's shoulders as she strolled down a well-kept sidewalk, a chill settled in her gut. She'd taken her time hooking up her RV in a nearby campground before walking the short distance to the townhome her mom and aunt had bought after moving to Florida. The closer she got to the picture-perfect retirement community, the more disconsolate she felt.

Visiting her mother was never high on her list of things to do. The two of them butted heads incessantly. No issue was too insignificant. They could, and usually did, fight over anything. However, Carol's outlook on life had changed recently, and she'd made this trip to the suburbs of Orlando hoping they could find common ground. If she was ever going to have a relationship with the woman who had brought her into the world, Carol was going to have to make the effort. Judith never would.

As Carol approached the porch to a smoky-blue

townhome, her aunt yanked the door open and gasped as if she wasn't expecting company, even though Carol had texted when she'd left the RV park. Ellen spread her arms wide, causing her teal and pink kaftan to flow like a kite flying above the beach. Carol had bought the dress for her aunt in Honolulu. Carol and her husband Tobias had vacationed in Hawaii a few summers before his death. Though they hadn't set foot on a beach due to Carol's aversion to water, they'd had an amazing time hiking the volcanoes and rain forest in between visiting museums.

Feeling happiness for the first time since arriving in Florida, Carol stepped into one of her favorite hugs ever. Aunt Ellen had always made Carol feel as if there was a special connection between them. Her aunt had been a ray of sunshine Carol would have spent her life basking in if Ellen hadn't lived so far away.

"How's my girl?" Ellen asked, squeezing her niece.

"I'm tired from packing up the house, but I'll survive. How are you?" Carol leaned back and her heart grew heavy.

The last time she'd seen her aunt and mom was at Tobias's funeral almost a year ago. The energy that had always radiated from Ellen seemed dimmer now. Age was taking a toll on her, as it was Carol's mother, reaffirming how necessary this trip was.

Ellen pressed her fingertips under Carol's chin as she looked her over. "You look like hell."

"Thanks."

"Are you sleeping?"

"As much as I can." Carol stepped into the cool air of the

open living area. The chill she'd felt earlier rolled through her again, but not because of the change in temperature. Being in the same house as her mother set her on edge. Knowing she'd come to confront a lifetime of emotional neglect made her blood run cold.

A painting on the wall caught Carol's eye, and a smile lit her face. The bright colors created an abstract image of mountains made of checkerboards and a waterfall filling a teapot. The last time she'd been in this house, her mother's bland taste had dominated. She was glad to see her aunt making room for her more eccentric style. "That's a great piece. When did you paint it?"

Ellen moved between Carol and the art. "Don't change the subject."

"What subject?"

"*You.* You're the subject. I was surprised when Judith said you were coming to visit, but now I have to wonder if there's more to it than you passing through. Are you okay?"

Carol nodded to reassure her aunt. "I've spent the last few weeks getting ready to live on the road. Like I said, I'm a little tired, but I'll catch up on sleep."

The way Ellen pursed her lips and cocked one brow suggested she hadn't believed Carol's excuse. Ellen always could see through her. "There's more."

There *was* more. Carol hadn't slept for days knowing she was on her way to visit her mom. She hoped to find a way to mend their relationship, though she wasn't foolish enough to think doing so would be easy. She was dreading the days ahead. "Where's Mom?"

"It's Sunday. Where do you think she is?"

Every Sunday for as long as Carol could remember, Judith made enough chicken and dumpling soup for Carol's father to eat leftovers for the week. That habit had remained, even though her dad had been gone almost four years. Carol followed the familiar scents to the kitchen, where she found her mom standing over a big silver pot, staring intently. Unlike the living area, Ellen's spunk hadn't migrated to the kitchen.

This was her mother's domain, and the neutral colors and clean, bare counters proved as much. Ellen tended to leave a mess in her wake, whereas Judith cleaned while she went. Despite making a homemade meal, Judith had left not even a trace of flour on the counter. The room was pristine. Sterile.

She hated to admit she'd kept her home closer to Judith's style than Ellen's. Carol had inherited her mother's need for cleanliness and order. She'd always hated that about herself but had never been able to change. Maybe now that her living quarters were barely bigger than a van, she could finally learn to live with signs of disorder. She doubted that, though.

"Hey, Mom," Carol said with a forced smile and more excitement than she felt.

Judith lifted her face and smiled, too, but the corners of her mouth wavered as a crease formed between her brows. Even though her mom was in her midseventies now, Carol could easily picture how she looked years ago with their piercing blue eyes, full lips, and narrow nose. Her age hadn't softened her heart or her sharp appearance. She still wore her long hair pulled back in a bun, though the strands were white now instead of the light brown she'd shared with her daughter.

"You're not sick, are you?" Judith asked.

And *that* was the extent of the warm welcome, which really was about as much as Carol was expecting. "No."

"You shouldn't be here if you're sick."

"I'm not sick. I'm tired. I've been on the road." She stepped closer, but the way Judith reared back caused Carol to stop. Her obvious aversion to embracing her daughter stung.

"Wash, please," Judith said.

Carol let the request sink in for a few seconds before turning toward the restroom. This wasn't anything new. Judith had never been warm and affectionate. Ever. In fact, if she *had* smiled and opened her arms like Ellen, Carol would have been the one pulling away with hesitation.

As she washed, Carol pictured the one thing she was counting on to keep her grounded over the next few weeks.

Tobias had filled their backyard in Houston with a variety of flowers. He would spend hours trimming and pruning and talking to the plants as she sat at the little wrought-iron table reading and sipping wine. If Carol cleared her mind enough, she could take herself back there. As a warm breeze brushed her cheeks, she could hear his deep, soothing voice and smell the sweetness of *Salvia dorisiana*, one of the varieties of fruit-scented sage he'd loved so much.

Those were some of the happiest moments Carol could recall, and she clung to them like the lifeline they'd become.

She was going to need that lifeline to get her through forcing her apathetic mother to face their broken relationship.

"What the hell am I doing?" she muttered, grabbing the pristine white hand towel embellished with her mom's signature needlework. Carol took her time wiping the water from her hands and face before staring at her reflection.

Part of her wanted to walk out there and announce she'd changed her mind about how long she intended to stay. She'd hang out for a day, maybe two, and then be on her way. But she was here with a purpose, one she couldn't walk away from. Facing the chasm between them was the only way to cross it. She couldn't run from her past forever.

The last few months had taught her a brutal lesson—the past *always* came back to be resolved. She had to work this out while she could. Life had shown her time and time again that people could be ripped away without warning. Her mother was older—time was running out.

"You can do this," she told herself before folding and rehanging the cloth precisely how it'd been before she'd dried her hands and face.

Back in the kitchen, Carol stopped at her mom's side. "It's nice to see you."

"You too," Judith said, though her attention remained on the soup.

"So you're one of us old retirees now," Ellen said, busying herself with fixing a pot of coffee. Though she hadn't looked at Carol as she'd spoken either, her lack of eye contact didn't feel nearly as deliberate as Judith's.

"I am." Carol tried to not overanalyze the slight she felt,

but her mother's cold shoulder was already irritating her. She hadn't been in the house for five minutes yet, not nearly enough time to start reading too much into her mother's behavior.

"And living in an RV," Judith stated.

Then again, the clipped tone illuminated everything Carol needed to know. She was getting a frigid greeting because her mother disagreed with her choices. As usual.

"For now," Carol said. "That will grow old eventually, and I'll settle down somewhere."

"Where, Carol? You're selling your house."

Carol cast a glance at her aunt, who diverted her eyes like a child trying to avoid trouble. From the moment Carol had filled her mom in on her plans, Ellen had likely been listening to all the ways Carol was messing up her life *this* time.

Judith turned and stared Carol down. "And what about your belongings?"

"I've sold most of them." She stood a bit taller—a matador bracing for the bull to attack. "Mary took the rest to St. Louis."

Her mom scowled as if she were already fed up with Carol's foolishness. "You burdened your mother-in-law so you could roam the country without a care?"

"I'm sure Mary didn't mind," Ellen offered. She was well-practiced at diffusing the tension between Carol and Judith before things erupted. For years, whenever Ellen was visiting, she would wade into turbulent waters in an attempt to calm them. She was rarely successful.

"No, she didn't mind." Carol's words were almost as sharp as her mother's. "I didn't send her home with anything larger than a few boxes of framed photos. Mary was happy to take them."

"You told me she drove home in Tobias's car." The slight smirk on Judith's lips seemed to imply that she'd caught Carol in a lie. "That's a bit larger than a box."

Carol bit the inside of her lip. Pictured flowers in the wind. Heard Tobias's voice in her mind.

Don't take the bait, she imagined him telling her.

"I gave Tobias's car to his mother," Carol said calmly. "She's not storing it for me. I *gave* it to her after *I* paid off the loan. All we had to do was switch the title. There was no burden passed to her. Thank you for being concerned, though." The last bit came out dripping with sarcasm, but Carol didn't care. For Judith to suggest Mary viewed Carol as the inconvenience her parents always had enraged her. She would never place undue stress on Tobias's family. They were the best thing in her life.

Judith narrowed her eyes into an accusatory stare. "Is this some kind of midlife crisis or...or...some kind of mental breakdown?"

Ellen carefully set three bowls on the counter before turning toward Carol. Where her mother had been direct and borderline harsh, her aunt offered Carol a concerned look and soft smile. "Honey, did something happen at that conference?"

Carol creased her brow with confusion. "What conference?"

"You went to a conference, and then, out of nowhere, you decided to retire and sell everything to live in your camper," Ellen said. "Why? What happened?"

John. John had happened. Her ex-husband had shown up and turned Carol's life upside down, as he'd always done.

Carol had loved being an executive at a pharmaceutical company. However, she'd clung to the monotony like a life preserver after Tobias's death. She'd stopped living— socializing was limited to work; her home became an extension of her office. When John resurfaced, he'd forced her to face that she'd put herself on autopilot and was in danger of never coming out. He had woken her from a daze and made her promise she wouldn't spend her life hiding behind her desk. She had the money and the means to travel. She only had to find the courage to leave the security of her self-inflicted prison—which she'd done without much of an explanation to her mom and aunt.

Though it pained her to concede so soon into her visit, she had to give this one to her mom. From Judith's point of view, Carol's abrupt redirection came out of nowhere. She didn't know where Carol had been or what she'd been going through because Carol had constructed a story about going to a conference rather than dealing with the fallout of her mother's reaction to her taking a trip with John.

Explaining to her mom and aunt where she'd been, as well as what she was planning to do after her visit, was one of the many reasons for needing to see them in person. This wasn't something she'd wanted to discuss over the phone.

"I wasn't at a conference," Carol said calmly as she sat at

the small round table in the corner of the kitchen. "I was on the road, but I didn't want you to worry about me."

Judith slammed down the wooden spoon she'd been using. Droplets of soup landed on her apron. "So you *lied*?"

Ellen waved a hand at Judith, as if to dismiss her anger, and stepped closer to Carol. "Why would we worry, sweetheart? Where were you?"

Carol took a second to brace herself, knowing the reaction from her mother was going to be over the top. "I was with John."

Judith visibly stiffened, straightening her shoulders and lifting her chin as she widened her eyes. "*John Bowman*?" She spit out his name as if the words tasted bitter on her tongue.

Carol supposed they probably did to Judith. Her parents never forgave her for falling in love with a man they hadn't deemed good enough. When she'd gotten pregnant and switched from premed to nursing, John became the bane of their existence. Though Carol and John's daughter, Katie, had been the best thing in Carol's life, her parents had never come to accept John.

On one hand, Carol didn't blame them. John's devil-may-care attitude had been an affront to everything they stood for. They'd warned her he was going to drag her down. They'd been right. He'd distracted her from her studies, seduced her into his bed, and spent the next eight years undermining every attempt she'd made to get her life back on track.

However, her parents had made things so much worse than they should have been. If they'd been kinder and more supportive, she might have felt she'd had the support system she needed to leave John long before she did. Long before staying with him had cost her everything.

Katie had died in a horrible accident weeks after her sixth birthday. An accident that everyone, including Carol, had blamed on John. She'd hated him for decades. She hadn't forgiven him until he'd reappeared out of nowhere and she finally came to understand he hadn't been the only one to blame. Something her mother would never comprehend.

"Oh, God," Ellen moaned. "Why?"

"He found me in Houston about two months ago and wanted to take that trip we'd planned for Katie."

Though Ellen was the calmer of the two sisters, her voice came out shrill, somewhere between disbelief and accusation. "And you went?"

Carol hadn't wanted to take that trip, but she didn't regret going. If she hadn't, she never would have found a way to forgive John and let go of the anger that had been holding her back. "He was sick." Her voice came out tense. John had so quickly gone from her archenemy to someone she could admit she had always cared for in some way. Losing him hurt. "He needed to make peace with the past before he died. So, yes, I went."

"*Carol*," her aunt said, sounding as if she'd been the one encumbered with nursing John for weeks. "No wonder you look so exhausted. Honey, are you okay?"

"I'm fine," she stated without hesitation. "Seeing him again was one of the hardest things I've ever done. I'd been hanging on to *a lot* of anger and resentment for so long, but he helped me realize I needed to make peace with the past too." She smiled as warmth filled her chest. "We went to all the places Katie had wanted to see."

"Mount *Hushmore*?" Judith asked softly.

Carol laughed at the reminder of the way Katie always mispronounced the national monument. "Yes. We went to Mount *Hushmore* and Yellowstone. Everywhere she wanted to go. He met Tobias's family when we went to the Gateway Arch. That was...interesting." Her smile softened. "He died the day after I got him home to Dayton. On the anniversary of when we lost Katie."

Ellen gasped. "Were you with him?"

An unexpected prick of tears stung the back of Carol's eyes. "Yeah, I was holding his hand. He said Katie was there too. I believe him because I swear, I felt her waiting to take him...wherever. It was very serene, and I'm glad I was there for him."

Carol was pulled from her moment of recollection when Judith let out a bitter half laugh. She glared at Carol, her eyes burning bright and hot with anger. The way she stood taller, shook her head, and pressed her lips tight let Carol know she was having an internal debate. If history proved true, she'd say what she was thinking, no matter how hurtful her words might be.

Judith's voice came out strained, as if saying the words cut at her throat. "He didn't deserve to die in peace after everything he did."

"Don't say that," Ellen chastised.

Judith didn't seem to hear her sister's warning. "Why in

God's name would you let him back into your life after all these years?"

Tightening her jaw, Carol waited until the urge to lash out eased. "I spent a good deal of the time reminding him of the role he played in Katie's death." Carol still felt shame over that, even though John had assured her he understood her anger. "He made so many mistakes, and I rubbed his nose in every one of them until..."

"Until what?" Ellen coaxed.

Twisting her wedding band, drawing on Tobias for strength, Carol said, "When John first showed up, all that anger boiled over. Everything he said gave me an opening to throw the past in his face. Then, one day I was lashing out at him, and I realized a very ugly truth."

"What truth?" Judith narrowed her eyes, as if daring her daughter to defend John.

Carol hesitated. "I carry as much responsibility for what happened to Katie as he did."

"No," Ellen stated firmly, "you do not."

"I knew his drinking was out of control, but I trusted him with our daughter anyway. I was wrong to think he could take care of her."

Ellen crossed the kitchen and put her fingers under Carol's chin, gently forcing her to look up. "You listen to me. You are *not* responsible for what happened to your little girl. You weren't even home."

Carol appreciated Ellen's attempt at easing her guilt, but she'd already come to terms with the truth. Katie's death was an accident. One that could have been avoided if she and

John hadn't been too young and naïve to face their problems head on. They'd both fallen into a cycle of denial about his addiction that contributed to a horrible outcome.

Clutching Ellen's hands, Carol said, "I knew John was an alcoholic, and I ignored it. I could have done things differently. I could have been stronger. I could have forced him to get help. But I never put my foot down because I was tired of always being the bad guy. I didn't fight when I should have."

Ellen shook her head. "*He* was the addict."

"And I was the enabler."

"You were a wonderful mother," Ellen said. "Don't you ever forget that."

Carol offered her a soft smile. "I haven't forgotten. But being a good mother doesn't make me blameless."

Judith interrupted the sweet moment with the same frigid voice she'd used before. "You always did let that man get into your head and twist you around."

As if reminded they weren't alone, Ellen stepped back, clearing the way for Carol to look at her mother.

The fire in Judith's eyes hadn't died, but she'd clearly put up the wall she was so good at hiding behind. She used that mechanism to keep the world, including her daughter, on the outside of her emotions. Carol had learned how to do the same. She'd hidden behind her walls for far too long.

The muscles in Judith's jaw flexed several times before she spoke. "God knows your father and I tried to talk sense into you. You wouldn't listen."

"You may not have liked John," Carol said calmly, "but

without him, I wouldn't have had Katie. I wouldn't change that for anything. Would you?"

Her words hit her mother's heart. Carol knew by the slight jolt that caused her to sway.

Judith threw up her hands before walking away.

Ellen frowned at Carol. "That wasn't called for, Carol. You know she loved Katie."

Shame made her lower her face. "I know. I'll apologize."

Carol pushed herself up and went in search of her mother. She found her in the living room, staring out the window, shutting out the world around her as she tended to do when she was frustrated with her daughter, which was most of the time.

————

Caroline had done everything she could to avoid what was about to happen. She finally had something good in her life. The last thing she wanted to do was share it with her parents. Their disinterested reaction to her announcement about inviting John to dinner had been more than enough to let her know this wasn't going to go well.

Her father had heaved the same loud, disappointed sound he'd done whenever she told him she didn't want to do what he insisted was best for her. The first time she'd understood the sigh was a reflection of his dissatisfaction with her was when she was in eighth grade and told her parents she didn't want to continue with piano lessons. She'd been going to lessons since she was seven and hated them just as much as the first time her parents had dragged her to old Mrs. Jackson's house, which was too hot and always smelled like burned toast.

Caroline wanted to learn to paint, to live in a world of imagination and fun, like her aunt. Her dad had pressed his lips together at her declaration and given her that unimpressed look he was so good at before informing her she would continue learning to play the piano.

Apparently, spending most of her schooling on the honor roll, winning science fairs, and constantly being praised by her teachers meant nothing if she didn't have the skillset to be a concert pianist.

"This is where you grew up?" John asked with the same amazed voice he used whenever he learned something new about her.

"Yeah," Caroline said, lacking his enthusiasm.

He laughed. "I can see you here. Running around the front yard with your hair in pigtails."

"I wasn't allowed to run," she said, looking through his cracked windshield at the brick ranch. "That's how accidents happen. And I never wore pigtails. Mom thought they were primitive."

"Primitive? Like cavemen wore them?"

She faced him. "Like uncultured simpletons wore them. Are you sure you want to do this, John?"

His smile returned. "Yeah. I have to meet your parents sometime. We've been dating for almost six months, babe. You can't hide me forever."

"I'm not trying to hide you. I'm trying to protect you."

He pulled her hand to his lips and kissed her knuckles, easing *some of her anxiety. He had a way of making her feel safe. She didn't want to lose that, but she couldn't deny how much she feared he'd run away from her by the end of the evening.*

"I'm the cop, remember?" he asked. "I'm the protector here. Come on."

He opened his door and climbed out. Caroline gnawed at her lip as she waited for him to rush around the front bumper and open the door for her. She'd told him a hundred times she didn't need him to do that, but John was a gentleman. So he said. She had come to think he insisted on opening her door so he could use the close proximity to steal a kiss. She didn't complain though. The little things he did made her feel more treasured than she ever had before.

True to his habit, he opened the door, reached in to help her stand, and then planted a kiss on her lips. She smiled and silently hoped he really did love her enough to deal with whatever her parents tossed at him. She'd never brought a boyfriend home before. She'd never had a boyfriend before.

"Shoes off," she whispered as she closed the front door behind them.

He looked down at the loafers she'd polished for him earlier. He thought she was being nice, but she feared her father would see the scuffs and add it to the list of reasons he'd find to disapprove of John. Appearance was everything to Dennis Stewart. If a man couldn't take the time to take care of himself, how could he be trusted to take care of anything else?

She skimmed over John's attire one more time. He had borrowed the sport coat from his father, so it was a bit too large, but Caroline thought that could be overlooked. He wasn't swimming in the material. She straightened his tie until the knot was centered.

"Come on," John coaxed, gently nudging her to leave the foyer.

They found her father on the light gray sofa reading the evening paper as scents of meatloaf filled the air. The scene would have been right out of a 1950s TV show if her parents had the capacity to be as nice as Ward and June Cleaver.

"Hi, Dad," she said tentatively. When he didn't respond, she continued. "I'd like you to meet John."

Dennis let out one of his big breaths before he even lowered the paper. A deep frown met them when his face became visible, reminding her that her life in this house had never been a lighthearted television show. Her father didn't even bother trying to smile when he looked at the man standing next to his daughter. John stepped forward and held out his hand, causing Dennis to fold his paper and set it aside.

"It's a pleasure to meet you, Mr. Stewart," John said.

Caroline couldn't see John's face, but she could picture his big smile clearly. The smile that made most people smile in return. John was so kind and approachable. Most people were drawn to him like bees to flowers on a bright spring day. Her father stared at John's hand as if it were contaminated before standing and puffing out his chest.

Caroline shrank inside, but John stood taller and kept his hand out. No doubt he was asserting his own brand of authority. He was a cop; he knew when someone was trying to intimidate him. He seemed to understand that if he showed weakness, her father would go in for the proverbial kill.

"It's a pleasure to meet you," John said again, more loudly, like someone might do to a person with a hearing impairment. Then he pushed his hand closer to Caroline's father.

In the most amazing display Caroline had ever witnessed, her father relented. He shook John's hand briefly.

"Caroline said she was bringing someone to dinner," Dennis said flatly.

"My name is John Bowman," he said, as if her father didn't know.

He did. She'd said she was bringing John to dinner. John Bowman. *The man she'd been dating for six months. The man she had come to care about very much.*

The fact that her father hadn't even cracked a hint of a smile wasn't lost on her. He'd already dismissed John. Already counted him as a lost cause. She didn't know why she was hurt by his behavior, but her heart ached in a way that was too familiar. She'd disappointed him. Again.

Even though John didn't seem fazed, she wanted to hug him and tell him he was worthy of her. Despite the way her father was frowning.

"Hello," Judith said from behind them.

Caroline turned, hoping her mother would be more civil. "Mom, this is John."

John crossed the room, hand out, and offered her the same proper handshake he'd offered her father. Her mother put on the frozen smile she tended to wear, but at least she'd smiled. However, she held up her hands and showed John the old oven mitts she was wearing. As if she couldn't remove them to greet him.

"It's nice to meet you, Mrs. Stewart," John said, once again seeming undeterred by the rude welcome he was receiving.

"You too," she said but then looked over his shoulder at her husband. "Dinner is ready."

Dennis bypassed John and Caroline to head to the dining room. The fact he hadn't even acknowledged his daughter wasn't lost on her. Apparently it wasn't lost on John either. He put his hand on her shoulder, gave her a squeeze, and nodded for them to follow.

At the table, John pulled a chair out for her like a perfect gentleman. She smiled her thanks and glanced at her mother, hoping to see her approval for John's behavior. Judith hadn't noticed. Her focus on the meatloaf exceeded what was necessary. Caroline got the message loud and clear. John wasn't welcome, and they were irritated with her for forcing them to entertain him.

Judith served dinner—Dennis first, then Caroline, and then she handed a plate to John—with a somber expression.

"This looks delicious," John said. "Thank you for inviting me to join you."

"Caroline invited you," Dennis clarified, causing his daughter's heart to drop.

The tension around the table went up about three notches, and Caroline's stomach twisted so tightly she couldn't possibly eat.

John, however, smiled as if her father hadn't all but said he didn't want this stranger at his table. "Yes, she did. Since we've been dating for a while now, we both thought it was time I met her parents."

"How long is a while?" Judith asked. "Our daughter isn't exactly forthcoming with information these days."

Here we go, Caroline thought. "Mom, I told you about John after our second date."

"And you've barely said a word about him since," Judith stated.

Caroline returned her hard stare. "I wonder why."

"Don't get sassy," Dennis warned.

"Stop being impolite," Caroline volleyed back. Her heart thumped against her chest as fear sent a surge of adrenaline through her. She could count on one hand the times she'd spoken up to her father.

Dennis tilted his head back, looking down his sharp nose at her with his steely gray eyes before focusing on his dinner. The tension grew, and Caroline felt like she was dying with every minute that dragged on.

John did his best to win her parents over. He asked questions about her father's company and complimented her mother on their home. He was met with curt answers and forced smiles every time.

They were about ten minutes into the awkward meal when Dennis said, "Caroline says you're a police officer."

"Yes, sir," John said, still smiling as if he were unaware of the thunderstorm brewing around him. "I've been protecting the great city of Dayton for a little over five years now."

"Five... How old are you?" Judith demanded.

"I applied to the police academy right out of high school, ma'am."

"That doesn't answer her question," Dennis stated.

For the first time, John seemed a bit shaken. "I'm twenty-four."

"Caroline is only nineteen," her father boomed. His pale cheeks turned red and his eyes narrowed. "She's a child."

"No, sir," John answered, calm and collected with the experience of an officer trying to defuse a situation before it started. "She's an adult."

Dennis threw his cloth napkin on the table as he glared at John. "Nineteen is hardly adulthood."

"I'm in college." Caroline couldn't think of any other way to validate her age and maturity but felt that should be enough.

"That doesn't make you grown." Dennis focused on John. "What are your intentions with our daughter?"

"Dad!"

John put his hand on Caroline's. "I love your daughter, Mr. Stewart."

"What do you know of love?" Judith asked with that exasperation she used when she was exhausted from trying to talk sense into Caroline.

John looked at Judith. "I know that I've never felt this way about anyone. I know that Caroline is the kindest, most supportive woman I've ever known. I know that someday, when she's ready, we'll start planning a future together."

John had said all those things to Caroline before, but for some reason, she hadn't really believed them until he'd shared his plan with her parents.

"Caroline isn't ready for that," Judith offered. "She isn't as mature as other girls."

Caroline jerked her face toward her mother. "What?"

"You're not. You're...shy and emotionally underdeveloped. You're not prepared for the things he might be prepared for."

The heat of humiliation rushed to Caroline's cheeks. Sex. Her mother was saying, in front of John, that Caroline wasn't ready for sex. "I'm in college," she said again.

"You're still a child," her father stated.

Caroline wanted to cry. Her parents had humiliated her plenty in her life, but this was worse. Way worse. They were intentionally undermining her in front of John. "Thank you for dinner, but I think we should go," she said as she stood.

"Caroline," her mother called, but she didn't stop.

"It was nice meeting you," John said from behind her.

By the time they reached the front door, hot tears had filled Caroline's eyes. John slipped his shoes on in silence and opened the door for her, as he always did. She was outside before she was able to inhale again. When she did, her intake was a gasping hiccup.

"Hey." John's voice came out so soft and soothing, Caroline nearly crumbled. He pulled her against him and enveloped her in one of his big bear hugs, reminding her that even if her parents rejected everything about her, he wanted her. He accepted her.

"I'm sorry."

He hugged her closer. "Don't be. You didn't do anything wrong."

"I told you it would be terrible."

"They'll come around," he said. "They're trying to protect you."

She pulled away from him. "No, John. They're trying to keep me locked in a box. They always have. I'm not stupid."

23

He used his thumbs to wipe her cheeks. "No, you're not, baby. I promise. You're great. Perfect. They're overprotective, that's all."

"No, John, they're autocrats."

That adorable lopsided grin curved his lips. "I don't know what that means."

She laughed slightly. "They're bossy."

"So say they're bossy, smarty pants."

The way he smiled made her believe he'd known all along what she was saying. He was trying to make her feel better. In that moment, she knew what she had already suspected: she was head over heels in love with this man, and nothing her parents did could change that.

———

"Mom," Carol said, keeping her voice soft and steady so her mother didn't feel attacked, "lunch is ready. Would you join us, please?" She was met with silence and had to remind herself not to play into the passive-aggressive behavior. They were too early into this visit to start hurling grenades at each other. "I would like for you to join us. Please."

Several more seconds passed before Judith turned her face up, acknowledging Carol's presence. "I tried to make you see that he was no good. I tried to protect you from him." Her voice was a mix of accusation and hurt, as if it pained her to bring up the past.

Carol knew, however, nothing brought her mother more pleasure than throwing Carol's mistakes into her face. "I was young and inexperienced and completely infatuated with

John. You couldn't have convinced me to break up with him."

"If he hadn't gotten you pregnant—"

"But I *did* get pregnant," she said firmly. "And never once, in all these years, have I regretted having a child with him. I loved my daughter."

Judith frowned but softened her tone the slightest bit. "I know that."

Carol let her defenses slip as well. "We had Katie for six beautiful years. It's taken me a long time, but I'm learning to focus on that instead of on what might have been. I'd love if you could too."

"He took her from us."

Carol took several steps, closing the distance between them. Where she wouldn't have hesitated in taking her aunt's hands, she looked at her mother's, debating, before finally sitting next to her and grasping her hands. She waited for Judith to meet her eyes before saying, "Blaming John tore me up inside for years. I'm not doing it anymore. I can't make you forgive him, but *I* did, and I need you to respect that."

Judith jerked her hands away and did the stiff upper lip thing she'd perfected long before Carol could recall. "Maybe some of us aren't ready to forgive and forget."

She walked away, leaving Carol to wonder who her mother wasn't ready to forgive. Because the cold stare and pointed words certainly seemed like they were directed at Carol.

Noticing her aunt standing in the doorway, Carol shrugged. "That went better than I expected."

The concern in Ellen's eyes didn't waver. "She still hurts over Katie's loss."

"So do I," Carol stated with more of an edge than intended. The following silence lingered long enough for her to regret her response. "I'm sorry. Touchy subject."

"For all of us." Crossing the room, Ellen gave Carol a weak smile. "I'm glad you feel more at peace, but your mother is right. You always did let John twist you around until you couldn't tell which way was up. Sounds like he did it again."

Carol wasn't surprised Ellen saw things that way. John had been a master manipulator, and Carol had been easy prey. She'd been starved for affection when she'd met him. He found her weakness and exploited it until she was in over her head, which hadn't taken long. But the John who'd resurfaced in her life had been truly repentant.

"I'm not the only one who changed over the last twenty-four years. John had as much loss and sorrow to work through. He wasn't the same man I divorced all those years ago. It's been twenty-four years. People change a lot in two and a half decades."

"People do change," Ellen said, "but not fundamentally, Carol. John was a schemer and a liar. He knew how to play you."

"We were both toxic back then," she said, "in different ways."

"You said he made you realize you're responsible for Katie's death. Seems like he was still pretty toxic to me."

"Putting the blame on him was easy," Carol said instead of trying to convince her aunt of something she would never believe. "Pretending I didn't have a hand in how things turned out was easy. But those were lies I'd told myself so I didn't fall apart more than I already had. Now that I've accepted the truth, I can finally grieve for my daughter in a healthy way. I can think of her without a burning ball of rage in my heart. I'd never been able to do that before. Crazy as it sounds, I needed to face John in order to accept responsibility for my mistakes and forgive myself."

"The only mistake you made was loving that son of a bitch too much."

Carol squeezed Ellen's hands. "He was a good man underneath his many flaws. I watched his drinking consume him, and then I blamed him for being weak." She shook her head enough to stop Ellen before she could protest. "I was a textbook enabler. I avoided, denied, and blamed. When I got fed up, I would set ultimatums, and he would pretend to meet them until the pattern started all over again. Every time. That was on me as much as it was John."

Ellen tightened her hold on Carol, as if begging her to reconsider her views. "Don't let that guilt eat you up."

Ever thankful for her aunt's tenderness, Carol smiled sweetly. "I'm not. We were young and had never dealt with adult problems. We both let things go too far, and it cost us our daughter. Neither of us ever expected to pay for our ignorance the way we did. I forgave him. And I forgive myself. Because of that, I've started to heal instead of ignoring how much pain I've been in."

"Your mother needs to hear that. She worries about you, even if she doesn't know how to show it."

Carol bit her bottom lip, bracing for another round of explaining herself. "Part of why I'm here is because I hate how distant we are. We always have been, and I want to change that. But I can't, not until I lay everything out there and find a way to forgive her and Dad for the way they've always treated me."

As expected, Ellen's concern visibly grew. "Oh, Carol, tread lightly. She's been through a lot too."

"I know. I'm trying to make things better, but we can't ignore the last fifty years."

"You can't push her. You know how she reacts when she feels cornered."

Carol rolled her eyes. "Like a feral cat?"

Ellen grinned. "Sometimes feral cats are better left alone."

"I've left this alone for too long. If we don't work this out now, we never will." Carol shook her head and let her shoulders drop with the weight of the burden she felt. She'd come to realize, probably too late in her life, she wanted to be close to her mother. "I can't tell you how sad that makes me. I want to know my mother."

Ellen gave another of her sympathetic smiles. "I understand, more than you can imagine, but she's a bit old to change her ways, honey."

"I have to try."

"Well, the first step is to convince her to join us for lunch. No more talk about John. Not right now. Enough has been said about that subject."

Carol preferred to pull the bandage off, so to speak, but

she understood where her aunt was coming from. She could only push her mother so far at once. Convincing Judith to change her views was better done in small steps, gentle nudges. Though she'd like to force her mom to sit down and hash everything out right then, Carol decided she'd nudged as much as she could. For now.

TWO

CAROL LOOKED across the small kitchen table when Judith let out a long, dramatic breath while staring at her breakfast. After an afternoon of working on a puzzle, a short walk, and then dinner at a local restaurant the night before, Carol had left her mom and aunt and returned to her motorhome. She'd been restless until the wee hours of morning when she'd gone to the park's guest center and taken out her aggression on the treadmill.

Even so, her mother's early morning play for attention was grating Carol's nerves before she'd even sat down for the bacon and eggs Ellen had prepared. "Are you okay, Mom?"

Judith eased her mug down and blinked several times. "No, I'm not. I'm exhausted. I didn't sleep a wink for worrying about you. I don't want you sleeping in that RV alone. It isn't safe. I told you that last night."

Oh boy, had she told her. They'd spent almost half an hour going around and around about Carol sleeping at the campground, as well as walking the short distance between there and the townhome.

"I'm in a secured park," Carol reminded her. *Again.* "People have to check in before gaining access, and there is an officer patrolling all the time. Like here in your neighborhood."

Pressing her lips together, clearly frustrated that Carol hadn't simply caved into her demands, Judith stared. "I suspect they use the term 'officer' loosely."

Carol focused her attention on buttering her toast. "The RV doors lock."

"Locks can be picked," Judith pointed out. "What would you do if someone broke in while you were sleeping inside?"

"I can take care of myself."

"*How?*"

Wiping her hands on a napkin, Carol pinned her mom with the same hard look she was receiving. "I have a gun."

Judith gasped and fell back in her chair as if Carol had pulled the weapon from her bag and aimed it across the table. "A gun? *Caroline!*"

"I've been thoroughly trained how to handle a weapon."

"I can't deal with this," Judith muttered as she walked away, leaving her breakfast barely touched.

Carol glanced at Ellen, catching the frown on her face. "*What?*"

Ellen didn't say a word. She didn't have to. Her face expressed her disbelief at Carol's confession.

"I'll apologize," Carol grumbled, leaving her coffee and breakfast on the table, knowing both would be cold by the time she returned. She found Judith sitting and looking out the window as she'd been the day before. "I was trained how to protect myself, Mom. Tobias made sure—"

Sitting even taller, clearly readying for a fight, Judith snapped, "It's a husband's job to take care of his wife."

"My husband *did* take care of me." Carol kept her voice as measured as possible. The implication that Tobias did anything less spiked her defenses. She took a lot from her mother, but she wouldn't tolerate attacks on her husband. "Part of which was making sure I could take care of myself."

"By teaching you how to shoot a gun?"

"I learned how to shoot a gun *after* my husband died. We lived in a gated community, but I'm not foolish enough to think nothing bad could ever happen. A single woman living in a big house in a fancy neighborhood made me a target. Traveling alone makes me a target too. I'm aware of that, Mom. I took steps to protect myself. As for Tobias, he taught me how to beat the hell out of someone." She grinned when Judith widened her eyes with shock once again. "You'll be happy to know that when John showed up unannounced, I punched him so hard, I knocked him out."

Judith smirked but forced the reaction away as if she refused to allow a moment of harmony between them. "Violence isn't becoming of a lady, Carol."

Sitting on the couch next to Judith, Carol chuckled. "No, but punching his smug face felt *really* good." Her mom did smile then, and Carol rested her hand on Judith's forearm. She hoped to put the conversation to rest. "I know you're worried about my safety, and I appreciate that. But I can take care of myself. Being alone doesn't scare me."

"It never has. You've always been brave."

Carol wasn't sure how to respond. Compliments from her mother were as rare as Halley's Comet. *Thank you* was on the tip of her tongue, ready to push through the shock.

"So much so, you bordered on foolish," Judith added, squelching the moment of amazement.

Yep. That was the mom she knew.

"I wasn't trying to upset you," Carol said instead of engaging further. "I wanted you to know that I can keep myself safe."

Judith gave her the same disbelieving frown Ellen had, and Carol had to consider if her motives had been as direct as she'd intended. She couldn't deny their long history of poking each other for no reason other than to get a response. That was the pattern she was hoping to break. In order to do that, Carol had to acknowledge she was equally as guilty of starting fights as her mother. She'd learned that behavior from her mom, who had likely learned it from hers. This type of generational cycle wasn't going to be easy for either of them to change.

Since Carol was the one who had decided to stop the cycle, she was going to have to be the one to step up and follow through. "I'm sorry I told you about my gun," she said. "I know you don't care for weapons. I apologize."

"Thank you."

"Will you please come finish your breakfast?"

Judith quirked a brow as her lips parted, looking shocked

at the request. "Are you even the slightest bit concerned that I couldn't sleep last night?"

"What do you want me to do, Mom?"

"Stay here. With us. Where it's safe. I don't think that's too much to ask."

Instead of reminding her mother she would be leaving soon, traveling and sleeping alone, Carol conceded. "Okay. If that will make you sleep better tonight, I will stay here. I'll go over and pack a bag today."

"Thank you."

She gestured toward the kitchen. "Can we finish our breakfast now?"

Judith huffed melodramatically as she pushed herself up. Carol stood, too, but came face-to-face with her mom, who hadn't taken a step. Clearly she wasn't done yet.

"You get upset when I don't worry about you," Judith said, "and you get upset when I do. I can't win with you, Carol. I never could."

She opened her mouth but immediately clamped her jaw shut. Taking a moment to envision the delicate pink hyacinths Tobias had grown soothed her so she didn't bark when she spoke. "I'm not upset. I told you I appreciate your concerns."

Pressing her lips into a thin line, Judith shook her head ever so slightly. "I don't know why you have to be so difficult."

Carol bit the inside of her cheek before asking, "How am I being difficult?"

"I am concerned about you, and you are mocking me."

Throwing her hands up, Carol said, "I'm not mocking you, Mom. I agreed to stay here, didn't I?"

Judith waved as if batting the words away. "If you keep this up, you're bound to get yourself into trouble."

Carol rolled her eyes and silently cursed. "Would you like to tell me what this is really about? Because I'm having a hard time believing you are this upset about my sleeping arrangements."

Several tense seconds passed before Judith stated, "I cannot understand why you went on a vacation with that man."

Furrowing her brow, Carol gawked at her mother. "This is about John? *Seriously?*"

Anger sparked in Judith's eyes. "After everything he did to you. To Katie."

Despite her attempts to stay calm, Carol's fuse was instantly lit. "That was *twenty-four* years ago."

"Twenty-four years that you have been without your daughter."

Carol's heart thudded. The statement struck more than one chord in her chest. Not only the reminder of Katie's loss, but the realization that before yesterday, she couldn't remember the last time she and her mother had discussed anything about Katie. Not her death, or how much she was missed, or memories of the short life she'd lived.

If nothing else, that was a clear sign of how distant from each other they were. She talked about Katie all the time with Tobias's family. Mary, his mother, considered herself Katie's grandmother and brought her up often as if she'd known her, even though Katie was gone before Carol and Tobias met. Her in-laws had never known Katie, yet Carol felt more comfortable reminiscing with them than with her own mother.

Sadness washed over Carol. More than sadness. The feeling was closer to anguish. This was a recognition deep in her soul at how disconnected she felt from her mother and that they may never have another chance to connect. Judith was in her midseventies. How much more time would they have to fix this? If not now, when?

This was the tipping point. Carol either played into their established cycle, or she broke it. Forcing her anger down, Carol counted to five. "Sit down," she said with a level of softness she didn't feel. She was met with her mother's usual defiance. "Mom, please, sit down."

Judith sat on the edge of a beige cushion but kept her eyes straight ahead, not willing to give an inch.

Carol eased down next to her. "I'm not going to ask you to forgive John. I'm not even going to ask you to understand why I did. You have every right to be angry at him."

"Well, I'm glad you think so," she snipped.

Biting back her response, Carol forced her voice to remain calm. "I forgave him because I had to find a way to forgive myself. Losing Katie was the most devastating thing I have ever been through. All of these years without her, and I'm just starting to heal. I'm starting to let go of the pain and anger. Do you have any idea how debilitating it is to carry that kind of guilt and grief for twenty-four years?" She scoffed as she shook her head. "I didn't even realize how much it was weighing me down. John helped me face a lot of things I had ignored for too long."

"Because he was acting as selfishly as he always had."

"I agree with you, one hundred percent," Carol said. "He showed up in my life without warning, without consideration for how I would feel about seeing him, and that was selfish. Believe me, I told him so. But he was right." She looked at her mother, who appeared unmoved. "John was an idiot. He was self-centered and foolhardy, but he was right about a lot of things. He was smart and compassionate."

Judith threw her hands up as she stood. "You sound as smitten now as you did then."

"I'm not smitten with him, but I do see him differently now. After letting go of my hatred for him, I can allow myself to understand him better."

"Understand what?" Judith eyed Carol with the kind of sympathy only a mother who had given up trying to get her child to see reason could. "That he was a monster?"

"He wasn't a monster, Mom. He was broken. From the day I met him, something was broken inside of him that needed to be fixed."

"Oh, I could have told you that. Actually, I believe I did."

Carol forced herself to let the I-told-you-so roll off her back. "Do you know he never remarried? He said he rarely even dated."

"I don't believe that for a second. The man was a cad."

"No. He was a drunk and a selfish fool, but he was never a cad. He left everything he had to me because he didn't have anyone else."

"If you're trying to make me feel sorry for him—"

"I'm not," Carol insisted. "I'm trying to make you understand that he realized what he'd lost, and he mourned for it. He mourned for the life he threw away. Not just Katie but me too. He was my husband, the father of my child, and I stood back and watched him fall instead of helping him. I made mistakes too. We were able to forgive each other before he died, and I believe that meant something. To me, to John, *and* to Katie."

Judith stood taller, obviously tapping into her defiance again. "He is the reason she's gone."

"It was an accident. He never meant for her to get hurt."

"She didn't get hurt, Carol. She *died*." Judith turned on her heels and headed for the door, muttering, "I'll never understand you," as she left.

———

Caroline slowed her steps as she walked into the living room of the small apartment she and John were sharing. His mother forced a smile on her face, and John shrugged, as if to silently communicate that whatever was about to transpire was out of his control. Though Frannie was a petite woman, the energy around her was so big she seemed to fill the room. The first time Caroline met his parents was two years ago, soon after they'd started dating. She'd felt a kind of belonging she'd never felt with her own parents. She'd already been infatuated with John by that point, but after spending an evening with his family, she'd been head over heels in love. With all of them.

Frannie was a delightful woman whom Caroline had grown to adore, but something about her behavior at the moment didn't feel right. The weekend before, while shopping for a wedding dress, Caroline had confessed to Frannie that her parents had all but disowned her for getting pregnant. Frannie had wanted to plan a church wedding and a reception, but Caroline couldn't face either. Not when her parents had already told her they had no intentions of celebrating what they saw as a failure on her part.

Caroline had done her best to avoid Frannie's sympathetic looks, but there she was, standing across the room with a sad smile on her face.

"Hey, honey," Frannie cooed with a bit too much sweetness.

Caroline glanced between mother and son and tried to return Frannie's smile but couldn't quite seem to make her lips work.

"I'll take that." John crossed the room and snagged the basket from Caroline. She watched him head into the bedroom and squelched the urge to grab it back. The last time he'd folded laundry, she'd spent hours ironing every piece of clothing he'd touched. His idea of folding was more like wadding and stuffing into a drawer.

"How are you feeling?" Frannie asked, bringing Caroline's attention back to her.

"I'm...fine." She drew the words out, unsure what she was really being asked. Though Frannie had always been kind to her, Caroline had years of experience reading between her own mother's lines. The way John and Frannie had abruptly ended their conversation when she walked in was a sign of trouble she had seen a thousand times. "How are you?"

Frannie seemed frozen at the island separating the kitchen from the living room. She usually rushed to give Caroline a hug. Something was definitely wrong. The prick of tears stung the back of Caroline's eyes. Without thinking, she rested her hand on her stomach, which was starting to bulge from the baby growing there.

She'd done something, but she couldn't pinpoint what. She'd tried so hard to do everything right—she'd altered her plans to go to medical school, she'd moved out of the dorm and into John's apartment when he'd asked...

Oh. That must be it.

They weren't married, and yet here she was—pregnant and living in his home. She wasn't working. She wasn't contributing to the financial burden she'd placed on him. They'd agreed she should focus on finishing her degree so she could get a job after the baby was born, but maybe... Maybe his parents didn't approve. Naturally they'd blame her instead of John.

The idea of losing Frannie's support crushed the little bit of happiness Caroline had managed to find.

"Don't look so scared, sweetheart," Frannie said with that same fake smile she'd plastered on the moment Caroline entered the apartment.

Caroline blinked but couldn't find her voice or the right words to say. Until she knew what was coming her way, silence was best. She couldn't defend herself against the unknown.

Frannie's smile faded into a frown as her face seemed to fill with concern. "Honey, I was talking to John about... Well, I thought maybe Mark and I should reach out to your parents and see if we can help make this easier for them. Grandparent to grandparent. John doesn't think that's a good idea. What do you think?"

Caroline's lip trembled. "I... No, Frannie, please don't. They're too disappointed in me right now."

"Well," Frannie said. Her smile returned—this time seemingly genuine. "I'm not. Neither is Mark. We're so excited to become grandparents."

Caroline tried to detect the hidden meaning, tried to find the trap Frannie was setting, but she couldn't figure out the game. She'd learned her parents double-speak long ago, how to hear what they were really saying when they lied through their forced smiles. She hadn't learned how to read Frannie yet. From what she could tell, Frannie was sincere in her excitement.

Frannie crossed the room and clutched Caroline's hands. "I can't wait to spoil my grandchild."

Caroline started to pull away, but Frannie held tight to her fingers. John had told her a hundred times how kind and generous his parents were. They were nothing like her parents, or so he'd said. She wasn't sure how long that would last after getting pregnant out of wedlock. Surely they thought less of her now.

"And you know what?" Frannie asked. "I can't wait to spoil you too."

Standing a bit taller, Caroline furrowed her brow. "Me?"

"Yes, you." Frannie released Caroline's hand and cupped her cheek the way John liked to do. "I've always wanted a daughter. Now I have you and a grandbaby. I can't remember the last time I've been so happy."

"Really?" Caroline asked, barely above a whisper. She so

wanted to believe her, but years of rejection from her parents kept her from trusting Frannie's words.

"Yes. Really. I'm sorry your mom and dad aren't being more supportive, but I'm sure they'll come around. Until then"— Frannie tucked Caroline's sandy-brown hair behind her ear —"you have me."

Caroline bit her lip hard, trying to stop herself from crying, but the moment Frannie pulled her into a hug, a little sob ripped from her chest. Frannie was at least six inches shorter than Caroline, so the hug was awkward until Frannie guided them onto the couch. She tucked Caroline's head onto her shoulder and rubbed her back. Other than John, no one had even attempted to ease her fears.

The show of kindness cracked her façade, and Caroline let loose the hurt she'd been burying deep inside. She was pregnant. Her life had been turned upside down. She was scared. And she'd never felt so rejected in all her life. She'd always known her parents could be cruel, but the last few weeks, when she'd needed them most, they'd turned her away. Abandoned her. She'd felt as if she were in a freefall with no one to catch her.

Until Frannie hugged her tight.

"I imagine you must be so scared right now." Frannie's voice was soothing and maternal. "Everything is changing so fast. You must feel like your head is spinning sometimes. When this all starts to feel like too much, you call me, okay? No matter what it is or how silly you might think it is, I'm right here, ready to help you sort through everything."

Caroline wanted to thank her, but she was crying too hard. She couldn't remember ever weeping like this. Her parents *thought this kind of emotion was a dramatic plea for attention, so Caroline had learned how to contain these types of outbursts long ago.*

Despite the embarrassment she felt, she couldn't stop herself. She clung to Frannie, ignoring how her sinuses were filling as she sniffed and snorted.

"Do you want to talk about what's going on with your parents?" Frannie asked after a few minutes. "I'm sure I can help."

Caroline shook her head. "They've wanted me to go to medical school since I was young. Now..." Sitting up, she nabbed tissues from the box on the end table and did her best to clean up her face.

"Do they know you're going to finish your nursing degree before the baby comes?"

She nodded as she wiped her nose. "We told them that, but it's not what they wanted."

Frannie brushed another strand of Caroline's hair from her face. "Well, you're an adult now. Your life can't always be about what they wanted. And that's okay, Caroline. I, for one, am really proud of you. You've shown the kind of forethought that is going to make you a great mom."

The compassion in her words, or maybe someone vocalizing that she'd done something to be proud of, melted her resolve again. She buried her face in her hands as her crying started anew.

Frannie ran her hand over Caroline's back for several moments before asking, "Honey, I have to ask. Is medical school your dream or your parents'?"

Caroline wished she could answer, but she wasn't sure. Although, she supposed, the why or how didn't matter now. They might have pushed her toward medical school, but she'd chosen her area of study on her own. "I wanted to be a pediatrician."

"You'll be an amazing pediatrician someday," Frannie said. "You'll get back to your plans. I promise. We'll find a way."

"We?" Caroline's voice came out as a cracked whisper.

"Of course." Frannie smiled wide. "We're family now. If my girl wants to be a pediatrician, we'll find a way. Together."

Besides her aunt Ellen, the only person who had ever called Caroline "my girl" was John. When he said those words, she'd swell with pride as if she was finally someone. Hearing them from Frannie, though, made her feel as if she'd found someplace where she belonged. She was someone's girl. John's girl. Frannie's girl. She was wanted here.

Caroline tried to stifle her reaction, but a soft cry left her anyway.

Frannie leaned closer, hugged her closer. "Caroline, unplanned pregnancies happen all the time. This is a distraction. A slight detour. Not the end of the road. Mark and I are here to help you. We want you and John to have an amazing life together, sweetie, and if that means pitching in to help you go back to school when it's time, then that's what we'll do."

Frannie's willingness to take her in, to help and support her, gave her a better understanding of what she'd been missing for so long. In that moment, Caroline came to resent her mother. More than resent her. The seedling of anger in her mind grew. As did her recognition that she could do this without her mother. She

*didn't need Judith Stewart's approval or help or...anything. She
didn't need a damn thing from her parents.*

*Though she couldn't have imagined willingly showing
Frannie weakness even ten minutes ago, Caroline leaned over
and put her head back on the woman's shoulder. Frannie hugged
her close, and Caroline leaned into the embrace, soaking up the
kind of maternal support she'd never had before.*

————

Carol loved seeing her aunt's work. Standing in the spare
room that also served as an art studio, she admired the many
paintings hanging on the walls as the late-afternoon sun
streamed in through the blinds. Ellen had left Dayton the day
after her eighteenth birthday and traveled the country,
working odd jobs to support herself. Judith, of course, had
shared that information as a warning of what not to do, but
Carol had spent her childhood dreaming of being carefree
like her aunt.

By her late twenties, Ellen had settled in Boulder, married
an incredibly sweet man, and become an art teacher.
Whenever Carol and her mother visited, Carol and her
cousins went wild with paints in the area Ellen had set up as
her studio. Watercolors were Carol's favorite, mostly because
she wasn't great at painting and watercolors were a bit more
forgiving. Even mistakes looked beautiful in watercolor.

She'd seen the same enthusiasm in Katie when she'd
colored. Carol had done her best to encourage her daughter's
love of art. Instead of steering her toward something else, as

her own parents had done, Carol bought more coloring books, crayons, and paints than one child could ever use up. She'd never been able to understand why her parents refused to let her pursue her own interests.

"Where's your mind?" Ellen asked from the doorway.

Carol blinked the memories away. "I was thinking about how you'd let us kids take over your studio when I'd visit. I loved that."

"Did you?"

Tearing her attention from a painting of a woman dancing in the rain, she looked at Ellen. "You couldn't tell?"

"Oh, sweetheart. You were such a serious child; getting a read on you was challenging sometimes. I do remember how hard you tried." Moving to Carol's side, Ellen slid an arm around her waist. "Maybe if you had relaxed and let the painting come to you, you would have had more fun. And been happier."

"I was happy when I was painting."

"It didn't show."

Carol shrugged. "Well, I learned how to hide my feelings at a young age. Hiding was safer."

Ellen gave her a light squeeze before stepping away and sinking into the plush red sofa. While the inside of the house was filled mostly with neutrals, the studio reflected Ellen's personal tastes with bright colors. "Why did you sneak away? And don't tell me it's to look at my art. I know you better than that."

"Mom's animosity toward me feels overwhelming at the moment. I needed a break."

Ellen gave a slight laugh. "Oh, I hate to break this to you, kiddo, but you're equally as bad. The moment she doesn't agree with you, your defenses go up and she responds in kind. The tension between the two of you is exhausting."

"I know," Carol admitted. "We've never been close, but we certainly know how to push each other's buttons."

Ellen didn't disagree. No logical person could. "If you're serious about mending fences, you're going to need a bit more patience than you've shown so far."

Carol considered her words for several seconds before facing her with a furrowed brow. "I'm not imagining things, am I? They always seemed so hostile when I was growing up and I never knew why. Was I seeing something that wasn't there?"

Ellen took a moment before answering. "Hostile is a strong word. They were strict. They were firm. Your father bought into an old-school authoritarian type of parenting. That isn't the same as hostility, Carol. I'm sure it seemed that way to you as a child, but they loved you. They hurt when you were hurting, and John hurt you a lot. You can't blame your mother for resenting him for everything he did to you."

"They were awful to him from the day they met him. They never gave him a chance."

"Did you ever consider they were awful to him because they saw through his charms a lot easier than you did?" Ellen clasped her hands and tilted her head to the side in the way she did right before agreeing with her sister instead of her niece. "She isn't wrong, honey. They did try to warn you about him."

Carol disagreed with a hard shake of her head. "No. They didn't try to warn me, Aunt Ellen. They tried to control my life like they always did. John wasn't *their* choice, therefore he was the *wrong* choice. Seeing them treat him like dirt made me want to protect him. That was probably how our entire enabling cycle started."

"Now *that*," Ellen said pointedly, "is definitely something you can't blame on your parents."

A wry laugh left Carol as she sank down onto the sofa next to Ellen. "No, I can't. I take full responsibility for that. My pride wouldn't allow them to be right, even when I saw they were."

"Sweetheart, you were in over your head with that man, and they knew it." Ellen's voice returned to her usual sweet tone as she gripped Carol's hand. "Your mom called me, so upset, after meeting him. She was worried he was going to ruin your future, which is exactly what he did in the end."

"But he didn't, and that is what Mom and Dad never seemed to understand. John was a detour. A brief hurdle I had to overcome. I had an entire life after I left him. I got my advanced degree, like they wanted. I had an amazingly successful career, like they wanted. I couldn't have asked for a better husband than I found in Tobias. None of that ever mattered because they never forgave me for altering the course *they'd* plotted for me." The burning fury took Carol by surprise. She hadn't realized how raw that old wound still was. "I wasn't strong enough to tell Dad how much he hurt me my entire life, but I'm going to tell Mom. I hope we can have some kind of relationship after I do, but if we can't..."

She shrugged, as if the idea didn't bother her much at all. "Then I will walk away from her knowing I tried."

Ellen blew out a long breath, and Carol realized how bitter she'd sounded. Hell, she *was* bitter. But she hadn't meant to let it show, especially with her aunt.

"That came out harsher than intended," Carol whispered.

"Anger tends to do that when you bottle it up too long. Starts taking over logic and spilling out when you don't expect it to." Ellen tenderly stroked her thumb over Carol's hand. "If you're serious about confronting all these old issues with your mother, you'd better be prepared for whatever she throws back."

"Meaning?"

"Meaning you have your grievances, and your mother has hers. I love you more than Nude Model Mondays at the art center," Ellen said, causing Carol to chuckle, "but you're not perfect either. You've done things that hurt them too."

"I know that."

"Are you ready to face them?"

Carol nodded. "If I can face the reality that I inadvertently played a hand in my daughter's death, I can certainly face whatever wrongs I've done to my parents."

"I hope so." Ellen kissed her cheek. "Take a minute to calm yourself and then come join us. We can work on that puzzle to give us all a distraction."

Carol squeezed Ellen's hand before she could leave. "I'm not trying to be cruel to her."

"She's not going to see it any other way. You know that, don't you?"

She did. She'd known the moment she'd decided to come to Florida that her mother was going to feel attacked. "I don't want to live the rest of my life wishing I'd done something to make this better."

"Confrontation isn't the right approach if you're trying to make this better, darling. You push her and she'll put up her wall, and then you'll never get in. You know this because you're the same way." Ellen kissed Carol's head before standing. "Take a moment and then come on. This puzzle won't put itself together."

Once alone, Carol closed her eyes and pictured Tobias's garden. She remembered how the butterflies flitted from flower to flower. The low baritone of his voice as he talked to his plants.

Even that wasn't enough to ease the knot in her gut.

THREE

AFTER A TENSE HOUR or so hovering over the puzzle, Carol walked out to the backyard and sank into one of the chairs on the patio. Clearly the two chairs and little round table had been her aunt's addition. Her mother never would have bought teal-painted wrought iron.

Unlike Carol's yard in Houston, with the endless varieties of plants, her mother and aunt hadn't done much landscaping. There were a few cannas with fiery leaves and bright orange flowers in one corner of the yard and a palm tree in another, but for the most part, the yard was empty. There were no sweet scents in the air. Just humid oppression.

Carol leaned over enough to slip her phone free from her pocket when it vibrated. Time stopped for a moment as she read the caller ID. Her real estate agent. Something inside her heart grew dark with dread. She hadn't been expecting a call, not exactly, but she wasn't surprised.

"Hey, Pam."

"Afternoon, darlin'," she answered with a Southern Texas drawl. "I wanted to let you know the bidding war is over. One of the buyers backed out. The price was getting too high for them. All that's left is for you to accept the remaining offer."

Tobias's garden flashed through Carol's mind. The flowers danced on the breeze. Their sweetness filled her senses. This time, Carol didn't feel calm. She felt the harsh slap of reality. All that stood between her and selling the house were a few signatures. A few scribbles, and she'd never see her husband's garden again. She had a thousand photos and videos. She had picked flowers and pressed them in Tobias's favorite book. She even had seeds he'd harvested from the plants so someday she could start a new garden in his memory.

Suddenly, that didn't seem like enough.

"Are you there?" Pam asked.

Carol inhaled and forced a smile in an effort to make her voice sound cheerful. "I'm here."

"You...still want to sell, right?"

Even if she didn't plan to spend an unknown amount of time traveling, keeping that big empty house wasn't logical. She had spent the last ten months avoiding as much of her home as possible. She could count on one hand how many times she'd been in Tobias's home office, the spare bedroom where she'd kept Katie's belongings, and the living room. Every day was the same—she would walk in through the kitchen and go up the stairs to her office or to her bedroom. The rest of the house was untouched.

But the garden... Was she truly ready to leave the garden?

"Carol?" Pam's voice had switched from cheerful to borderline panicked.

"Yes," she said, her tone flat without the forced cheer. "Yes, I still want to sell."

Pam laughed dryly. "You scared me there for a second."

"I'm sorry. It's real now, isn't it?"

"I know this is difficult." Pam's drawl took on a maternal tone. "You and Tobias made so many memories there."

Though she was certain the little speech was one Pam had given to a thousand different widows or widowers or grown children who were selling their parents' homes, Carol appreciated the attempt at comfort. "Yes," she said, "we did. I know the new owners will too."

"Oh, darlin', they will. I'll email you the papers with instructions for your signature. If you can get them to me by the end of the day tomorrow, I'd really appreciate it."

"I will. Thank you, Pam."

"You're welcome. And as hard as this is, I want you to know the biggest selling point was your husband's garden. The buyers love what he did with the yard."

Carol closed her eyes and swallowed down the sob welling in her chest. "I'm glad. We'll talk soon." She hung up as she lost the strength to hold back the sound any longer. Tears fell and she choked out a miserable sound as she dropped her phone into her lap.

"Are you okay?" Judith asked from behind her.

After wiping her cheeks, Carol glanced back to where her mom stood holding two glasses of iced tea. She sniffled as she dried her hands on her shorts. "I will be."

Judith held out a glass. "You're upset." Her comment was flat, emotionless.

Carol knew from experience that her mother would never intentionally delve into her problems. Where Ellen would have rushed to sit and ask what had happened, her mother simply made an observation that was left for Carol to acknowledge or ignore.

Carol accepted the drink, even though she didn't care for her mother's tea. Though she didn't eat candies or cakes much anymore, she did prefer her tea made southern style—with a hefty dose of simple syrup and a pinch of baking soda to heighten the sweetness. Yet another thing they disagreed on that didn't warrant pointing out. She'd drink the bitter tea without remark.

"One of the potential buyers backed out. It's a done deal." Her voice cracked as she said, "I've sold the house."

"Oh." Judith eased down into the chair on the other side of the small table. "I remember how heartbroken I was when I decided to leave Ohio."

Carol let the words sink in. For some reason, she'd never considered how upset her mother must have been to sell the home Carol had grown up in. She had few memories in that home that warmed her heart, but certainly her mother hadn't shared her misery. Carol had been so selfishly relieved that she wouldn't have to settle the estate someday, she hadn't considered what her mom had gone through.

Even when she'd returned for her father's funeral, she'd checked into a hotel since Ellen was staying with Judith. Ellen had assured Carol there was room for them all at the house, but the last thing she wanted was to be stuck there, especially since she and Tobias had agreed she should go to Dayton alone.

Her father hadn't been any fonder of Tobias than he'd been of John. Neither Carol nor her husband had to wonder why. Dennis Stewart would never come right out and say so, but he was less than thrilled that his son-in-law was Black. Carol couldn't say if her mother held the same prejudice or if she simply never pushed back against her husband's.

That didn't change how Carol hadn't been there for her mother when she'd been widowed or when she'd sold her home. Guilt and shame overshadowed her pain. "I didn't...I guess I thought you wanted to move here with Ellen."

Judith was quiet for a few seconds. "I was lonely, Carol. I had friends in Ohio, but most of our family moved away years ago. Or died. There was no reason for me to stay after your father died." Ice clinked in her glass as she took a drink. She set it on the ground beside her and wiped her hands on her dress.

Carol suspected her mom was waiting for some kind of response to her comment, but now wasn't the time to inform her that had she at least tried to make Tobias feel welcome, they may have visited. Instead, her parents had been very clear that, like John, they didn't approve of Carol's second husband.

Tobias had been everything they'd said they wanted her to marry—smart, kind, and successful. Yet, they'd never even attempted to make him feel part of the family. Of course, they barely made Carol feel like part of their family. Maybe she had expected too much of them. If they couldn't be open and warm toward their own daughter, she shouldn't have expected them to be that way toward an in-law.

"I suppose you started to feel lonely in your own home too," Judith said after several long seconds of silence. "There's no reason to keep that big house, but parting with it is...difficult."

Carol swallowed around the pain in her chest. "That house was perfect for a family—the right size, the right neighborhood, the right school district. When that didn't happen, we adjusted and made it the perfect home for the two of us. The last few months, it felt more like a museum. I was afraid to change anything because I didn't want to lose my ties to the past. I could pretend Tobias was still alive if nothing changed."

"That's not healthy," Judith said with a strain to her voice that almost sounded like concern.

"I know. There were too many times I really did forget he was gone. I'd fix two cups of coffee or get out two plates for dinner without even realizing what I was doing. I'd call out to him and listen for his response before remembering. Then everything would come crashing down on me, and I'd be a mess all over again."

"Your father has been gone three years, and I still fix him a pot of chicken and dumpling soup every week. Drives Ellen crazy, but it's a habit I've had for fifty years. I can't stop now."

Carol smiled as she imagined the spat the sisters likely had every Sunday afternoon.

Growing up, Sundays were when her mother would ban

everyone from the kitchen so she could chop vegetables and roll out homemade dough to cut into dumplings while the chicken boiled on the stovetop. There were few memories Carol could conjure that didn't bring a hint of resentment to her heart, but picturing her mother in a short-sleeved dress and her white apron with cross-stitch embroidered flowers on the pockets around her waist was one she could count on.

She hadn't been allowed to help, but she remembered the scents, the sounds, and her mom humming as she worked. As she grew older, Carol realized being alone in the kitchen was the one time her mother ever seemed to be at peace.

Her father spent that time preparing for the upcoming workweek by polishing his shoes and checking that his suits were crisp and ready to be worn. Both her parents were too busy to micromanage what Carol was doing, so in a way, Sundays were her most peaceful time too.

Though her mother never taught her the recipe, Carol had learned to make a similar soup on her own. Tobias said the dish was one of the things that had won him over. Carol never fell into the habit of cooking soup weekly like her mother, but he'd always lavished her with praise when she did. Of course, he offered his compliments about everything she did. He had known how empty she was inside and spent their twenty-two years together filling the void.

"Tobias has only been gone for ten months." Carol's voice was thick with emotion. "Do you think I'm letting him go too soon?"

"You aren't letting him go any more than you let Katie go," Judith said. "Moving on, trying to have some kind of life, isn't letting go. I can't say I agree with, or even remotely understand, your choice to live like a vagabond, but the living can't stay stagnant and wait to join the dead. Moving on hurts, but you have to do it. Tobias would want you to."

The surprising show of solidarity from her mother choked Carol up again. She bit her lip to try to stop from crying but had to turn her face away to hide her scrunched nose and tightly closed eyes from her mom. At some point, she'd have to explain her choice of living in her RV—her promise to John, a man her mother hated—but now wasn't the time. She didn't have the strength to have that fight right now.

Her house was gone. Tobias's flowers were gone. Another piece of her life with the man she'd loved more than anything else in this world was gone. She couldn't fight right now if she wanted to.

Judith stood and put her hand on Carol's shoulder. "Come inside when you're ready. Ellen is determined we're going to finish that damned puzzle of hers."

"I, um...I need to go to my RV and pack some things if I'm going to be staying here. You two work on the puzzle. I'll help when I get back."

Her mom didn't argue as she moved around her chair.

"Mom?" Carol turned and looked up through her tears. "I am so sorry I wasn't there for you when you sold the house. It was selfish of me not to consider how hard that must have been on you. Now that I'm going through the same thing, I see how much my indifference must have hurt you. I'm sorry."

Judith nodded slightly. "I appreciate that."

Once she was alone, Carol sat back in her chair and looked up at the blue sky. She couldn't recall the last time she felt like she was on the same page as her mother about anything. This felt nice. This felt like progress.

Though she was still devastated about closing a door on her past with Tobias, calm settled over her heart. She'd taken the first, albeit small, step to finally connecting with her mother.

Good job, she told herself. She smiled as she looked at the tea in her hand. Then, with a quick glance behind her to make sure her mom was gone, Carol dumped the bitter drink into the grass. After she entered the house through the kitchen, she put her dirty glass into the dishwasher and went to put her shoes on.

"I brought this for you," Ellen said, coming into the living room. She held out an absurdly large straw hat with a bright-pink bow that caused Carol to giggle. "Take it. You need more protection than that baseball cap provides."

Carol opened her mouth, wanting to reject the offer, but the sternness on her aunt's face made her concede. "Thank you." After slipping into her sandals, she pulled the hat onto her head and chuckled as she dropped her head back to peer from under the floppy brim. Ellen laughed and situated the hat on Carol's head so she could see.

"Did you steal this from Scarlett O'Hara?" Carol asked.

Ellen gave her a conspiratorial grin as mischief lit in her eyes. With a wink, she whispered, "That bitch has enough, don't you think?"

"More than enough," Carol agreed.

Ellen's face grew more serious. "Your mom told me the house is sold. I know that's tough, but please remember you aren't alone. We've both been through this. We know how hard it can be, and you can lean on us as much as you need."

"Thank you." She let a smile curve her lips. "I'd hug you, but I'm afraid this hat might put your eye out."

"Oh, you think you're so clever." Ellen nabbed her keys off the wooden hanger by the door.

As Judith came into the room, she frowned at the monstrosity of a hat Carol was wearing. "You look foolish."

"I agree." Carol started to reach for the oversize brim, but her aunt caught her hand.

"Leave it," Ellen instructed. "I'd rather you look foolish than get skin cancer."

With her signature theatrical sigh, Judith removed the hat from Carol's head and tossed it onto the sofa. "She's not going to get skin cancer from one short walk."

Ellen exhaled with equal displeasure. "If you say so. She's your daughter."

"She can wear sunscreen if you're so concerned," Judith countered.

"We should all wear sunscreen, actually," Ellen said, her voice distant as she scanned the room, likely trying to spot a bottle of lotion nearby. "Where did I put it?"

"It's probably with the remote control you lost this morning," Judith offered.

"Why would you need sunscreen?" Carol asked.

"We're going with you." Ellen turned her attention back on her niece.

Carol immediately faced her mother, who didn't seem nearly as interested. "You don't have to."

"We're going with you." This time Ellen's voice was firm, but she was looking at Judith, as if daring her to disagree.

Carol knew better than to intervene with whatever had transpired between the sisters. Her mother didn't seem pleased. Neither did Ellen. Carol wasn't going to ask why. Pulling her baseball cap on her head, she followed the women out into the afternoon sun.

"It's too hot," Judith said. "We should take the car."

"It's not too hot," Ellen insisted.

"You can stay, Mom," Carol offered. "We won't be long."

Ellen dipped her chin and eyed Judith with one eyebrow quirked, as if to silently warn her against even considering the idea.

Judith shook her head. "No, I'd like to come along."

Carol was quite certain she wouldn't, but she appreciated the effort none the less. Even if it was made under the stern stare of her younger sister. The muggy air enveloped her as they left the shade of the townhouse porch. Carol glanced back at her mom, trying to get a read on her, but the woman was stoic as usual.

As they walked the mile or so to the RV park, Ellen chatted about the clear sky, the flowers, and shared gossip about their neighbors. Carol responded at the right times, but she wasn't really listening. As she tended to do when she was near her mother, she was tuned in to the vibrations radiating from Judith. Right now, she was picking up on the tension and frustration rolling off the woman beside her. In turn, that fed Carol's tension and frustration, which were always churning right below the surface when they were together.

Even though they'd been on the same page fifteen minutes ago, a fight was brewing. She didn't know why or when, but one of them was sure to say the wrong thing and light the other's fuse. That was how things went between them. That was the cycle Carol had come here to break.

"Doing okay, Mom?" she asked.

Judith pulled a cloth from her pocket and dabbed her forehead. "We should have taken the car."

"It's August in Florida," Ellen said with a light, dismissive tone. "Bound to be a little warm."

"Which is why we should have taken the car," Judith said again.

Ellen lifted her arms, and the breeze made her short-sleeve shirtdress flap like a flag in waves of bright pinks, yellows, and oranges. "The sun is shining. The birds are singing."

"The sweat is running down my back like a river," Judith chimed in flatly.

"I have air conditioning and cold water in the RV," Carol assured her. "We're almost there."

Judith didn't seem satisfied. She scowled as her sister continued holding her arms to the sky. "I wish you'd listen to me, Ellen. Just once."

Carol smiled as she shook her head. How many hundreds of times had her mother said those exact words to her?

Though Judith had given up overtly trying to tell Carol what to do long ago, there was little doubt Judith thought a million times that she wished her daughter would listen. Apparently Ellen needed to listen to Judith's wisdom as well.

At the walk-in gate to the campground, Carol entered the code she'd been given at check-in. The lock clicked, and she opened the panel, gesturing for the bickering sisters to go first.

Ellen stepped in and turned with a bright smile. "Well, isn't this lovely."

The park was well-kept and quiet. Several picnic tables were set up where the three women had entered. On the other side of that was a small play area. There were a few kids on the swings, but most had converged at the pool, both of which, thankfully, were far from the lot assigned to Carol.

"I can see why you are drawn to this life." Ellen wrapped her arm around Carol's.

Carol was going to have to come clean at some point. She wasn't drawn to this life. She was using this opportunity to face the wounds that had never healed. This would be okay for a while, but eventually, she'd long for the stability of a home.

"This isn't a life," Judith offered. "This is a permanent vacation and it's ridiculous."

"She's worked hard for years," Ellen said. "She's earned this permanent vacation."

"This isn't a vacation," Carol said as her stomach rolled. "I'm on a...mission of sorts."

Judith scoffed. "What kind of mission?"

Ellen gave Carol a slight tug, a silent warning that now wasn't the time. Carol looked at her aunt and received the same grim stare given to Judith when it seemed she was about to back out of the walk.

"I'm trying to find myself now that Tobias is gone," Carol said. "I don't know who I am without him."

"And you think you'll find yourself in some park for nomads?"

Carol stiffened at the sardonic tone her mother used. She'd heard that voice her entire life. Judith had used that attitude to dismiss her daughter's feelings over and over again.

"No," Carol countered, "I think I'll figure out what things I need to face in order to make peace with myself. I'd like to enjoy what's left of my life without this constant sense of guilt and dread."

"You've been dealt some difficult blows in this life," Ellen said. "I think it's wonderful that you are taking time to reflect on things and get your balance."

"Well, I think it's childish," Judith said.

Carol rolled her shoulders back. She'd tried. She'd tried so hard not to let her mother light the fuse, but there she went. She could run down the list of things in her life that had left her broken, from her parents' indifference to Katie's death to the two miscarriages she'd suffered during her marriage to Tobias to finding out he'd been hit by a truck so hard his spine had snapped and his skull had fractured. Fire burned in her belly as she narrowed her eyes at her mother. "Are you kidding me?"

"Okay," Ellen interceded. "This isn't the time or place to hash this out. Judith, don't dismiss what Carol has been through. She's suffered more loss than any one person should deal with."

"I didn't say she hadn't."

Ellen lifted her hand before Carol could add her input. "Everyone heals differently. Carol, it's okay if this is what you need to do right now. But it is also okay for your mom to worry about you."

Carol filled her lungs and counted to five. The fight wasn't worth the stress. For any of them. "I'm parked right over there."

The rest of the walk was silent. And tense.

As she unlocked the side entry door of her RV, Carol said, "Watch your step. The first one is a bit high." Once Ellen and Judith were safely inside, Carol looked up at the clear blue sky. "Give me patience, Tobias," she whispered. "Please."

Walking inside, she'd barely finished climbing the stairs before she was met with her mother's horrified stare.

Judith's jaw was slacked, her lips parted, and her eyes wide. Carol was about to ask what she'd done now, but she didn't have to. She followed her aunt's gaze to the little dinette table where she'd sat looking over her trip plan the night before. A folded map sat tucked between two urns—John's and Katie's.

"What in God's name is going on with you?" Judith asked with a strained voice. "Have you lost your mind? Why are there...*urns* on your table, Caroline?"

Carol had to bite back the sarcasm begging to rush forth.

The words nearly spilled from her lips. *Why, who else would I dine with, Mother?* Instead, she took the vessels and carried them to a cabinet.

"Cremation is a very common choice—" Ellen started.

"Stop," Judith insisted. She huffed out a breath and shook her head. "You left those on your table with...human...bodies inside?"

"Human remains," Carol said flatly. "Yes."

Judith looked like she was going to be sick as she put one trembling hand to her lips and the other to her stomach.

After Carol secured the urns inside a cabinet, she gestured toward the table, silently asking them to sit in the bench seat. Ellen took the cue, but Judith stood, ramrod straight, as if she had no intention of moving at all.

Carol tugged her hat off and slid into the empty bench seat at the table. "John asked me to spread his ashes with Katie's."

Judith, as expected, reacted by taking a sharp breath and swaying on her feet. "You have," Judith said definitively. "You've lost your mind. You need help."

"No, I don't."

Judith shook her head. "This isn't normal."

"*Mom.* For God's sake, listen to me." She glanced at her aunt for help, but the way Ellen's lips were pressed into a scowl made it clear she wouldn't be getting any. "I promised John I would spread his and Katie's ashes together in places they would have enjoyed visiting."

"You don't owe him—"

"I do," Carol stated, cutting Judith off. "I do owe him,

Mom. And I owe Katie *and* myself. I'm not rehashing this with you. We've already fought about it."

"You've let him manipulate you again."

Carol swallowed the kneejerk response, the urge to engage. Instead, she softened her face and did her best to look amicable. "The next stop on my list is Disney World. I was planning to ease you into this, but... I would like for you to join me and maybe say a few words for Katie."

"Oh, for the love of all that is holy," Ellen muttered.

Judith fell back two steps until she hit the kitchenette with her lower back. The pans in the cabinet below clinked from the vibrations. Though the RV was one of the compact models, there had always been ample space for Carol and Tobias. However, with her mother looming inside, the RV suddenly felt *too* small. The dark floor and cabinets had never seemed overpowering to Carol before, but being in this place with her mother, the living area made her feel borderline claustrophobic.

"You cannot dump human remains at an amusement park, Caroline!" Judith said, clearly horrified.

Carol fought the urge to roll her eyes at the dramatics. "I'm not going to take an urn on a rollercoaster, Mother. I'll take a little bit of the ash—"

Judith's eyes grew even wider. "Stop! This is insane."

"No, it's not. People do this all the time."

Judith furrowed her brow. "And how do you... How are you... She's in an urn. How are you..."

Carol lifted her hands, recalling all too well how queasy she'd been the first time John scooped Katie's ashes into a small container. She couldn't say she was any more comfortable with the process now, but at least she didn't want to vomit when she had to fill the containers. "That's not important," she said. "What's important is that Katie would have loved going to Disney. I won't leave them anywhere that someone might accidentally come into contact with them. I'll find a nice grassy spot outside the park and—"

"Enough!" Judith closed her eyes and pressed her fingers to her forehead. "Oh, my God, Carol. Is this what you've been doing with your life?"

"Letting go is part of the healing process, Mom."

Dropping her hand, Judith gawked at her. "I don't think 'letting go' was meant to be taken so literally."

Carol nearly giggled at her mother's observation. Judith would never be known for her sense of humor, but that comment had been amusing.

"Do you think this is funny?" Judith whispered.

Grinding her teeth to stop from smirking, Carol looked across the small space. "No. I think your overreaction is funny."

"*Overreaction?*" Judith repeated, as if she couldn't believe what she'd heard.

"This is not nearly as unusual as you seem to think it is."

"That is your daughter in there." She gestured wildly at the cabinet where Carol had put the urns.

The delight Carol had found left in an instant. "You think I don't know that?"

"How can you be so nonchalant about this?"

"I ran away from *this* for twenty-four years. I don't

consider that being nonchalant." She rubbed her fingertips into her temples, reminding herself to be patient, before dropping her hands on the table and clasping them together. "Mom, this is how John and I planned to say goodbye to her all those years ago. This is how he wanted me to say goodbye to him. I'm honoring them by taking them to places—"

"It's wrong," Judith said.

"No. It's not. They both wanted to see the world. I'm doing what I can to make that happen for them."

"They aren't seeing the world, Carol. They're *dead*."

She hadn't expected her mother to understand, so she didn't know why those words stung her. Carol swallowed her anger, more than ready to tell her mother to burn in hell, but Judith threw her hands up and marched out of the RV. Carol had forgotten her aunt was there, watching the entire scene unfold, until she looked across the table. "I'm not apologizing for spreading my daughter's ashes."

"And she's not going to apologize for disagreeing with you. So where does that leave you?"

Carol shrugged. "With no middle ground. As usual."

Ellen didn't seem to have anything else to say. She pushed herself up and started for the door. "Dinner is at seven. I expect to see you there."

———

Caroline couldn't quite understand what her mother was saying. She was beyond numb. She was discombobulated. Her mind was outside her body, and nothing felt real. A nurse had given her a shot within minutes of learning that Katie had died. The drugs were still coursing through her veins, making her mind swim in a cloud of nothingness.

John and Caroline had waited what seemed like a lifetime to find out if their daughter would be okay. But Caroline was a nurse. She knew it had been mere minutes that doctors had tried to revive Katie before pronouncing her dead. They'd been led to a room where Katie was lying on a bed. Caroline had held her daughter and cried until John had pulled her away. She didn't know how much time had passed. Everything was a blur.

Caroline wasn't thinking clearly enough to even realize their parents needed to be told. All she could think was that Katie was gone. Katie was never going to wake up again. Katie was never going to laugh or sing or beg for one more bedtime story again. Katie was never going to sneak into her bed to cuddle again.

Katie was never going to do anything again.

John had driven them straight to her parents' house. He said he wanted to get this over with. Caroline hadn't argued. She couldn't. Her throat was raw from screaming. Her mind was outside her body. She hadn't even realized where he was going until he parked behind her father's car. She couldn't really remember walking into the house, but there she was, in the sterile living room she'd avoided as much as possible all her life.

Judith grabbed Caroline by the arm and pushed her onto their sofa next to John.

"Caroline, what is going on?" Judith demanded. "You're scaring me."

John sniffled, and Caroline looked at him, waiting for him to answer. He didn't. He wiped tears from the side of his nose as she watched, thinking it was the first time she'd ever seen him cry. At least when he was sober. He'd cried plenty of times when he was drunk off his ass and she'd threatened to leave him.

"Caroline!" Judith screamed.

She jolted, turned her eyes to her mother, and noticed the fear on Judith's face. Opening her mouth, she tried to find the words. Katie died. Katie's dead. Katie... She couldn't say it. She couldn't.

Dropping onto the couch beside Caroline, Judith stared at her. "What happened?"

"She... She's gone," Caroline managed to say.

"Who's gone?"

Caroline knew the moment her mother figured out what she was saying. Tears sprang to Judith's eyes. Odd. Caroline had never seen her cry, either. Her face, the one that always seemed so filled with animosity, sagged and her cheeks lost their color.

"Who is gone?" Judith demanded.

"K-K-Katie." The word tumbled from Caroline's lips, and her eyes started to fill as well. "Katie's...gone."

"Gone where?" Judith whispered.

"She..."

"She died," John spit out. "Katie died."

Judith stared at Caroline, as if she expected her daughter to counter what John had said. A fat tear fell from her right eye and rolled down her cheek. Caroline was mesmerized by the light shining from the little stream. But then she sensed the shift. The concern and shock switched to anger so quickly it would have shocked anyone who hadn't grown up anticipating these abrupt changes in the woman.

Instead of unleashing at her daughter, Judith turned her rage to her son-in-law. *"What did you do, you bastard? What did you do?"*

"I didn't—"

"What's going on in here?" Dennis boomed from the doorway of the living room.

A heart-wrenching sob left Judith. A sound Caroline had never heard before, hadn't known her mother was capable of. A sound that was so human it took her by surprise. Was that how she'd sounded when she'd heard the news? She remembered screaming. She remembered her knees buckling and falling. She remembered someone catching her before she hit the floor and voices trying to calm her.

Had she sounded like that? So...raw? So broken?

The sound reverberated around her, cut through the numbness of the drugs, and made the fist around her heart clench again. Made her tears return.

"What have you done?" Dennis demanded, rushing to his wife.

"Katie," Judith sobbed. "Oh my God. Katie."

Caroline couldn't look at her father. All her life, she'd cowered before him. Now was no different. Now was worse. She had failed a thousand times in their eyes, but nothing could compare to this. Nothing could compare to this failure. Her failure to keep her child alive.

Judith said something, but Caroline embraced the numbness again. She embraced not hearing, not feeling. She tapped into that void she'd learned to disappear into when she was a child. Her father couldn't get to her there. His hateful words couldn't break her there.

Not that there was anything left of her to be broken.

Her father spoke. She didn't hear the words, but his voice vibrated through her like a tornado. The deep timbre was familiar. He was displeased, unhappy, furious. And he was directing that rage toward her. But she wasn't listening.

She had her own rage brewing inside her.

Turning to John, for the first time, she realized how deeply her hatred for him ran. How every fiber of her being wanted to crush him with her rage.

That must be how her father felt. The ire that he was barely containing all her life. That must have been how she'd learned to contain her hatred for John for so long. Like she'd learned to hide behind a wall by watching her mother, she'd learned from her father how to bury her hate.

John said something. He glared up at her parents and said something, but Caroline wasn't hearing them. She was so incensed herself. He grabbed her hand and pulled her from the sofa and out the door. He took long strides, half dragging her behind him, until he helped her into his beat-up car.

He muttered something and hit the accelerator so hard his tires screamed as he backed out of their driveway. Caroline didn't know what had happened. Actually, she did. Her parents had happened. She hadn't heard the details, hadn't needed to. She understood the gist.

Her parents were placing blame without even knowing the full story.

"It's not our fault," John said. "It was an accident. Do you hear me, Caroline? Do you hear me?"

She nodded, muttered a response even she didn't understand.
Then sank into the darkness of her mind again.

———

The tension inside the townhouse was unmistakable. The air was alive with anxiety the moment Carol walked inside. Her stomach turned sour as she set down a backpack of clothes and personal belongings. She didn't know if her mom and aunt would still want her to stay at the house, but if she showed up emptyhanded, she'd be setting them up for another round of arguments.

Part of her wanted to slink to the room her aunt used as a studio, the one where she'd be sleeping, and hide until she could leave again. But that's what *Caroline* did. *Caroline* hid inside herself and avoided confrontation. Carol couldn't run away anymore. She was here to face the ongoing issues, and that couldn't be done from the shadows.

"Hello?" she called out.

"We're in here, sweetheart," Ellen answered from the back of the house.

Carol found the pair in the kitchen. This time Ellen was standing at the stove and Judith was getting plates from the cabinet. Ellen glanced over her shoulder, as if verifying Judith was behaving.

The smile Judith offered couldn't have been more fake, but Carol silently applauded her mother's effort. The cycle they usually found themselves in wouldn't have allowed for Judith to give even that much. At least not until she felt she had given enough cold shoulder to drive her point home. Whatever she thought her point had been.

"I'm sorry we fought earlier, Mom," Carol offered.

A smugness, as if Carol's apology meant she was saying she was wrong, caused Judith's smile to appear more sincere...and cocky. "Apology accepted."

But none returned. Not that Carol had expected an apology. Judith never had been good at admitting when she was wrong. Ellen opened her mouth, as if intending to set her sister straight, but Carol waved her hand dismissively. She hadn't been met with the anticipated animosity. That was going to have to be enough. Besides, even if Judith had said the words, she wouldn't have meant them.

"I'm sorry to you, too," Carol said to her aunt. "We were having a lovely walk."

"There will be time for more walks. Help set the table."

Carol took the hand-painted ceramic plates, likely her aunt's handywork, from the counter and added them, as well as napkins and silverware, to the table. As she did, her mother busied herself with fixing three glasses of ice water. Her aunt carried a bowl filled with what were obviously store-bought noodles and chunks of beef covered in rich-smelling gravy.

Her aunt was a wonderful cook but had never gone the extra mile like Judith. Ellen's life had always been fun but chaotic. Judith was the one who spent hours in the kitchen every day, planning meals and making homemade bread and noodles. For some reason, Carol had expected Judith to naturally take over cooking responsibilities, but they'd settled on a rotation with two nights designated to leftovers.

She had to give her mom credit. Though the noodles were premade and the gravy likely came from a jar, she didn't point out either. Then again, maybe she was still too focused on her anger at her daughter to point out what she certainly perceived as her sister's laziness in the kitchen.

"This looks so good," Carol offered.

"Thank you," Ellen said.

Judith didn't say a word as she grabbed the spoon and added a scoop to her plate. She selected a slice of bread and focused on spreading the top with butter. Then she took her time spreading a pink cloth napkin across her lap and taking a sip of water.

Her silence was so pointed and intentional, Carol wanted to scream but was determined to resist the bait her mother was dangling in her face. Instead, she asked her aunt about the painted plates as she served herself. Ellen smiled and started talking about blending and brushes and something else that Carol tried to focus on.

However, her mother's bitterness was louder than Ellen's excitement. Like a moth to a burning building, Carol couldn't help glancing across the table at her mother's stiff posture. Nor could she stop the tension growing in her jaw. She was being drawn in. The urge to respond grew every second. She hated how the temptation to engage always consumed her, but damned if she could stop the need to react.

Finally, she focused on the cold front coming from the

other side of the table. "You're going to throw your back out if you don't relax, Mother."

Judith lifted her face, narrowed her eyes, and flexed her jaw. The battle was on.

"Perhaps I could relax if I hadn't just learned my daughter is insane."

"What do you mean, you *just* learned?" Carol asked with a forced smile. "I've been crazy my entire life, thanks to *you*."

Judith threw her hands up. "Here we go. Poor Caroline was handed everything—"

"Everything that *you* decided to give me. Nothing I asked for, nothing I wanted."

"Nothing you wanted?"

God, she hated when her mother started repeating what she said, as if she couldn't believe the words coming from Carol's mouth.

"We gave you the best clothes, the best piano teacher—"

"I *never* wanted to play piano! How many times did I tell you that?"

"Oh, every time your poor father had to physically drag you to a lesson."

Carol scoffed. "My poor father? Let me tell you something about my poor father—"

Judith's smirk turned into an evil scowl. "You're as spoiled now as you were as a child. The difference is, I don't have to tolerate you anymore."

The words hit their target, as they usually did. A poisoned arrow to Carol's heart. But, as always, she was ready to shoot her own. "You never tolerated me, Mom. You were too busy trying to keep up appearances for your precious social status to even pay attention to me."

Ellen slammed her fists on the table. "Enough! Both of you. I don't know why I bother with either of you. You are both making *me* crazy!" She shoved her chair back as she stood and stormed from the room, leaving Carol with a cloud of shame hovering over her.

Carol looked at her mother, not the least bit surprised that Judith wasn't at all humbled. She was furious, and the glare on her face made it clear she blamed Carol for the entire scene.

"Clean up dinner," Judith ordered, "while I console my sister, and then you come and apologize to her for ruining this dinner she worked so hard to make for you."

"Sit down," Carol stated, outright defying her mother.

"Excuse me?"

"Sit. Down. Aunt Ellen will be fine. You and I, however, need to settle a few things."

Judith remained standing. "I don't think that's a good idea. I'm very upset with you."

"Give me a break," she barked. "You've been upset with me for as long as I can remember."

"Because your defiance is exhausting."

"Where do you think I learned it?"

Judith seemed to consider the question. "I can be stubborn at times."

Carol resisted the urge to snort. Her mother had given an inch, which was more than she usually gave. Ridiculing her for it would be a step in the wrong direction.

"But you…" Judith straightened her shoulders in the way she did to prove she was right. "You're traveling around the country with human remains, Carol. What am I supposed to do with that?"

"Try to understand. Try to be supportive of what I've been through."

Judith shook her head. "Please clean up dinner."

Carol didn't prevent her mom from leaving this time. She looked at the uneaten meal, wondering why the hell she was so determined to put herself, her mother, and her aunt through this. Maybe it was better left alone, like Ellen had said. Maybe she needed to accept that she would never have the mother-daughter connection with Judith that she'd been looking for all her life.

Maybe she needed to give up and put her energy into fixing other broken parts of herself. God knew there were plenty of them.

FOUR

THE TEMPTATION TO return to her RV, to get on the road to her next destination, had Carol tossing and turning all night. In the past, she'd always kept her distance from her mother, stayed away so things couldn't escalate. When they did spend time together, no more than once a year, she'd smile and pretend that her mother wasn't intentionally cutting her to the bone with her snide comments and hard looks. Then she'd be relieved she'd survived and could go another year or so without going through the ordeal again.

However, Carol couldn't think of a time when her broken relationship with her mother was more apparent. She'd always known they were on shaky ground, but having John wake her up from her most recent bout of emotional isolation made her understand how deeply the cracks beneath them ran. If she left Florida without making amends, she likely never would.

After a restless night on the too-soft couch in Ellen's

studio, Carol rolled to a sitting position and debated if she wanted to go for her morning run. With her mood already dark, the deliberation reminded her of another time she chose to sleep in instead of getting up to exercise.

The morning Tobias had been hit by a truck.

He'd tried to wake his wife, but she'd pulled the covers over her head as she rolled away from him. She'd been restless the night before, stressing about a big presentation for work she wasn't prepared to give. Instead of resting, her brain had been distracted by incomplete slides and points she hadn't wanted to forget.

That morning, sleep was more important to her than going for a run before work. She hadn't opened her eyes. She hadn't looked at him one last time. She hadn't even said goodbye to him.

Tobias had smacked her behind through the plush comforter, told her she was lazy, and then he left. He took their morning run without her.

And he never came home.

He'd left their bed, their home, and this world without her.

She should have been there.

The familiar guilt and depression filled Carol. Tears burned her dry eyes. Hurt pressed down on her chest until inhaling became difficult. The images she had created filled her mind—Tobias running, a truck speeding through the fog, the sound of metal hitting his body, his bones cracking as he slammed to the ground. Him lying there twisted and broken. She didn't want to see the scene she'd created play out in her mind, but she couldn't stop it. Her memories, even those she'd invented, had a way of playing on repeat.

Biting her lip until she could no longer ignore the self-inflicted pain, she used the sensation to reconnect with the present. The pain would help her ward off the anxiety that was starting to make her heart race. If she didn't focus on the apprehension, the feeling wouldn't consume her.

She'd felt this way a thousand times since losing her husband. Some days the loss punched her gut harder than others. But this gut punch was followed up by a second—an acknowledgement that despite her mother and aunt being so close, she felt as alone in her grief as she had when she'd walked into Tobias's hospital room and known he'd never recover.

Instead of seeking reassurance from her family, she crossed the hall to the half-bath. After brushing her teeth, she splashed water on her face and stared at her drawn and pale reflection. The lack of sleep and the stress of fighting with her mother had left dark circles and bags under her eyes. She looked older than she should, more haggard. And broken. She looked so incredibly broken.

Carol wiped her face and returned to the spare room. Mary Denman wasn't her birth mother, but she was the closest maternal connection Carol had. The woman had taken her in, loved her unconditionally, and had never failed to be there for her. From the time Tobias had introduced Carol to his family, they had treated her like one of their own.

So Carol didn't hesitate to grab her phone and dial Mary's number, despite the early hour.

"Hey, baby," Mary said, her voice clear but concerned. "You okay?"

Carol swallowed, not wanting to answer until she could force away the sob building in her chest. "I woke up with it again."

It didn't need a name. *It* was the survivor's guilt her court-appointed therapist had tried to help her process. *It* had been the reason she'd needed a court-appointed therapist.

After a particularly bad day, Carol had taken a tire iron to the road where Tobias had landed after being slammed by an oversize pickup truck. Someone witnessed her violent breakdown and called the police. She'd been arrested, but her attorney managed to get the charges dropped with Carol's agreement to attend three months of grief counseling.

Three months hadn't been long enough, but she hadn't gone back. By then, she'd managed to work her way into the void that had always provided empty comfort. The disconnection she'd managed to slip into gave her the ability to watch her life from the outside but never fully engage. She was safe in that dark place.

Facing John had yanked her from her detached state, and she was determined not to sink back there, despite how the old coping mechanism was calling to her. The quiet solitude of numbness was beckoning her back. She could put up walls the way her mother had taught her to. She could turn off her emotions, walk away from all this struggle and pain, and simply...*exist*. She could exist. Peacefully. Without confrontation. Without the hurt.

However, she'd come to realize that existing wasn't the same as living.

Tobias would want her to live. Living was filled with challenges and conflict. And her mother.

"I'm sorry," Mary said. "I know how hard that is for you. Where are you?"

Carol scanned the room. The colorful paintings that usually caught her attention were mere hangings on a wall. "I'm visiting my mom."

"Oh." The short sound was a mixture of sympathy and understanding. Mary was more than aware of the prickly relationship Carol had with Judith. "How are things going?"

Tears hit Carol as she laughed wryly. "Guess."

"Honey—"

The tone—half warning, half pleading—was one Carol recognized. Mary was going to try to talk her into giving up, into putting her mental health and inner peace first. She didn't expect Mary to understand why she couldn't do that. Mary saw this situation from her maternal point of view. She didn't want to see Carol hurt.

"I have to do this, Mary. I have to leave here knowing I did my best to fix this."

"Can it be fixed?"

Carol debated before answering, "I don't know. She's my mom. I have to try."

Mary didn't disagree. "Don't break yourself trying, Carol. You've come a long way in your recovery."

Recovery was code for coming to terms with being a widow. They hadn't consciously agreed on the term. The word had evolved in a way they'd both silently accepted and understood without ever defining. Recovery might indicate healing from an addiction or an injury to most, but for Carol recovery meant learning to live without the other half of her soul.

"I know," Carol said softly.

"I commend you for trying, baby, but don't let anyone undo the progress you've made. Including your mother."

Carol gave in to a hint of a smile. Mary would never say a bad word about Judith, but the clip she used when she said "your mother" made her feelings clear. "I wanted to make things right, but as soon as I'm around her... God, she gets under my skin."

"She always has. What's going on?"

Leaning back on the couch, Carol frowned. "She pokes me. I poke back. Then things blow up, and I apologize because she's incapable even when she should. And then we start all over again."

"Something triggered this setback. Something bigger than poking. What happened?"

The wound Judith had inflicted the night before started to throb. "We were bickering, and she told me that I'm spoiled and she doesn't have to tolerate me anymore."

Mary was quiet, and Carol suspected she was considering her response. "Now that you aren't a child, you have the power to push back when she makes you feel less than you are. That's not you being spoiled. That's you standing up to her. You're allowed to stand up for yourself."

"I'm not standing up for myself as much as simply sinking

to her level and lashing out. I let her goad me into behaving like a spoiled child, and then she can feel better about herself because I've proven her right."

"Recognizing the pattern is the first step to breaking it."

Carol grinned at the statement. "That sounded incredibly clinical."

"Fine. Old habits are hard to break. How's that?" Mary's soft laughter filtered through the phone.

The light moment didn't last. The cloud of depression hovering over Carol was too thick to be so easily dismissed. "I want to break it," she said. "I do, but I can't do this alone. She has to meet me halfway."

"Have you told her that?"

"No."

"Well, you have to," Mary said. "You can't expect her to read your mind, and you know damn well she's not going to take the first step. If you want to make this better, you have to do all the work until she reciprocates."

"I know."

"I wish I could give you a hug."

Carol's smile returned. Mary's hugs were the best. Getting a hug from Mary was like being wrapped in a warm blanket fresh from the dryer on a chilly morning. Very few things brought that kind of comfort to Carol these days. "I wish you could too." Sitting forward, she rested her forehead against her hand. "I wish a lot of things, you know."

"I know," Mary said.

Neither had to go down the list. She wished Katie were still alive. She wished she and Tobias could've had a family.

She wished her husband hadn't gone for a run that day or that she'd been with him. She wished she could go back in time to when things felt right. And good. And she had love and happiness and hope in her heart.

They didn't have to go down the list. They'd done so many times before.

"When will you come see me?" Mary asked, distracting her.

"Soon. I won't be here much longer. I had planned to travel up the East Coast, but I don't have a schedule. I can head your way if you want."

"You know I want you here. I'm worried about you."

"I know. I'm sorry. But I am doing better than I was six months ago. I promise."

Again, there was a long silence. "We're coming up on a year soon. That's going to be hard for both of us. I have Elijah to get me through."

Carol closed her eyes as she pictured Tobias's younger brother. Elijah had stepped up and become the rock she and Mary were missing now.

"Who's going to take care of you?" Mary continued.

Carol had managed to stop counting the days she'd been without Tobias, but Mary was right. The year anniversary of his death was closing in, likely contributing to the raw nerves her mother was so easily grating. "We'll see where I'm at."

"I don't want you to be alone on the road."

Taking a cleansing breath, Carol let it out slowly. "I agree. That wouldn't be good for me."

"So come home, baby. I'll get your room ready."

Carol closed her eyes against the newest round of tears forming in her eyes. Her room used to be Tobias's room. He'd grown up sleeping in that room, and when they went back to St. Louis to visit his mother, it had been their room. Now it was *her* room. The room where Mary had put the boxes of photos and keepsakes Carol couldn't part with when she'd packed up the house.

Her room, which had felt so empty the last few times she'd slept there. Even so, that room was far more welcoming than where she'd slept the night before.

"I have to do my best to fix things here, Mary. If I leave without resolving the issues I have with my mother, I don't think I'll ever come back. I don't want to resent her like this forever. I have to try."

"Okay," Mary whispered. "Okay. But if that woman drags you down any further than you are right now, I'm coming for you myself. You hear?"

A light laugh left Carol, mostly because she didn't doubt for a moment that Mary would show up at the door, demanding she leave. "I hear. I love you so much, Mary."

"I love you."

"I am glad that I have you. You've gotten me through some really tough times. I wish...I wish I could have grown up with a mom like you. I wish I'd had you when I was younger. I wouldn't be so screwed up."

"You have me now, baby. I'm gonna take care of you."

Carol knew that to be true. Mary always took care of her. "I'll see you soon."

"Bye-bye."

She ended the call and wiped her face again. As she turned, intending to set her phone on the end table next to the couch, she froze. She hadn't heard her mother enter her room, but the anger on Judith's face implied she'd been standing there long enough to hear at least part of Carol's exchange with Mary. She replayed the conversation in her mind, confirming that she had indeed wished she'd had a different mother growing up.

Judith had a mug in her hand. The scent of the hot drink drifted toward Carol. Coffee.

Judith didn't drink coffee. She drank tea. However, Carol drank coffee by the gallon. Her mother had been bringing her hot coffee and, in turn, overheard her daughter wishing someone else had raised her.

Damn it.

"Mom—"

"I brought you..." Judith started. "I wanted to..." Instead of finishing, she turned and walked away, leaving Carol alone with even more guilt.

———

Carol was hoping this wedding would be different. She and Tobias weren't rushing to the courthouse to get married before anyone realized she was pregnant. He'd proposed to her when they'd moved into an apartment together after graduation. He'd told her he wanted to plan for their future.

She'd spent months finding the perfect dress and the right ballroom for the reception. She had friends to be her bridesmaids.

This was a real wedding. Yet, her parents still held the same lack of enthusiasm now as they had years ago when she'd married John. She supposed she should be happy they'd accepted the invitation this time. Neither had bothered to show up when she'd exchanged vows with John. They'd been too disappointed in her to offer the support she'd needed.

Though, the way her father rigidly stood next to her made Carol wonder if she'd have been better off without them at this wedding too. Looking down the aisle he was supposed to walk her down during the mock ceremony, she did her best to ignore his discontent. One more sigh from him, though, and she was going to come unglued. She had enough stress on her mind without her father doing that disapproving exhale of his.

"This won't last much longer," she said out of obligation.

"I don't understand why you had to do this," he said.

She jerked her face to his. "Get married?"

"Have this fiasco. You've been married before, Caroline. Carol," he said, sounding even more frustrated. She'd started going by the shortened version of her name almost four years prior, but he still struggled to use it. "There's no need for all this."

Her heart ached. She hadn't believed for a moment he was excited to be there, but this dismissal hurt. Weddings were celebrations of love and happiness. This was important. "This is what Tobias and I want, Dad."

"You've been married before," he stated again, as if her first marriage invalidated the life she'd built since leaving Dayton.

She forced her anger down. "Tobias hasn't. This is for him and his family."

That long exhale of his raked over her nerves again. Part of her wanted to tell him to leave. Take his frigid wife with him and go. Judith hadn't been any more enthusiastic than he had. When she'd told her parents Tobias had proposed, a long pause filled the air before her mom clicked her tongue and asked if Carol thought that was a good idea.

Carol had been taken aback. She hadn't been expecting that reaction. But then her mom went in for the kill.

"You didn't do so great at your last marriage," Judith had said. "Do you really think you should try again so soon?"

Carol jerked as if she'd been slapped by her mother's words. "I've been divorced for almost four years."

"That's not so long, really."

"Tobias isn't like John."

"Thank goodness," Judith muttered. "What about school? You said you were going to finish your doctorate."

"I plan to. So does Tobias."

"Perhaps you've forgotten how quickly plans change when you have kids."

Katie. She was taking this moment to remind Carol she'd dropped out of premed to have Katie.

"I haven't forgotten anything. We haven't talked about having kids. We both want to finish school."

"Well," Judith said. "At least this one has plans for his future."

A dig at John for being a lowly policeman. Carol had been foolish enough to think her mother had gotten over all that mess. She should have known better, and she should have known then she would be better off not inviting her parents to her wedding. They wouldn't have even had to know she'd had this big ceremony. Other than her aunt Ellen, no other members of Carol's family had been present. Her side of the church would be filled with the friends she'd accumulated since moving to St. Louis.

"Bring in the bride," someone called.

Dennis frowned and took his spot next to Carol. She put her hand on his arm and did her best to focus on the happy faces, the faces excited to be there practicing for the ceremony.

She thought she'd hidden her hurt well, but as soon as the rehearsal broke up and Mary started directing everyone to the basement for the reception dinner that had been organized, Tobias pulled her aside.

"What's going on?" he pressed.

She smiled and shrugged as if she hadn't a clue what he meant. "Nothing. The stress and—"

"Carol?" Furrowing his brow, he dipped his head enough to stare into her eyes. He did that when he knew there was more to what she was saying. When she was trying to hide her feelings or slip inside her mind. He knew the signs, and he never let her get away with them.

She loved that about him. Sometimes his persistence drove her crazy, but overall, she needed him to push her to open up. She'd spent so much of her life closed off from everyone else, feeling the need to protect herself from the constant disappointments she caused those around her—particularly her parents. Tobias's gentle nudges were required, more times than not, to prevent Carol from shriveling in on herself.

She looked over her shoulder to where her father was waiting for her mother to get her things. "My parents don't want to be here. Did you see them? Neither has smiled once."

"Maybe they're tired from traveling."

"My dad reminded me that I've already been married. I didn't need this fiasco, as he called it."

The concerned crease between Tobias's brows grew deeper. "You don't need it, but you deserve it. We both do. This isn't about them, Carol."

"I know."

"Do you?"

"Yes," she said.

Tobias rested his hands on her hips and pulled her closer, smiling enough to ease the worry on his face. He lowered his voice. "Do you really?"

Carol smiled too. "Yes."

He put his lips to her forehead. She loved when he kissed her there. Forehead kisses made her feel so cherished. She didn't know why, but whenever he did that, her heart seemed to swell. Sinking into his arms, she rested her head on his shoulder as he hugged her against his broad chest.

"This isn't their wedding," he said. "It's ours. This is about what we want. Don't let them take that away from you."

"Okay."

"Yeah?" Tobias asked.

"Yeah."

Draping his arm around her shoulder, he turned her toward the basement. "Good. Now let's get downstairs before Elijah eats everything."

Though the heaviness of her parents' negativity hung in the air, Carol did her best to pretend she didn't know they hated *every minute of their time at the dinner. She pretended they were laughing and enjoying themselves like everyone else.*

As she made her way to the table reserved for the bridal party, she noticed her aunt whispering to her mother. If she had to guess, she'd say Ellen was reminding Judith to act human, but Carol wasn't going to press or try to please her parents. Tobias was right. This was their evening, their wedding. She couldn't let someone else ruin it.

After dinner, Carol was gathering plates when Tobias's mother pulled her aside.

"I know it's supposed to be something borrowed, something blue," Mary said, holding out a box, "but I think this wedding calls for something pink."

Caroline opened the gift and found a silver chain with a little pink heart pendent perched against the satin lining.

"For Katie," Mary said with so much love that Carol almost forgot the woman had never met her daughter. "So she can be here with you tomorrow."

Tears sprang to Carol's eyes at the reminder that she was loved and supported. "Thank you," she whispered, her voice thick from emotion. She wrapped her arms around her soon-to-be mother-in-law and embraced her for a long time. When she pulled back, she sniffed and touched the little heart. "Thank you for always thinking of her."

Mary put her hand to her heart. "I didn't know her, but I'm her grandmother as much as I am your mother. Forever."

The wide smile on Carol's face froze when she noticed her mom standing a few feet away, watching the exchange. "Hey." She lifted the box, ready to show her mother the gift.

"Your father and I are leaving. We're tired," Judith said, her voice clipped.

Rejection. A feeling Carol was used to from her parents but, for reasons she couldn't understand, still had the ability to sting. She felt her smile begin to sag before forcing it back into place. "Okay."

"What time should we be here in the morning?"

"No later than ten, please."

Judith nodded, turned, and walked away.

Determined not to let her mother's cold shoulder ruin the moment, Carol returned her attention to Mary and asked for her help putting on the necklace.

———

As Carol entered the living room, Judith straightened her spine and jutted her chin out. The move was subtle but said so much about where she and Carol stood with each other. They both tended to put up their defenses before the other even spoke. Seeing her mother stiffen her posture, readying for attack, nearly brought tears to Carol's eyes.

"I'm sorry for what I said."

Judith shook her head, as if to dismiss Carol's apology. "You and Mary have always been closer than you and I could ever be. I know that."

Carol stared, saddened by the way her mother tried to be indifferent, as if her daughter having a stronger maternal connection with someone else was normal. There was underlying hurt in that casual brush-off, and for the first time, Carol considered her relationship with Mary might be painful for her mother. Judith had never seemed to have time for her daughter, but putting herself in her mother's shoes, Carol imagined how heartbroken she would be if Katie had wanted someone else to be her mother.

The knife she'd unintentionally shoved into her mother's heart must have felt more like a machete.

"Mary is very important to me," Carol said. "So are you, Mom."

Judith lowered her eyes. "I can understand why you'd rather have her as your mother, Carol. We can't ever seem to see eye-to-eye for more than a minute, can we?"

Carol watched her mother continue to stare at her hands.

This was the part where she had to take the extra steps. "I don't want to keep doing this," she said gently. "I love you. We've never had much patience for each other, but I do love you."

Judith hesitated before saying, "I love you, too."

Carol crossed the room and sat on the other end of the couch. "We don't have to keep going around and around like this. We can break this cycle. But we both have to try. We both have to want this to work."

Judith looked up. Her eyes were as sad as Carol had ever seen them. "I don't know what to do. I don't know how to reach you. I never did."

"I feel the same way. Our entire relationship has been two steps forward, five steps back. I want us to find another way. After losing Tobias and watching John die... Mom, I've lost too many people."

"I know you have." Judith's bottom lip trembled. "I don't know how you've been so strong."

"I'm not." The tears she'd been struggling with since waking burned her eyes again. "I'm so broken inside, and I don't know if I will ever feel whole again. Sometimes I wake up, and the first thing I think about is how I should have been with him. I should have been there beside him. The feeling hits so hard, I can't breathe."

"That feeling isn't because you weren't with him," Judith said. "I was with your father, you know. I wake up feeling the same way sometimes. Wondering how I'm supposed to go on."

"Still?" Carol whispered.

Judith nodded. "Did missing Katie ever go away?"

"No."

"This won't either, but missing him will get easier. Some days dinnertime comes around before I remember. But I always remember."

"I should have been here for you, Mom. I didn't know how."

"I haven't made it easy for you. I'm aware of that."

Rather than acknowledge her mother's failing, Carol offered her a weak smile. "I am doing everything I can to heal, but I could really use my mother right now."

"I...I don't know how to be there for you either, Carol. I never did, did I?"

Moving closer, Carol leaned over and rested her head on Judith's lap. She couldn't remember the last time, if ever, she'd done that. When she was overcome with nausea during her pregnancy with Katie, Frannie would ease her down and stroke her hair until her stomach settled. She'd suffered two miscarriages after marrying Tobias. When she'd cried, Mary would cradle Carol's head on her lap and speak soft, soothing words.

But Carol couldn't remember ever sitting like that with her mother. Judith seemed surprised, hesitating for a few moments before putting her hand to Carol's hair.

Instead of hiding her feelings, as she tended to do in front of her mom, Carol let them go. She let the pain that had been building in her chest rip free as she gripped her mother's robe, crying like a child. Like the child she'd never been allowed to be.

"I don't know how to stop hurting," she said after some time. "I don't know how to fix this."

"Oh, Carol." Judith lightly brushed her hand over Carol's hair. "You can't fix this. You have to learn to live with it. You know that. You've been living with Katie's loss for all these years. You know this pain will never heal, not completely. There will always be something that comes along and reopens that old wound. You have to stop hiding. You've spent so much of your life hiding from everything and everyone. Sometimes you have to face what is."

"I can't keep hurting like this. It's about to consume me."

"And you think driving around the country with two urns is going to make it better?"

Carol fought the surge of frustration she felt at how far Judith had to go to connect those particular dots. "Mom. This isn't about that. This is about how I miss Tobias so much I can't think sometimes." Turning enough that she could look up at her mom's face, she swallowed hard. "I would normally run with him, but I didn't want to get out of bed that morning. I couldn't sleep the night before, so I told him to go without me. I should have been there."

"What would be different if you'd been there?" Judith asked.

Tears slid from the corners of Carol's eyes. "I used to be a nurse. Maybe I could have saved him."

"Maybe. But the likelihood is you would have been killed too. Have you considered that?"

Carol nodded. She had. She'd considered it a million times. Because that seemed like a better alternative than the reality she was living. "I would have rather I'd been killed than go on like this without him."

A choked sound came from Judith's lips. Part gasp, part hiccup. "*No*. That would have devastated me, Ellen, Mary. Imagine what it would have done to Mary to lose both of you. I saw her at the funeral, Carol. Taking care of you was the thing that kept her going."

Carol put her hand to her face as she started to cry again. The image her mother conjured broke her heart. Mostly because Judith was right. Mary had become focused on getting Carol dressed, fed, rested, hydrated...and anything else she could think of. Carol had appreciated the help but hadn't realized her need for Mary's care had been helping Mary as well. In fact, she'd spent these last months embarrassed that she'd leaned on her mother-in-law so much, knowing how hard it was to lose a child. She'd considered her actions selfish, but perhaps the need had been mutual.

Rolling onto her side, Carol buried her face in Judith's stomach. Part of her expected the woman to shoo her away. This was not a normal practice for them. She'd learned long ago that raw emotions made her mom uncomfortable. However, Judith brushed her hand over her Carol's back and hushed her.

"I'm sorry I didn't do a better job taking care of you when you lost Tobias," Judith said. "I... I guess I thought I should let Mary do it."

Carol bit her lip as she considered the situation. "I don't know how receptive I would have been, to be honest. Angry as I was, I think I would have taken that out on you without meaning to."

Judith let out a wry laugh. "Carol, we *always* take things out on each other. It wouldn't have been anything new, would it?"

"No. I guess not. But my anger during that time was ugly, Mom. It's best that Mary was there for me then, but I really need you now."

Though the few pats that Judith put on Carol's shoulder were stiff, she appreciated them. This was probably the most maternal moment they'd ever had, and she was going to soak it in because, given their turbulent history, this might never happen again.

FIVE

NO MATTER HOW MANY DEEP, cleansing breaths Carol took, she couldn't clear her mind. Sitting in half-lotus, inhaling and exhaling, she did her best to focus on nothing. A breeze caused a few strands of her hair to dance across her cheek, tickling her until she swiped them away. The grass beneath her began to feel prickly and made her exposed calves itch. The chatter of neighbors enjoying the outdoors on the other side of the privacy fence distracted her.

Focus, damn it, she told herself.

A bug buzzed dangerously close to her face, as if to mock her attempt at ignoring the world around her.

As much as she hated to admit it, she knew why she was having a hard time clearing her mind. She and her mother had taken a huge step forward earlier in the morning. For the first time she could recall, she had hope that they could find a way to connect. Hope, however, could be dashed in a heartbeat. If she could find a way to dismantle the rest of the wall between them before the old cycle started up again, they might be able to have a good relationship. One that wasn't based on bulldozing each other's feelings.

"How long are you going to sit like that?" Judith asked, her voice rife with impatience.

Then again...

Carol opened her eyes and blew out yet another failed attempt at mindful breathing. "I was trying to meditate."

"Ellen and I want to go to the store. We've been waiting for you to come in. And you're just"—Judith gestured with her hand—"*sitting* there."

"That's what mediation is, Mom." Carol pressed her palms into the grass to push herself up to stand and then brushed her hands together. There was nothing to clear away; she needed the distraction to remind herself not to be snippy. She hadn't slept well, she'd had a minor meltdown, and she'd yet to find a way to stop her thoughts from racing back to Tobias's death.

However, she wasn't going to backpedal on the progress she and her mother had made so quickly.

"It wasn't working anyway," Carol said, heading toward the screen door where Judith had appeared.

"What you need is a midmorning margarita," Ellen suggested as she joined Judith.

The scowl that caused Judith's lips to turn downward nearly made Carol laugh. At least she could still find amusement in the nonstop antics of her aunt.

"Only alcoholics drink in the morning." Judith stepped

aside so Carol could slide the screen door open and join them inside.

"And retirees with nothing better to do." Ellen looped her arm around Carol's. "Come on, sweetheart. We'll add limes to the shopping list. I haven't had a fresh margarita in ages."

"She doesn't need a drink," Judith insisted. "It isn't even noon yet."

"She's had a rough morning."

This back and forth would continue, and likely escalate, if someone didn't put an end to it.

"Perhaps with dinner," Carol suggested. "I believe it's my turn to cook. How about chicken fajitas and fresh margaritas?"

Ellen clapped her hands and let out a little squeal, but Judith didn't respond.

"Would you like something else?" Carol asked.

"I don't like spicy food. Or margaritas. You know that." Judith reached for her bag, turning her back on the pair. "You *both* know that."

Instead of pointing out that the fajitas didn't have to be spicy or that no one would force her to drink a margarita, Carol conceded. "Okay. How about steaks and red wine? You like red wine."

"We should get a few potatoes for sides," Judith said.

"And bacon," Ellen added. "I love bacon on potatoes."

When Judith remained silent, Carol tilted her head, waiting for her mother to disagree. Instead, she made a point of skimming over Carol's attire. Glancing down at her gray cropped yoga pants and fitted pink T-shirt, Carol confirmed nothing about her outfit was inappropriate or shocking. Nothing sordid was visible. But she knew that look. Mother didn't approve.

Part of her wanted to push back. She looked fine. Certainly good enough to go to the store. Her outfit was perfectly acceptable. However, for the sake of the growth they'd had, she said, "I'll be right back," and headed toward the spare room to change.

"She looks fine," Ellen said as Carol left the room.

"She looks like a mess."

Carol closed the door on the sisters' debate. Yesterday they'd bickered about the straw hat. Today it was yoga pants and a fitted shirt. Maybe she'd shave her head tomorrow and see what they had to say about that. She could imagine. Her mother would be horrified, and even Ellen would likely have a hard time finding words defending the choice.

After changing into a sundress and sandals, Carol went to the bathroom to freshen up. Though she didn't have much makeup in her arsenal these days, she did add mascara and lip gloss. She brushed out her shoulder-length hair and then took a moment to scan for the ever-encroaching gray strands. She did her best not to obsess, but she was aware of how her eyes were getting more crinkled and a few more age spots had settled on her pale skin.

Thanks to a regular exercise routine, she was fit and trim overall, but her fifty-one-year-old body was starting to show a few undeniable signs of...*maturing*. That was a good word for the subtle changes taking place. The increasing freckles, the deepening lines, the softer waistline, the graying of her hair were all signs of *maturing*.

Carol gave her head a firm shake, intent on dislodging the negativity taking hold. She'd been around her mother for two days and old insecurities were resurfacing already. Her father used to tell her that the dumbest person in the world could seem smart if he wore the right suit. Judith kept the house immaculate on the off chance a neighbor might stop by unannounced.

Cleanliness was no joke in the Stewart household. Outward appearances were taken seriously. Carol had grown up wearing the best clothing her parents could afford. Unfortunately for her, that didn't mean they were the most stylish clothes available. Not that she would have known what to do with stylish clothing during her geeky and awkward youth.

Though she'd done her best to rebuff her parents' ridiculous standards, she'd never quite shaken the need to pay special attention to her appearance and her surroundings. As the years went on, she and Tobias collected beautiful things. Their home was impeccable. She made certain they always had the right suits in the right colors. She knew how to dress to impress, even for casual events, and spent far too much of her budget on salons and shopping.

She'd never considered that might have been because of her parents' expectations of her. She and Tobias had both been executives with big companies. They'd had important jobs and had to look the part. Standing there now, however, less than a month into retirement and already criticizing her unpolished appearance, she had to consider the need to look perfect had been engrained more deeply into her that she'd wanted to admit. That maybe the effort she'd put into her appearance all these years was Caroline whispering in the back of her mind that she still wasn't enough.

"Piss off," she told the nagging voice before walking away from her reflection.

———

Carol's life was finally getting back on track. She was engaged to a wonderful man and had been accepted into a doctorate program. She was going to be a doctor. Like her parents always wanted. For some foolish reason, she thought her mother would be happy for her. She'd called to share her good news as soon as she'd read the congratulatory letter from the school dean, but the silence on the line was tense. Even from several hundred miles away, Carol could sense her mother's disapproval.

"I don't understand," Judith said.

"Don't understand what?" Carol asked.

"You were going to be a pediatrician. I've told everyone how you were going back to school to be a pediatrician."

Carol furrowed her brow with confusion. "Mom, I told you two years ago I needed to change direction."

Carol had been a pediatric nurse for years, but the first time she'd had to treat a patient after Katie died, she'd frozen. The guilt of not being able to save her daughter kept her from even treating someone else's. She'd been transferred to helping adult patients, but she no longer had what it took to be a pediatric nurse. The stress of having young lives depending on her was too much following the trauma of losing Katie.

"But... I thought you'd change your mind, Carol. You always wanted to be a doctor."

"I'm still going to be a doctor," she said.

"Of medical science. What does that even mean?"

Carol sank onto the couch in the apartment she and Tobias were sharing as the excitement faded. Like a child watching her balloon float away, a sense of disappointment settled over her. However, the disappointment wasn't directed at her mother. She was disappointed in herself for letting her mom do this to her again and so soon after discounting her engagement to Tobias.

She had recently told Tobias about Katie and the loss that haunted her every thought. Once she'd opened up to him about that, she was able to tell him about her marriage to John and how he'd spent years thwarting her every attempt at going back to medical school. But after losing her daughter, Carol no longer wanted to be a doctor. She didn't know what she wanted.

Tobias had encouraged her to finish her doctorate, even if she could no longer be a pediatrician. He'd told her that even if the direction had changed, the goal hadn't. She would have thought her parents would be thankful to him for that.

Carol had overcome so much in the last few years. For the first time since leaving Dayton, she believed she could have a future, no matter how empty it might feel without her daughter. She'd found her footing. One might think that would be enough. However, she could hear in her mother's voice it wasn't. Nothing was ever enough.

Why had she bothered making this call in the first place?

"Nothing, Mom," she said softly. "It doesn't mean anything."

"Don't be like that," Judith snapped. "I just don't understand. What are you going to do with an advanced degree in medical science?"

"I don't know." Even if she did know, she wouldn't have shared her plans so her mother could disapprove of them. "Mary is planning an engagement party next month. Do you want to come?"

Judith's dramatic exhale filled the line. "All the way to St. Louis? For a party, Carol? We can't drop everything because you ask us to. I would think you'd understand that by now."

Carol picked at a string on the couch pillow. "I do, Mom. I wanted to ask, that's all."

"If you want us involved in your activities, you should come home," Judith stated.

"My activities? This isn't the debate team. It's a celebration of my upcoming marriage."

Silence.

Carol rolled her head back, knowing what was coming. She closed her eyes and steeled herself. Her parents didn't approve of Tobias. They hadn't outright said they didn't want her to marry him, but she had anticipated the reaction. After the first time they'd met him, her mother chastised her for not warning them ahead of time that she was dating a Black man. Now she was marrying him.

Ever since that first meeting, her mom had been dropping subtle hints that Carol was making yet another mistake. Accepting Tobias's proposal had increased the instances of her mom telling her she needed to come home. She didn't seem to *understand that Carol was home. For the first time in her life, she had a home where she wanted to be. Where she fit.*

"I understand how difficult things have been for you," Judith said. "But that doesn't mean you have to rush into another marriage."

"I'm not rushing."

"How long have you and Tobias been a couple?"

Falling back on the sofa, Carol looked at a crack in the ceiling. "Over a year."

"How long were you with John before you married him?"

John. *Everything always came back to John. They would never let her forget the mistakes of her past. Even when she was making strides to have a better life.* "I have to go, Mom."

"Carol," *she called.*

Carol hung up the phone. Almost immediately, her mother called back. She knew it was her mother. Calling to lecture her for the rude goodbye. Carol didn't answer. She'd had enough of her mother undermining her for one day. Putting her hand to her head, she ground her teeth and forced her tears away. After inhaling to the count of five and exhaling the same way, she read the letter of acceptance again.

Once the phone stopped its second round of ringing, she lifted the handset and punched in the numbers to call Tobias's mother.

"Hello?" *Mary's sweet voice sounded.*

Carol smiled, instantly soothed by the tenderness. "Hey, it's Carol."

"How are you, baby?"

The difference between this and the greeting she'd received from her mother was night and day. Light and dark. Love and obligation.

"Tobias is out with Elijah, but I have to tell someone before I burst," Carol said. "I guess you get to hear the news before he does."

Mary gasped. "Did you get into your program?" Her excitement was real and reignited the pride Carol had initially felt. Before calling her mother.

Closing her eyes, Carol forced away the lingering disappointment from the last call. "I did."

"Oh, Carol! I am so proud of you. Are you home?"

"Yeah."

"Don't you go anywhere. I'm on my way over. We're going to go celebrate."

Carol laughed. "I'll be ready when you get here."

She put the phone in the cradle, and her smile faded. Why couldn't her mom be like that? Why couldn't her mom, just once, be happy for her without judgement? She was tempted to call her mom back, tell her how shitty she was, how she always ruined everything.

Even when Carol had told her about her engagement, her mom had thrown John in her face. Every time Carol brought up Tobias, Judith brought up John. John was in the past. John was a mistake she'd walked away from years ago. She was trying to be better now, do better now. That would be a lot easier if her mother would stop flinging the past in her face.

She'd hoped, by now, her parents would have accepted her ability to do what was right for herself. They hadn't. They never would. Instead of being happy for Carol, they were still trying to *dismantle her so they could put her back together to suit their needs.*

She'd never be a pediatrician, she'd never go back to Dayton, and she'd never walk away from Tobias. She couldn't be what they wanted, and she had to stop trying.

For her own sake.

———

"Why are you still up?" Judith asked as she walked into the living room.

Carol finished topping off her third glass of wine—which was two too many. "Couldn't sleep."

Easing onto the other end of the sofa, Judith watched her take a drink before asking, "Thinking about Tobias again?"

"Always," Carol said with a wry smile. "It was almost a year ago now. Seems like yesterday."

"I'm sure you know this, but time does make this hurt a little less."

Unfortunately, she did know that. While she never got over the loss of her daughter, time did help ease the crushing pain.

"Is the TV too loud? Did I wake you?" Carol asked, hoping to redirect the conversation before she got even more depressed.

"You're the only one in this house who doesn't need hearing aids. I couldn't hear it if I wanted to."

Carol grabbed the remote. Even if Judith couldn't hear the rerun of *The Golden Girls*, she turned the volume down. Carol hadn't been listening anyway. The TV was on for noise. For pretend company. Now that her mom was sitting with her, she didn't need the sitcom.

"It's late, Carol," Judith said. "You should try to sleep."

"Why are you up?"

"Call it mother's intuition. I suspected I'd find you sitting here."

Carol sipped her wine. It wasn't mother's intuition as much as knowing Carol had suffered from restlessness most of her life. Even as a teenager, her problems would fill her mind the moment she tried to sleep. She'd roll things around and around until she'd give up and crawl out of bed to write in her journal. Sitting here was pretty much a given after the way she'd started the day.

"What's on your mind?" Judith asked.

"Too much, I suppose."

"Well, that's vague. Perhaps if you could narrow it down, we could find a way for you to let it go enough that we can sleep."

Carol thought that was her mom's attempt at being light. The slight curve on the woman's lips was almost a smile. The oddity of the moment almost silenced Carol, but the memories that had been nagging overruled and the words tumbled out of her. "Did Dad ever get over the fact that I married a Black man?"

Judith jolted slightly, clearly surprised by the directness of the question. "Oh, Carol." She used that same dismissive tone whenever her daughter presented her with a truth she didn't want to see.

"I'm serious, Mom. He never accepted my marriage. He never liked Tobias, and I have no idea why. Tobias was a wonderful man."

"Tobias was a very good man. We never denied that. Your father was..."

"An asshole?" she said without thinking.

Judith scowled at her. "Don't speak about him like that. No matter what you think about him, he was your father and did his best to give you a good life."

Carol pressed her lips into a frown too. "I've had too much to drink. My filter isn't in place."

Judith looked at the wineglass in Carol's hand but didn't comment. She didn't have to. They'd selected a nice Cabernet Sauvignon to go with their rib eyes. Ellen and Judith each had a glass with their meal. Carol had just poured the rest into her glass. Though her day had gotten tremendously better, Mary's reminder that they were creeping up on a year without Tobias had echoed around her brain all day. Catching up to her when she least expected it.

Reminders that Katie had died tended to do the same. Carol would be perfectly fine, and then she'd feel as if a fist had squeezed her heart, Katie's sweet voice would fill her ears, and grief would overcome her without warning. Tobias's loss was like that sometimes. She'd hear his voice from the other room and her heart would drop to her stomach. Then she'd realize she couldn't have heard him, and her tears would start.

"I was going to say that your father was old-fashioned," Judith said, pulling Carol from her thoughts. "He had strong ideas of how things should be, and you always went against the grain. He thought you did it to spite him."

"Dad thought I married Tobias to spite him?"

"No. But I think..."

"What?" she asked, though she wasn't sure she really wanted to know.

Judith focused on the TV and shook her head. "I think you were too strong, even as a child, to conform to your father's demands. What he saw as defiance was you trying to be your own person. You were never a bad child, Carol. You were just...strong-willed."

Carol snorted. "Never a bad child? Are you kidding me, Mom? I couldn't have been a *better* child. Nothing was ever good enough for him."

"That's not true."

"It is true. Everything I did set the bar higher, further out of my reach. He was never satisfied."

Her father's scowl had been a permanent fixture in their home. A constant reminder to do the right thing or face his wrath. When he'd died, part of Carol was relieved. Not that he was gone but that the weight of his constant disappointment in her could start to fade. However, she'd soon learned that Dennis Stewart's discontent was engrained in her DNA. She hadn't escaped it even after he'd left this world. The fear of displeasing him hung over her, even now.

"He was proud of your accomplishments," Judith said. "Each one proved to him that you could do more, be better. If you'd tried harder."

"That's the point," she stated, focusing on the woman next

to her. "I don't think either of you realized how hard you pushed me to reach unrealistic standards. When I eventually broke free, you acted like I lit your world on fire because I refused to continue playing your game. John—"

"I've heard enough about John, young lady." Judith exhaled that preemptive-argument sigh, the one filled with so much frustration she barely seemed able to contain it. "You had so many talents. You succeeded at everything you tried. Everything came easy to you. Your father saw that too, and he wanted better for you. He wanted you to want better for yourself."

Carol shook her head. She didn't need to be better. She had been happy. She'd found a good life. In fact, she'd found more happiness than a lot of people, despite the traumas she'd been through. Her parents had still tried to make her feel bad about herself and the choices she'd made.

"I envied your strength, you know," Judith said after a few moments. "The reason you two could never get along was because you're so stubborn, just like him. I've never seen two people more determined to fight each other than you and your father."

Carol lifted her glass in a halfhearted toast. "Don't cut yourself short, Mom. You'd disagree with me if I said the sky was blue."

Judith reached across the length of the sofa and took the glass from Carol's hand. "I think you've had enough of that. Your tongue is getting away from you." As she put the glass on the end table next to her, she said, "We've had a good day. Let's not ruin it."

That was a statement Carol couldn't disagree with. They'd spent the day together without too much bickering. They'd eaten dinner and even had a few laughs. This day had been a rarity, and she didn't want it to end in a fight. "We did have a good day. I hope we have more days like today."

"Me too," Judith said.

Without a wineglass to distract her, Carol looked down at her wedding bands. "Dad didn't want to be at my wedding," she blurted out without thinking. "I remember that. I remember how much he didn't want to be there."

"He was never comfortable in those types of settings. All the people and the fuss. That wasn't about you."

"My marriage wasn't acknowledged in his obituary," Carol pressed. "Tobias wasn't even mentioned. Why did you leave him out?"

Judith tilted her head. "You think your husband was deliberately omitted from your father's obituary?"

"Wasn't he?"

Another heavy exhalation drifted from the other end of the couch. "I asked a friend from church to take care of the obituary while Ellen helped me plan the funeral. She didn't know anything about you besides your name. By the time I got back to her with more information, she'd already sent the obituary off to the paper. She did me a favor because I was beside myself with grief. No one deliberately left Tobias out, Carol. You were so far removed from our lives for so long, our friends didn't even know you. Even before you moved away, we rarely saw you."

"Dad didn't want to see me, Mom. He made that clear."

Judith stared at her for several seconds. "I know we were hard on you growing up. We could have been kinder, but you were loved. Even when we didn't approve of what you were doing. You and Katie had dinner with us at least once a week until you started working nights. We would have had you over more, but your weekends were always about John."

"Well, he was my husband."

Judith clutched her hands in her lap. "You can try to deny it all you want, but he changed you, and not for the better. You had a bright future ahead of you, and he dimmed it."

"Oh, Mom. The only thing John did was make me realize there was more to life than trying to be something I wasn't. It's taken me fifty *freaking* years to start to peel away the layers of my life and realize that..."

"What?"

Carol shook her head. "Nothing."

"Spit it out," Judith stated. "It's taken you fifty years to realize *what*?"

Did she dare say it? Put voice to the sad understanding she'd recently started to make? "That you didn't know how to be...a mom."

Judith stiffened and pressed her lips together.

"I'm not saying that to be mean. I know you tried, but you took your cues from Dad, and he was...*cold*. He was rigid and kept himself at arm's length my entire life. I never really knew him. You know that? He's gone, and I never knew him."

Turning enough to look right at her daughter, Judith said, "Your father wasn't cold. He kept his emotions in check because that's what he was taught. Men were supposed to

117

provide for their families and be pillars of strength." She hit her fist on her knee for emphasis. "He grew up in a time when men weren't supposed to show feelings, Carol. Do you know I was with that man through so much, so many ups and downs, and the one time I saw him cry was the night Katie died? His heart was so broken, he wept. He *wept*. He loved that little girl so much."

"We all loved her," Carol said softly.

"He was devastated when you took her urn and disappeared. I don't think he ever recovered from that. You were gone for days before even calling us. We didn't know what had happened to you. We were worried sick. You were in no state of mind to be on your own, and you vanished without a trace. Mark and Frannie were beside themselves with worry. They deserved better than that, Carol. We all did."

Carol lowered her face. She hadn't considered anyone else when she left. She'd been in so much pain, so scared of what the future held without her daughter, that she'd had to get away. From everything. Especially John. But also because she didn't have the strength for what she knew was coming— her parents would have put the blame on her. They may not have vocalized it, but they would have made certain she knew they held her responsible for Katie's death. She couldn't handle that.

When John resurfaced months ago, he made her face how selfish she'd been to slip away in the night with Katie's remains. Even after he'd pointed out how wrong she'd been, she'd never felt ashamed of her decision. She'd always felt justified in leaving John like she had. But, even then, she hadn't considered the ripple effect to the rest of their family.

"All we knew," Judith continued, "was that you'd taken Katie's urn and left. You didn't even give us a chance to see her. You didn't give us a place to visit her. How do you think that made us feel? Katie was our grandchild. No matter what you and John had been through or what you were going through, she was *our* grandchild. And we didn't get to mourn her. You took that away from us."

Tears welled in Carol's eyes and fell before she could blink them away. "You're right. I didn't think about what that would do to anyone else. I needed to get away, so I left. I'm sorry, Mom. I was in a *really* bad place."

"I know that. And your father knew that, but he..."

"He what?"

"To be honest, he never found a way to come to terms with what you'd done," Judith said softly. "I don't think he handled it well."

After wiping her cheeks, Carol dragged her hand over her pajama bottoms. "So it wasn't Tobias he couldn't stand the sight of, it was me?"

"That's a harsh way to put it," Judith said.

"But accurate?" When Judith didn't agree or disagree, a lump formed in Carol's throat. "I snapped when Katie's urn arrived. John opened the box and unwrapped this little silver container. All I could think was that my daughter was in there. My daughter that *he* took away from me, and I broke. If I had stayed in the house with him one more minute, I would have... My God, Mom, I think I would have literally killed

John. I think I would have slit his throat and watched him bleed to death and not done a thing to help him."

"Well, if anyone ever deserved to be mercilessly murdered, it was that bastard."

Looking at her mom, Carol didn't voice her shock at hearing the anger in the words. For the first time, she was starting to understand why Judith couldn't fathom her willingness to forgive John. "Maybe some of the anger you're dumping on John is actually at me. Have you thought of that?"

Judith blinked before meeting Carol's eyes. "I admit there were times I thought that if you had only listened to me…"

"She would still be alive?"

"Yes."

"I've thought it too." Carol gnawed at her lip for a few seconds. "Even if I'd left John, he would have had visitation. I couldn't have stopped him from seeing her. There is no way to know what would have happened. If she'd still be with us. I've played this game a thousand times. I've nearly lost my mind playing this game. The only thing I've realized is that I've always felt guilty and ashamed for the role I played, even if it was passive."

Judith visibly sagged. "I understand why you did what you did, but we all felt her loss, Carol. You were the only one who got to be with what was left of her, and that wasn't fair to us."

The reality of how selfish she'd been hadn't really sunk in. She felt bad she'd taken Katie's remains from John. That he'd had to hunt her down in the last weeks of his life to properly say goodbye to his daughter. But Carol hadn't allowed herself to think beyond John. To his parents. Both of whom died years ago, having never seen Katie's urn. And her father. She'd never—not once—thought about how her father must have felt. She'd always considered him too shut off, too cold to care.

The cool and aloof Dennis Stewart sobbing over the loss of his granddaughter had never occurred to her. The image in her mind broke her heart.

"I'm sorry," she choked out. "I'm so sorry, Mom."

Judith scooted closer and put her hand on Carol's. "I'm not trying to make you feel bad. I just want you to know that despite his flaws, your father wasn't a hateful man. You two never saw eye-to-eye on anything. You both went in different directions simply to spite the other. From the time you were little, you were like that. But he loved you, Carol. You know that, don't you?"

She closed her eyes against the sting of fresh tears. "I don't think I do. I don't think he loved me very much at all."

"He was a difficult man to understand, but he did love you. And he was so proud of you. He didn't show it well, but you meant the world to him. I know you loved him, too, even if you spent most of your life frustrated with him."

Frustrated was a vast understatement. She spent most of her life infuriated with him. However, yes, sitting there with her mother, having a real heart-to-heart conversation with her, Carol felt love for her father, maybe even the first hints of forgiveness. She wiped her face, but fresh tears fell as she reached for a tissue. She couldn't remember the last time she'd cried in front of her mother before today, now she couldn't seem to stop. "This is all coming to the surface now that I've lost Tobias, and I'm trying to process it. I don't know how. I have too much pain, and I don't know how to find the way out."

"Oh," Judith sighed. "Come here."

Carol leaned over and, much like she'd done earlier in the morning, rested her cheek on her mom's thighs as she cried. She closed her eyes and bit her lip, trying to regain control as Judith stroked Carol's hair from her wet cheeks.

"Is this going to be our new normal?" Judith asked.

A mix of a cry and a laugh pushed from Carol's throat. "If so, we're going to need more wine."

"And tissues. Come on. Let's get you to bed."

"No, Mom. Please. Don't...don't push me away."

Judith froze for a moment. "I'm not pushing you away. You need to get some sleep."

Carol didn't sit up. "I don't want to go back there."

"Go back where?"

"Where I was when John found me. Alone and hard and angry. I'd rather be like this than like..."

Judith frowned. "Than like me?"

"I was going to say like Dad."

"I wish you could find it in your heart to go easier on him, Carol. Maybe someday you'll see how hard he worked to give you what you had."

"I know he did. But I didn't want all those things, Mom. I wanted him to be proud of me."

"He was." She brushed Carol's hair. "He may have had faults, but he was proud of you and he loved you."

Carol sniffled. "I hope so."

Judith grabbed the blanket from the back of the couch and tucked it around Carol. "Close your eyes. Try to stop overanalyzing everything."

"Oh, that's never gonna happen," Carol said even as she let her eyes drift shut.

SIX

CAROL KNEW BETTER than to drink too much. She hated how too much wine made her head throb the morning after. She had a low tolerance for alcohol on a good day, but three glasses of wine mixed with the high amount of emotions she'd been feeling lately had left her with a harsh hangover. Her entire body felt the vibrations of each heartbeat.

Ellen set a cup of coffee on the table in front of her and leaned down to kiss her head. "Another restless night?"

"Drank too much."

"I assumed you were the culprit behind the empty wine bottle on the end table."

She offered her aunt a weak smile. "I'll clean it up."

"Already did," Ellen said. "What brought on this round of gluttony?"

"My brain is my worst enemy. But the upside is Mom and I had another good chat."

"That's wonderful, Carol. I'm happy for you." Ellen sat

across from her and lifted her brows. "What was this one about?"

"Dad. Tobias. Katie. Katie's urn, to be more specific." Now that she was clearer minded than the night before, shame settled into her soul. "How I took Katie without letting anyone grieve."

Ellen nodded. Clearly, she'd heard about this particular resentment long before Carol had. "That was hard on your parents."

Damn it. The day was too young to start stirring up Carol's emotions. She mentally stepped back from the guilt and depression trying to take hold. "I see that now. I was too caught up in my own pain to think of anyone else. I had to save myself before I went insane."

Reaching across the table, Ellen rested her hand on Carol's. "No one ever blamed you for doing what you had to do during that time, sweetheart, but others were impacted by your choice to leave in ways you probably didn't realize. We all hurt for Katie's loss. Not nearly as deeply as you, but we hurt too. We were scared for you and what you were going through. Nobody knew how to be there for you."

Carol turned her palm up and entwined their fingers. Her aunt's hands were thin, the skin soft as Carol ran her thumb across it, mesmerized by how close to the surface the blue veins seemed to be. She traced one vein before bringing herself out of the trance with a few rapid blinks. "I had a lot to work through before I could open up to anyone about what had happened. Tobias and I were together for over a year before I even told him about Katie. I was scared he'd judge me, hate me as much as I hated myself. Even after I told him, I had such a hard time sharing her with him. I felt like she was a secret I had to keep so I didn't lose her."

"I understand that. Sometimes sharing feels like letting go."

"I'll never forget John's reaction to seeing her urn again." Her voice sounded flat to her ears, but that tended to happen when she dissociated from her feelings. "He was so shaken he fell to his knees crying. Seeing him like that broke my heart."

"I'm sure that wasn't easy. Nothing about what happened was. There was no right way for you to recover. You did what you had to. I'm sure even John understood that in his way."

Carol nodded enough to show Ellen that she'd heard her reassurances. "Looking back on things now, I have to consider that I didn't run away simply to recover. I think part of me was punishing John. He took her from me, so I took her from him. That wasn't right."

"There was no right or wrong. There was just a whole lot of pain. If John were still alive, I'd hunt him down and kick him square in the ass for putting you through this again."

Carol laughed wryly. "Oh, Aunt Ellen, he didn't put me through anything I wasn't already going through. I'd never come to terms with losing Katie."

"You never will, Carol. But if you keep finding ways to blame yourself, you're going to lead yourself to a very dark place."

"I've been in a very dark place for a long time," Carol admitted. "Part of me never left that place, not even for Tobias. I put the darkness away, found a place in the back of my mind to keep it, but I never left. Without him here, keeping me going forward, it's been pulling me back. I think that started even before John showed up."

"This sounds an awful lot like depression, Carol. Maybe it's time to talk to someone." Ellen spoke softly, gently, as if she expected the suggestion to ignite a fire.

"I'm talking to my favorite aunt."

"I meant a professional," Ellen said, unmoved by the flattery. "I think you need to talk to a therapist, honey. There's no shame in that, especially after what you've been through in this life."

"I know there's not, but..."

"You can stay here with us. Let us help you process all this grief. I'll keep your mother at bay as much as you need."

"Aunt Ellen—"

"I'll take care of you so you can focus on getting well."

Carol squeezed her hand to stop her from rambling. "I must seem pretty far gone to you."

"That's not what I'm saying—"

"I know what you're saying, and I understand where you're coming from. I appreciate your concern, which, by the way, is completely founded. I'm not saying you're wrong. I probably would benefit from speaking to someone." Sitting back, Carol considered what to say next to try to ease the worry on her aunt's face. "Forgiving John changed me in ways I still don't understand. He made me take a good look at myself, and I didn't like what I saw. Not just how frozen in time I'd become, but how..." She laughed lightly and then whispered, "How much I'd become like them."

Ellen tilted her head, confused for a moment before whispering back, "Your parents?"

Carol nodded. "I was completely dissociated. I'd been going through the motions for so long, I didn't even recognize myself anymore."

"Grief does that."

"It wasn't all grief, Aunt Ellen. That's how I was raised. Stand back, don't get invested, don't feel too much, don't show emotion. I was able to break free from that when I had Tobias, but once he was gone, I fell back into the same old behaviors. I was losing myself behind the wall Mom taught me to build. Behind the numbness Dad instilled in me. I don't want to be like that, but that's exactly where I was a few months ago. A shell going through the motions, angry at the world for betraying me."

"Carol," Ellen said, her voice almost a plea. "You lost your husband in an unexpected and tragic way. You're allowed to be angry. What you can't do is let the grieving process consume you, and honey, you are being *devoured*. I'm worried about you. So is your mother."

"I don't mean to make you worry. I know this must look incredibly destructive to you, but I swear, I'm okay. I'm going through some things, but I'm okay."

"Going through some things? You're putting yourself through a meat grinder, expecting to come out whole on the other side."

Judith had said something similar the night before. Carol was going to have to find a way to explain herself if she expected to ease their minds. At the moment, however, all she could think was to ease the concern in Ellen's eyes.

"The best cheeseburgers in the world have gone through a meat grinder a time or two," she said lightly.

"Don't be a smartass," Ellen said, even though her lips twitched with a hint of a smile.

Sitting back, releasing her hold on her aunt, Carol swirled the coffee in her mug. "Mom said that Dad never forgave me for leaving like I did. I wish he would have said so. Maybe we could have mended things."

Ellen rolled her eyes and waved her hand dismissively. "Don't count on that. You know how he was. If he'd told you, it wouldn't have been to mend things. He would have been trying to hold you accountable for something that he would never have let go of anyway. You would have been worse off if he'd said something."

Her aunt was right. That was the man Carol knew. The one who kept a mental ledger of all the ways he'd been wronged. He didn't hold a grudge, he never wanted people to suffer, but he certainly never forgot. People who crossed her father were never given a clean slate. Their misdeeds were always there. She probably knew that better than anyone.

"Why was he like that?" Carol asked her aunt. "Why was he filled with bitterness all the time?"

Ellen shrugged. "Honey, he had a hard life. He lost his parents when he was young and had to take care of his brother. I don't think he ever learned how to relax and take it all in. He was a hard worker and took his responsibly as a provider seriously. You never went without because of that."

"I never went without *material things* because of that," Carol corrected. "But I never had a father. Not really. I think that's why I allowed myself to overlook so much of John's bad behavior. He drank too much and was irresponsible, but he was an attentive father. He was always there for Katie, never hesitating to play with her or read to her." Even now, Carol could remember a thousand different times John had made Katie laugh. Her little cheeks would turn red from giggling so hard. He'd blow raspberries on her belly or lift her up and spin her like an airplane as she squealed.

Carol didn't have a single memory like that with her father. She couldn't even recall a time when he'd sat on the floor and played with her. There wasn't a single memory she had that humanized him.

"I can't remember ever hearing my father laugh," Carol said sadly. "Not once. Not even when I was younger. He was always so stern. So...cold."

"Dennis wasn't the father you wanted," Ellen said, "but he was there. He provided for you and took care of you in other ways."

Yeah, he was there. Scowling. Judging. Making sure she was too scared to step out of line. He never raised a fist, but his raised brow was equally as frightening. Psychological warfare left wounds too, and Carol had plenty of scars to prove that.

"And Mom?" she asked softly. "Why was she so... compliant? He wasn't any kinder to her. I remember her scurrying around the house, making sure everything was in its place before he got home. I think she was as intimidated by him as I was."

To that, Ellen chuckled. "You keep using these terms like hostile and intimidated. Maybe that's how you saw it as a child, but you're older now. Surely, you must see things a little differently. Your mother wasn't intimidated by him. She felt it was her job to make him happy, and he was happy when things were in order. They both were. That's how they liked things. She still likes things in order. You know that."

Carol did know, but she couldn't understand. There had to be more to her mother than what she'd seen all her life. That was the part she was starved to know. After taking a sip of her coffee, she asked, "How is it that the two of you are so different?"

"You think your parents were tough? They had nothing on our parents. When we were growing up, being hard on your kids was far more acceptable than it is these days. Judith got the brunt of it, being the eldest. I learned how to let their disappointments and harsh words roll off my back, but those things cut her. Like they cut you when you were younger. I don't know why some people are more easily hurt than others, Carol, but you were one of those sensitive souls, like your mother. So easily broken."

Carol scoffed. She'd never use *sensitive* to describe her mom.

Ellen continued. "You said you learned how to hide your feelings when you were young because it was safer. Your mother did the same thing. That cycle started long before you were born. I'm sorry you were subjected to it, but because you were, you developed the same coping mechanisms your mother used. Hiding all the hurt away so no one could use it against you. So you couldn't use it against yourself. Your mother's life was easy compared to yours. Stuffing her feelings down works for her. That approach isn't working for you any longer, is it?"

Lowering her face, Carol shook her head. "No. This is the cycle I'm trying to break. I can feel it—that old way of shutting down. Life is so much easier when I don't have to feel anything, but I can't keep hiding like that."

"I'm glad you see the cycle. But you have to remember, just because you've come to this point doesn't mean your mom has too. She's clung to this way of thinking her entire life. She can't change simply because you want her to."

"I know that, but I..."

"You want to be close to her and you feel like you can't because she keeps the world at a distance."

Carol let the words sink in before nodding. "Yeah."

Ellen smiled. "Maybe one of the lessons you need to learn is that being close to her isn't the same as being close to someone else. You and I, we can talk. We can laugh. I can hug you and show you that I love you because that's who I am. I'm comfortable giving affection. Judith never has been. That doesn't mean she doesn't *feel* affection. I wish you could understand the difference."

Rubbing her fingertips into her temples, Carol frowned. This was a fairly heavy conversation to be having under the weight of her hangover. "I do understand the difference. I do. But I guess I always hoped for more, and losing Tobias like I did, facing John, watching him die... We're all on a clock, Aunt Ellen, and we run out of time eventually. I don't want her to run out of time before I know her. *Really* know her."

"That's a wonderful thing to want, and we all need hope. However, we have to accept reality. Judith might not show you love the way you want, but she feels it. Deeply. Stop looking for affirmations the way you want to see them and start looking at the ways she gives them."

Carol dragged her hands over her face. "I wish I could, but her distance hurts me. She makes me feel unloved. Unworthy of her time. Why have I spent my entire life being punished because *she* wasn't loved enough as a child?"

"You're not being punished, Carol. I'm sorry it feels that way. You know that she loves you, don't you?"

She laughed softly. "I know, but I want better for us than this habit we have of showing affection by tearing each other apart. Is that wrong?"

"No, it's not. Just remember things can't always be on our terms, Carol. If you could forgive John and learn to be at peace with him, you certainly can find the same ground with your mother. You simply have to give a little more than you may want to. Can you do that?"

"Yeah, I can do that."

The sound of light footfalls headed toward the kitchen signified the end of the conversation. Ellen pushed herself up and grabbed a loaf of bread as Judith entered the room.

"I wasn't expecting to see you up this early," she said.

Carol sipped her coffee before answering. "I don't like to sleep in."

Judith tilted her head as if considering what she'd said. "Is that because of... Because you blame yourself for not getting out of bed that morning?"

That morning was clearly a reference to Carol's confession to wishing she'd been with Tobias when he'd been killed. "I don't know. Maybe," she said quietly. "I think when I sleep in, I tend to feel more stressed, so yeah, I guess it is." She almost laughed at how surprised she was at her mother's insight. "Sleeping in is a reminder that I wasn't with Tobias."

Judith frowned. However, it wasn't the judgmental scowl Carol usually saw. She looked frustrated, but not at her daughter. At the situation, perhaps. But not at Carol. "You can't change what happened. Depriving yourself of sleep won't help."

"I know. I'm working on accepting that, Mom."

Judith took an apple from the fruit bowl and cut it into slices before sitting at the table. "Do you have plans for today?"

"I think today's the day," Carol said.

"The day for what?"

Carol hoped this wouldn't lead to another battle but braced for one all the same. "I want to take Katie to Disney."

As she anticipated, the air felt as if it had been sucked out of the room. Judith stiffened. Ellen turned, wide eyed, waiting for her reaction.

"I'd like you to be there," Carol said, not waiting for the bomb to go off. "I know you don't agree with spreading her ashes, but I think you'll be surprised how cathartic it can be."

Judith shook her head. "I don't think so."

Carol finished the last of her coffee, letting the conversation linger before continuing. "The first time John and I released her ashes was at the Grand Canyon. Neither of us knew what to do. I'd done a ton of research, of course, because that's what I do. But when the moment came, I was at a loss. We sat on this overlook, staring at this huge canyon, and all I could think about was what Katie would be doing if she were there with us. I could almost hear her talking a mile a minute, asking about everything. So, I asked John to tell her about it. That became our thing. Every stop, he would try to answer all the questions she might have had. How was it made? Why was it made? How big?"

Judith smiled slightly. "She never stopped asking questions, did she?"

"No," Carol said. "You don't have to go, but I want you to know that I would like for you to be there. You can say something if you'd like, but you don't have to."

She pushed herself up and carried her empty mug to the sink. As she passed her mom on the way out of the kitchen, she stopped and put a kiss to the top of her head. "Think about it."

———

Katie was three weeks old. Three weeks. And Caroline's parents still hadn't come to see her.

For some reason, she had expected the birth of her child to be the thing to mend her strained relationship with her parents. She thought they would come to their senses and realize that being disappointed in her wasn't worth holding on to any longer. That hadn't happened. They hadn't called or visited. They hadn't even acknowledged they were grandparents. Caroline tried to blow them off as they had done to her. Tried to brush away the hurt. However, there was a storm brewing inside her. When she woke up after another long night of changing diapers and soothing Katie while John did his best to avoid any responsibility, she was ready to unleash it.

This wasn't about her anymore. She had a child. An innocent baby. Their grandchild!

Yet they couldn't set their pettiness aside long enough to even visit her? No. That was unacceptable.

Marching toward their house with her infant daughter in the carrier, Caroline told herself to be calm. She was a mother now; she couldn't act like a child, despite the urge to stomp her feet and cry out at the unfair treatment she was getting from her parents. That would play into their mentality, anyway. She wasn't going to prove them right. She wasn't going to sink down and play their stupid games anymore. However, she was going to call them out on their behavior.

She reached the door, but instead of walking right in as she'd done all her life, she knocked.

When her mother opened the door, her brow creased with confusion. "Why are you..." Her words faded as she looked down, noticing her granddaughter. The slight quirk of her brow gave Caroline hope that, for once, she had the upper hand.

"Her name is Kathryn. Kathryn Elizabeth Bowman. She was born June fifth. Three weeks ago. We use Katie because Kathryn sounds too proper for a sweet little baby. She sleeps most of the

time, but when she cries, she sounds like a kitten. She lets out these high-pitched squeaks and her face turns red. Sometimes we call her kitty cat because that's what she sounds like, a little kitten. She is your grandchild, and she is amazing. If you would like to meet her, call me to schedule a visit at my home. The one I share with my husband and my daughter." With that, she turned and walked away.

"Caroline," her mother called.

She didn't stop. Her parents had made their point. Now she was making hers. They could be cold and aloof and uncaring. So could she. She'd learned from the best.

She was securing the carrier to the car seat base when she sensed her mother behind her. Turning, she glared as bitter tears stung her eyes. "You don't deserve to know her, but I want you to and you should want to. She's your granddaughter."

"I..." Putting a hand to her stomach, Judith seemed to be searching for how to respond. "I...I..."

"You what?" She waited, hoping her mother would apologize but knowing she would never admit to being wrong.

"This situation has been challenging for all of us."

Caroline shook her head. "No. It hasn't. John's mother really stepped up when you turned your back on me. She took care of me when I was scared and sick. She was there for my wedding and my graduation. You were invited to both, but you didn't show up at either one. She called you when I went into labor. Do you remember that? She was the first person besides John to come see Katie and me. Frannie has been there for me every step of the way. The only challenging thing for me was learning how to balance school and morning sickness, but I did okay because I had John's mom there to help me."

Judith lowered her face. "You never made it easy—"

"It's my fault that you chose to sit on your high horse looking down your nose at me all these months? Really, Mom?"

"Your father... He's still upset."

"If you wanted to see me, you would have. No matter what Dad said." Turning back into her car, she finished securing Katie's carrier into the car seat base.

When she shut the back door and turned, Judith was still standing there. Her shoulders were slightly bowed, her face sagged with what appeared to be concern. Caroline was tempted to back down. She almost said she was sorry for getting angry, for lashing out and making such a scene.

But she wasn't sorry.

Her mother had all but abandoned her, which sounded silly considering Caroline was an adult. The feeling of desertion, however, was strong and it was turning into a burning resentment, building on years of other resentments. If her mom couldn't see how wrong she'd been, if she couldn't find the courage to apologize and to make things right, then to hell with her. To hell with both of her parents.

"Whether you approve of John or not," Caroline said coolly, "he's my husband. The father of my child. I'm going to make a life for us. It's up to you and Dad if you want to be a part of that. If you do, you have to accept that John is family now too. If you can't accept him or the decisions we've made for our life together, then don't bother." She jerked the driver's-side door open, ready to leave.

"Caroline."

Hesitating, she turned enough to look over her shoulder.

"Would...Would you... Does John like pot roast?"

Caroline almost laughed at how difficult saying his name seemed to be for her mother. However, olive branches from her mother were rare, so she held back her sarcastic response and nodded.

"I'd like to... You look tired. I remember how difficult those first few weeks were after I had you. You're juggling a lot, so... I'd like to bring you dinner tomorrow. If that's okay."

"I would like that. Thank you."

Judith peered into the back seat and smiled. "And if it's okay with you, I'd like to meet my granddaughter properly."

Part of her wanted to crumble, to fall into her mother's arms and thank her. She didn't. She didn't trust herself or her mother enough to jump into a reconciliation. She had to tread lightly, step-by-step, to see what path she was being led down.

Instead, she nodded her agreement and climbed into her car. Her tears didn't start until she'd turned the corner and was far enough away that her mother couldn't possibly see how relieved Caroline was that she hadn't been turned away.

By the time she reached the parking lot outside her apartment building, the relief was giving way to something else entirely. Dread.

She looked up at the old building and saw the brick façade through her parents' eyes. While she and John understood their little apartment was temporary, her parents were going to look down their noses at their home. Caroline had worked hard to transform the space from John's bachelor pad to an accommodating home for them. With Frannie's help, she'd cleaned the carpets and the furniture. She'd scrubbed floors and counters until everything was clean.

However, there were dents in the walls from previous tenants. Stains on the carpets that would never come out. The space was small and quickly filling now that they had a baby. Her parents weren't going to see this as a starter home for their daughter. They were going to see this as yet another failure. And she had brought this on herself.

Sitting in the car, with her baby sleeping in the back seat, Caroline rolled her head back and started to quietly laugh. She certainly knew how to screw things up. She should have left the situation alone. Let her parents go on with their lives feeling superior and justified in turning their backs on her. Undoubtedly, that would have been easier in the long run.

However, as soon as her ironic laugh died down, fresh tears formed in her eyes. These weren't with relief that her mother hadn't openly rejected her. These were because they had been right. They'd tried to warn her that her life was going to be a disaster if she stayed with John, and here she was. Her plans for medical school were on hold indefinitely. Her husband had spent half their rent money at the pub and had to crawl to his parents for a loan—one they all knew would never be repaid. And less than a month after she'd given birth, Caroline was scouring the help wanted ads looking for a nursing job that would work with John's schedule because they couldn't afford daycare.

Her parents were right. This was a disaster, and she had walked right into it.

Carol led her mother and aunt through a resort lobby as if they belonged there. Ellen seemed to be excited for the adventure, but Judith hadn't stopped reminding them that they shouldn't be there since the moment Carol parked her aunt's car in the guest parking lot.

"Half an hour, Mom," she'd explained as she'd killed the ignition. "We'll be here for half an hour."

Judith had sat staring up at the fancy resort before climbing from the car and straggling behind. "We're breaking the rules."

"And doesn't it feel good?" Ellen asked with a laugh. She snagged Judith's hand and pulled her along as they walked to the other side of the resort lobby and out to a walkway.

Carol glanced up at the bright blue sky and smiled. Katie had loved sunny days like this. This was the perfect day to leave her at Disney World.

"I don't know about this," Judith said.

Slowing her pace, Carol waited for her mom and aunt to close the small gap between them. "I've looked into this a dozen times. There's a nice walkway between here and another resort. Once we get away from here, there shouldn't be many people."

"We're going to..." Judith's voice faded.

Carol shoved her right hand in her pocket and gripped the little container she had hidden there. Inside was a small amount of Katie's ashes. She'd left John's urn sealed when she'd gone into her RV to collect the remains. Her mom was there for Katie, not John, and Carol respected that. There were plenty of stops she intended to make along the way where John would be included, but this stop... This one was for Carol and Judith to share in saying goodbye to Katie.

"Mom, I promise you, we're not going to be disrespectful to Katie or to anyone here. We'll find a nice place to leave her remains that won't interfere with anyone's vacation. I don't want to harm anyone."

Judith looked around at the families laughing and enjoying themselves. "I know you don't, but this doesn't feel right."

"Would you like to stay here?" Carol gestured toward the resort. "You can find a seat inside and wait. I promise it's okay if you don't want to do this. I know this is hard."

Ellen gave her sister a gentle nudge. "At least walk with us until we find a place, Judith," she said softly. "If you want to walk away while we sprinkle her ashes, you can, but you should see where we leave her."

They began walking again but didn't speak until they were away from the resort, strolling next to a lagoon. Carol smiled as she looked out at the calm water. She'd come a long way in the last few months. In June, when John had found her, she couldn't look at the little manmade pond outside of her office without dread. Now, she was walking next to a lagoon and couldn't help but notice how serene the water was. She didn't feel the dread she'd always felt before.

"She would have loved it here," Carol said.

"This is too close," Judith said, almost sounding panicked. "There're too many people."

Carol resisted the urge to laugh. "I know. I was remarking how much Katie would have loved to be here, in this place."

As they moved away from the rocky shore and around another building, the sounds of children playing grew quieter. The smooth path led them away from the buildings to a path surrounded by greenery and palm trees.

"I remember the first time I held her," Judith said out of nowhere. "She was so tiny. I don't remember you ever being so small."

"She was on the smaller side of average," Carol said. "Until she started eating solids, and then she grew like mad. I swear, she doubled in size in less than a month."

"As soon as she started walking and talking, that child never stopped," Judith said with a shadow of a smile. "She was so much like you, Carol. So strong and determined."

"And here I thought you were going to say smart and adorable." She smiled at her mom to let her know she was kidding. "But you're right. She was very strong and determined. Too much so, unfortunately."

Ellen looped her arm through Carol's. "We're not going to talk about that. Not right now."

"No, we're not," Carol said, lifting her face to the sky again.

The path took a sharp turn, and they all stopped. They could continue along the path to a sandy beach or go straight to where a metal bridge crossed the lagoon. There was also a grassy area. Any of those would be a nice, tranquil, out-of-the-way place to leave Katie's remains.

Carol looked at her mom. "What do you think?"

Judith's lip trembled and she sniffled.

"From the bridge," Ellen quietly suggested. "Katie would have loved that bridge. Don't you think, Judith?"

She didn't answer.

"Mom," Carol whispered, "you don't have to—"

Lifting her chin, Judith straightened her shoulders and seemed to tap into her stubborn side—the one that usually signified the start of a fight. "The bridge." Without another word, she moved forward until she stopped in the middle and gripped the rail.

Carol leaned on the railing beside her and looked out at the water. She took the container from her pocket and held tight as she rambled off the fun facts she'd memorized about Disney World—the park was the size of San Francisco and visited by about one-hundred-fifty million people each year. All those people ate over ten million hamburgers every year.

"Oh my," Ellen said lightly, but Carol could hear the strain of emotion in her voice.

"And nine million hot dogs," Carol added.

"Well, people like to eat," Judith offered.

Carol nodded. "You would love it here, Katie."

"Yes, you would," Ellen whispered.

Judith cleared her throat. "I personally find giant rodents used for entertainment to be horrific. For the life of me, I'll never understand why they chose mice."

Carol pulled her lips between her teeth, determined not to laugh. However, when Ellen let a chuckle slip, Carol followed suit.

Judith gawked at one and then the other. "I'm serious."

"I know," Ellen said. "That's what makes it so funny."

Judith exhaled dramatically, as she tended to do, but her lips curved up into the smallest of smiles. Shaking her head, she looked at Carol. "Now what?"

Opening her hand, Carol showed them the small container with Katie's ashes. "Now we open it and let her go." She gauged Judith's reaction. When her mother didn't recoil or walk away, Carol made sure there was no one else in the vicinity before twisting the top off. Turning the bottle on its side, she lightly tapped until the ashes danced out. She watched them blend into the water and disappear. Once they were gone, she swallowed the lump in her throat and said, "We miss you, kitty cat."

A quiet sob left the woman next to her, drawing Carol's attention. She put her arm around her mom and hugged her from one side while Ellen hugged Judith from the other. Judith pulled a tissue from her pocket and dabbed her eyes. "Grandma loves you, Katie," she said with a trembling voice.

The three women stood in silence for several long moments before Judith shook her head. "You're wrong, Carol. That wasn't cathartic at all. I feel absolutely miserable."

"When don't you feel miserable?" Ellen asked and offered a wink to her niece.

"This was awful," Judith continued, ignoring Ellen's question. "I don't know why you're doing this to yourself."

Carol took one last look at the scenery, committing this moment to memory. "Because it's what she would have wanted, Mom."

"Well, don't do this to me when I'm gone. Put me in the ground next to your father and be done with it."

"Fat chance," Ellen said. "Now that I know how much you hate giant mice, I'm bringing you right back here. I'm going to get a year pass so I can leave little Judith droppings all over."

"Go to hell, Ellen," Judith muttered.

Ellen's laugh filled the air, and they started back toward the path.

Catching up to them, Carol grasped Judith's hand and pulled her to a stop. "Thank you for doing this, Mom. I know it wasn't easy, but this was important to me. I'm glad you were here."

Judith pressed her hand to Carol's cheek. Something unspoken passed between them, something Carol didn't quite understand. A truce, perhaps? A hint of understanding?

"I love you," Judith said.

"I love you too."

Judith lowered her hand and walked away as if she hadn't shaken her daughter to the core. The exchange was brief but pivotal. A huge piece of Carol's heart seemed to have fallen back into place with that simple touch, those simple words.

Looking back at the bridge, she smiled. She didn't know if Katie was watching over her, though she liked to believe so. If she were, she'd undoubtedly had a hand in what had transpired.

"Are you coming?" her mother called.

"We're going to be okay, kitty cat," she whispered before turning away and joining her companions as they discussed where to stop for lunch on the way home.

SEVEN

CAROL STABBED at the potato salad on her plate. Rather than any of them cooking after their emotional day, they'd stopped at the grocery store on the way home and bought lunchmeat, potato salad, and chips to have for dinner. Carol intended to replenish the wine she'd finished the night before, but when her mother frowned at her suggestion, Carol dropped the idea and walked by the wine aisle without so much as a glance.

"Don't you like the potatoes?" Ellen asked.

Carol blinked a few times before setting her fork aside. "I'm not very hungry."

"You're too thin," Judith commented.

The urge to argue about her weight wasn't even a blip on Carol's radar. She knew better than to go down that road. Besides, her weight was fine. Her blood pressure was probably slightly elevated after staying with her mother the last few days, but her weight was fine. Instead of replying to her mom's observation, Carol carried her plate to the trash and scraped what was left of her dinner into the bag. As she was putting her plate into the dishwasher, her phone vibrated where she'd left it on the counter.

Though she was no longer an executive with a demanding job, the habit of immediately checking her notifications hadn't broken. As soon as she dried her hands on a towel, she pressed her finger to the sensor on the back of her phone to unlock it and found a new email from the contractor in Ohio with several photos attached.

"That's one heck of a smile," Ellen commented.

Carol tore her attention from the images she was scrolling through to face her mom and aunt. "Remember when I told you John left me the house in Dayton?"

Tension instantly filled the room. Her mother sat taller; her aunt's eyes darted from Carol to Judith, waiting to see what was about to happen.

"You should burn it to the ground," Judith muttered.

"Considered that," Carol said brightly. She wasn't going to let this devolve into an argument. This was good news. Happy news. "Instead of committing arson, we agreed I'd have the house remodeled and donate it to the children's hospital. Families who are dealing with long-term care for their kids fair better emotionally in houses rather than hotel rooms. Especially if they have other children."

"That's nice, Carol," Ellen said.

Judith didn't respond. She kept her attention on picking at her sandwich. Carol didn't know why she bothered putting tomatoes and pickles on the bread. She always picked them off after a few bites. Carol thought she'd developed the habit because her father wanted those items on his sandwich, and much like making chicken and dumpling soup ever Sunday, she'd never stopped.

Instead of getting sidetracked, she forced away her annoyance at her mother's eating habits and said, "I hired a contractor soon after John died. Once the title was in my name." She opened the attachments and held the phone out so her mom and Ellen could see. "Look at what they've done."

Judith wiped her fingers on her napkin but didn't look up. "That house was always a money pit. I can't even begin to imagine how much this is going to cost you."

"That's not important, Mom. Look at the pictures."

"I'd rather not," Judith said.

A bit of Carol's excitement faded, but Ellen put a wide smile on her face and leaned closer as if her extra attention could make up for Judith's dismissal. Carol scowled but scrolled through for her aunt.

"They added a play set to the back. Isn't that nice?"

"It's delightful."

"And look at the color. I couldn't believe John still had that ugly yellow paint—"

"Enough," Judith stated. "I don't understand how you can just... A nice play set in the back? A play set, Carol? She died there. In that yard."

Carol's heart rolled over in her chest. "I'm aware of that, Mother. I'm the one who found her there."

Judith's eyes changed from hard to sympathetic. "I know

that." Her voice filled with confusion. "Why are you doing this to yourself?"

"Because—"

"Don't you dare say it's what Katie would have wanted," her mother warned. "She was a child. She didn't know what she wanted."

"I disagree," Carol said solemnly. "Katie was smart and compassionate. Whenever she was given an opportunity to help someone, she took it. This is going to help people, Mom. People who are watching their children suffer through medical crises. Things parents should never have to watch. We're giving them a place to call home while they go through something horrific. Katie would want that. She would want that very much."

"She would," Ellen said barely above a whisper. "It's a wonderful thing. *Judith*. It's a wonderful thing Carol is doing."

Judith pursed her lips. "How can you... How can you even look at that house after what happened there?"

Carol scrolled to the first photo that she'd opened. A sign had been placed in the front yard. The design Carol had selected replicated building blocks with bright letters that spelled out *Katie's House*. Beneath that was the logo from the children's hospital to let people know the home belonged to the medical community.

Squatting down next to her mom, Carol showed her the picture. "Look at this. This is what I'm doing. I'm making a safe place for families who are terrified of losing their child. I know that pain, Mom. If giving them this space, even for a few weeks, makes that better, it is worth me facing the past."

Judith exhaled loudly, but this wasn't one of her fed-up-with-the-world sounds. Her breath trembled as it left her. "She would like that," Judith whispered.

Carol smiled up at her as yet another step toward healing was made. "Yes, she would. Once the remodel is done, there will be a small ceremony where I hand the keys over to the hospital. It won't be anything fancy, but I thought you might like to be there. Both of you," she said, glancing at her aunt.

Ellen stared at her sister, but the two older women remained silent.

Carol kissed her mom's cheek. "Think about it. I need to call the contractor and see if he has any idea when they'll wrap up construction so I can set a date with the hospital."

They sat, unspeaking, as she left the room. Sinking onto the sofa, Carol connected a call to the contractor. The man she'd hired had been so kind and considerate while discussing the project that Carol hadn't hesitated to leave him in charge when she left Dayton to go back to Houston. She hadn't seen any of his work in person, but he sent an email update every week or so and had been diligent in calling with questions or concerns. He'd taken this project to heart, which had eased her worries.

When he answered her call, his cheerful voice made her smile. "I thought I'd be hearing from you soon. What do you think of that backyard?"

"It's amazing, Daryl. You're doing a fantastic job. Thank you."

"Everything is coming together nicely."

"I was wondering if you had any idea when I would be able to set the ceremony with the hospital."

"I think three to four weeks would be a safe bet," he said. "That puts us right around—"

Her heart dropped to her stomach. "The end of September," she said flatly.

He was quiet, as if he had felt the change in her. "Right around then. Is that a problem?"

Carol took a deep breath and forced a smile to her face. "No. No, that's...perfect. I'd like to get this done before the weather turns."

Returning to his upbeat self, as if the drastic change in her tone hadn't happened, he said, "Go ahead and set the date and then let me know. I'll make certain everything is ready."

"Thanks, Daryl," she said with forced happiness.

"You're welcome."

He ended the call, and she lowered the phone. The end of September. Oh, how she'd been dreading the end of September.

"Carol?"

She blinked and noticed her mom standing in front of her.

"You were so excited a few minutes ago," Judith said. "What happened?"

"Um. The house will be ready around the end of September. It'll be a year since..."

"Tobias," Judith finished in a softer tone.

Carol fell back into a slouch on the sofa as her mind filled with images of her husband. The end of September. She laughed flatly. "This year is like...one kick to the shins after another, you know? I can't ease from one thing to another. Everything seems to happen at once."

"So don't set the ceremony in September. Put it off."

"If I put it off, we'll be getting into autumn. It'll be cold. Rainy."

"*Carol.*" Though Judith didn't call her daughter out on being ridiculous, her tone did.

"I know," she murmured. "I could wait until spring if I wanted. There's no rush. It's only..." She smiled slightly. "This seems serendipitous somehow. Mary wants me to be with her when the year anniversary comes around. His family wants to be there for the ceremony to hand over the house. Maybe this is Tobias's way of making sure that happens. Maybe..."

"Maybe you're reading a whole lot into a coincidence."

Carol grinned. "I do that a lot more these days. I try to see signs in everything. That started after John and I visited Yellowstone. This flock of birds flew up as we spread Katie's ashes, and it felt like she was telling us she was okay. Ever since then, I find myself looking for hidden meanings in everything."

The concern that filled her mother's eyes was becoming as familiar as the frustration Carol had grown up seeing.

"I'm okay, Mom," she insisted. "Stop looking at me like I've lost my mind. Please."

"I fear you have, Carol."

"I haven't. I'm a little lost right now, but I'll be okay."

Judith was quiet for several moments. "Ellen said she talked to you about seeing a therapist."

Carol sighed. "She did."

"Have you considered it?"

Rather than drag out the debate, Carol took her mom's hand. "I'll look into. Later."

"Later? You mean after you drive around the country leaving human remains in your wake?"

She couldn't help but smile at her mother's description of her plans. "Yeah. After that."

"Carol—"

"Mom." Her voice held a firm but gentle warning. "I don't want to keep talking about this. I'm at peace with this. Katie and John are at peace with this. I know that in my heart. Maybe what I'm doing doesn't make sense to you, but it does to me. Spreading their ashes is the right thing. You don't have to agree with it, but please don't try to tell me I'm wrong. I'll never agree with *that*."

"I don't disagree. I can see why you're doing what you're doing. Today was hard, but knowing Katie got to be someplace she would have loved does make me happy. In some...odd way."

Warmth, maybe even a touch of serenity, filled Carol's heart. That was probably as close as her mother would ever get to understanding Carol's need to spread Katie's ashes. She gently squeezed Judith's hand. "I know going back to that house is difficult. I had to take John back there. I had to look out at that yard. That day played over in my head, moment by moment. Like a nightmare I couldn't wake up from."

"That must have been horrible," Judith said.

"I vomited," Carol admitted with a scoff. "It'd been twenty-four years, but nothing had changed. John had updated the furniture, but everything was the same—even the photos on the wall. Walking into that house was so jarring, I ran to the kitchen and puked in the sink. But then I went to her room and..." Carol's voice grew thick as tears filled her eyes. "I sat there and remembered tucking her into bed and kissing her good night. I swear I could hear her chattering away to her stuffed animals, making up stories for them like she used to."

Carol closed her eyes as those memories washed over her again. Katie's sweet voice swinging from high to low as she pretended to be a doll or a teddy bear. "Going back there wasn't easy for me, Mom," she said, dragging her mind from the past, "and it won't be for you if you decide to go. But if I hadn't gone, that place would still haunt me. I could never forget, but now, I can look at pictures of that place and see a home, a safe place for a family, instead of the terrible things that happened there. I can see how happy Katie would be if she knew what we were doing to honor her."

"The last time I was there was..."

"Her sixth birthday," Carol finished when her mother couldn't seem to.

Judith snagged a tissue and dabbed at her nose. "Your dad and I gave her that little kitchen play set, remember?"

Another memory—a flash of Katie playing with the set—made Carol smile. "She loved that, Mom. She really did. She pretended to make pancakes for her teddy bear every day."

"I remember. She was so happy."

"Yes, she was."

Judith stiffened. "And then you and John got into a fight at the party."

Carol lowered her face. "You knew?"

"Everyone knew. The way he stormed inside, and you rushed after him like you always did when he got mad for no reason," she said bitterly. "We tried to stop Katie from following, but she was determined to get you so we could have cake. She slipped away when we weren't looking."

A familiar sense of shame washed over Carol. "We tried to protect her from our problems. We really did. I know we weren't successful, but we did try. Things were so out of control by then."

Judith shook her head. "He was so—"

"Addicted, Mom. He was an alcoholic, and his addiction had taken over our lives. He was about to hit rock bottom. He would have crashed even if we hadn't lost Katie. Things were bad. Incredibly bad. I see that now. I didn't then, but I do now. I should have made him get help."

Judith pressed her lips together but didn't push the issue.

Another sign of progress.

"This isn't about John," Carol said, redirecting the conversation. "None of this is about John. This is about making sure Katie's memory lives on. Her life and her death will be tied to the house for as long as it stands, but now people will know about her. They'll see her picture and know she's the reason the hospital was able to give them a place to call home during their trying times. Don't make this about John or his drinking or our fighting. This is for Katie."

"I don't know if..."

She squeezed her mom's hand. "If you can't be there, I understand. I hope you'll think about it though. It's early, but I'm going to get ready for bed. I need to think about the timing of the ceremony." She pushed herself up, feeling like the weight of the world was pressing down on her.

"Carol," Judith called before Carol could leave the room.

Turning around, Carol waited as her mom seemed to debate what to say.

"I'm glad you were able to resolve your past with John," Judith said before hesitantly meeting her eyes. "Forgiveness is an important step. I can't forgive him. Not just because of Katie's accident but because of how much he hurt you. I saw how much you loved him, and he... He wasn't a good husband to you, Carol. He drank too much. He was never around when you needed him. You couldn't rely on him, and you suffered because of that. He made your life hell. I'll never forgive him for what happened to Katie, but more than that, I'll never forgive him for hurting you." Judith jutted her chin out in that defiant way she'd perfected long before Carol had been born. "You may not have believed it, but your father and I loved you more than anything, and seeing John hurt you over and over was one of the hardest things we ever went through. He's still making you suffer after all these years. I'm not going to forgive that."

Carol could have used this opportunity to point out that no one had hurt her as much as her parents, but she couldn't poke her mother. Not when she was being so open. "I'm sure that was difficult," she said instead. "I'm sorry you had to see me hurting. I know you tried to warn me that I was walking into a hurricane and I didn't listen. But Mom, John wasn't solely responsible for the things that happened back then. We both had issues that played into our marital problems. I brought plenty of baggage to the relationship. Maybe you need to work on forgiving all of us for things in the past." That was as close as she was going to get to pointing out that Dennis and Judith Stewart had played a hand in how messed up their daughter was.

Judith lowered her face, and Carol thought maybe she'd finally broken through her mother's anger. Or at least cracked the surface.

"Good night, Mom. I love you."

She walked away without waiting for a response. This was a good place to end the conversation. For both of them.

———

"That's it," John said, setting a stack of boxes on the floor of the living room.

Caroline inhaled deeply. The scent of carpet shampoo and cleaning supplies lingered in the air. Though the older house was run-down, she and Frannie had scrubbed every corner the day before. Now that the carpets were dry, boxes had been piled in every room, ready to be unpacked.

Smiling, she turned, hugging Katie a little bit closer. "I can't believe it," she said to John. "Our first house."

His face broke into a brilliant smile, the one that always warmed her heart. Crossing the room, he rested his hands on her hips and pulled her closer before putting a soft kiss to her lips. "We're going to be so happy here, baby. Wait and see."

"I know," she said.

He put another kiss on Katie's little head before turning away and clapping his hands together. "Let's get started."

"I think we should put Katie's room together first," Caroline said. She looked around at the boxes, debating how long it would take to unpack. "And then the master bedroom so we have a place..."

Her words trailed off when she heard the telltale sign of a beer can clicking open, followed by the familiar hiss of carbonation. Next, she'd hear the obnoxious sound of John chugging. "Stop," she warned before he could get the can to his lips.

He looked at her, his blue eyes wide behind the shaggy brown hair hanging in his eyes. He was overdue for a haircut, but Caroline hadn't had time to trim it for him. Rather than go to a barber on his own, like any normal adult would, he'd let it go until his sergeant or his wife intervened. However, his wife had been working extra shifts at the hospital to help earn enough for a down payment on this house and was too tired to worry about his hair. So, until his supervisor told him to get a cut, his bangs would continue hanging in his eyes like a rugged schoolboy. He probably thought the style was cute, but Caroline simply saw a reminder of how irresponsible he could be.

"You are not drinking right now," she warned him.

He looked at the beer in his hand. "I'm thirsty."

"*Have some water.*"

The smirk that crossed his lips let her know the battle was on. They'd had this particular one too many times in their young marriage. However, before they could get started, someone knocked on the front door. John slammed his beer on the counter and eyed his wife in a way that told her this discussion wasn't over, merely on hold.

He opened the door, and sarcasm oozed from his words as he turned and said, "Look, honey. It's your parents. How exciting."

Caroline focused on the little bundle in her arms and was able to calm herself, despite the rage boiling inside her.

"Come on in, folks," John said, his voice still sardonic. "Have a look around. I was heading out, but I'm sure Caroline would love to tell you all about our new place. Wouldn't you, sweetheart?"

She fought the urge to tell him to go fuck himself but was certain the words were plainly written on her face. Her mom and dad walked in, and the tension rose another three or so notches. Once they were inside, John stormed out. She wished the stress had gone with him, but she was still itching to unleash her fury. So much so, she wasn't willing to let him go without letting him know how angry he'd made her.

Caroline forced a smile as she handed Katie to her mom. The baby was six months old now and squirming constantly. Caroline made sure her mom had a good hold on Katie and then stepped back.

"Excuse me." She pretended not to notice the frustrated glance that passed between her parents as she followed John outside. Despite the cold December weather, she didn't bother

grabbing her coat on the way out. "Where are you going?" she demanded before he could get to his car.

He didn't stop walking as he said, "We both know it's best for everyone if I don't hang around with your parents."

"John—"

"They get upset and then you get upset and we end up fighting. Let's avoid all that."

"Dad came over to help you set up the crib," she said as he opened his car door.

"Your mom can watch Katie while you help him." He gave her a cocky smile as he winked at her. "It'll be a good bonding experience for you."

"You're going to the pub, aren't you?" She didn't need to ask. She knew where he was headed. "In the middle of the afternoon. When you're supposed to be helping me move into our new home."

"I'm not going to have your parents looking down their noses at me in my own house."

"Then stop giving them reason to." She turned to go back inside, but John grabbed her hand. He was likely going to apologize. This was the part of their fight when he realized he'd gone too far and tried to talk his way out of being on the receiving end of her wrath.

She jerked her hand free and waved him off. "Go to the bar, John. Get drunk. But be aware that if I have to choose between paying the mortgage and bailing your worthless ass out of jail for drinking and driving, I won't miss a mortgage payment. Ever."

As she marched off, he climbed into his car and the door

creaked as he slammed it. His car engine clicked and whined as it came to life moments before he peeled out of the driveway, but she didn't look back. To hell with him. Useless bastard. She would get more done without him there anyway. Whenever he was around her parents, she spent all her time trying to keep everyone from starting a war. She didn't have the energy to play peacekeeper at the moment.

At the front door, Caroline forced a fake smile, as if nothing was wrong. Her mom was still holding Katie, patting her little back and bouncing her to keep her content. When her mother faced her, Caroline could see that Katie was the only one content.

The scowl on Judith's face was one of the many reasons John couldn't stand to be around her parents. Caroline couldn't really blame him for not wanting to be subjected to such blatant disapproval. She had been looked at that way her entire life, but he'd grown up seeing Frannie's big smile. He'd never had to develop thick skin the way Caroline had. She could understand why her mother's silent judgement ate away at him. After two years together, the calm and confident man who wanted to win them over was gone, and she couldn't blame him for that.

But to hell with him for leaving to get drunk in the middle of the afternoon on their first day in their new home.

He could burn for all she cared. So could her parents. She was so sick of walking this high wire. Nothing she did was good enough for them. Or for John. Trying to please them all was exhausting. Trying to be the bigger person all the time was exhausting.

She *was* exhausted. Emotionally tapped out. She had nothing left to give them. She had a baby now, and everything *she had left was going to go to her daughter. The one person who didn't look at her like she was a huge mistake.*

Why couldn't they...

Why couldn't any of them...

Caroline swallowed hard, trying to force the surge of emotion down. If she had learned anything in this life, it was that showing her parents the slightest bit of emotion would cause more problems. Putting on her best stone face, she looked around the room. "Where's Dad?"

"Putting the crib together. As you asked him to."

Her mother's pointed words hit their mark, but Caroline didn't react. She wouldn't react. Doing so would give her mother a sense of twisted pleasure Caroline had vowed to never give her again.

"I'll see if he needs a hand." She knew he wouldn't accept her offer, but she stopped in the doorway of the small bedroom she'd designated as Katie's. "Need help?"

"No," he said without looking up from the parts he was sorting.

She didn't offer again. She turned away and went into the master bedroom, closing the door behind her. And then she went into the bathroom, closed that door, and let her tears flow.

———

The following afternoon, Carol carried three glasses of lemonade into the dining room to where her mom and aunt sat staring at puzzle pieces. The image of a rundown barn in an overgrown field was starting to come together. There were still a few hundred pieces to place, but Carol thought by the next afternoon, her aunt would have to find a new activity to distract them...unless they agreed to the idea Carol was about to spring on them.

"Mary texted me while I was in the kitchen," she announced.

Ellen leaned back, leaving plenty of room for Carol to ease the glasses onto the table.

"Tobias's family is on board for having the ceremony at the end of September." Carol stood upright and looked at her mom. "What about you? Have you put anymore thought into attending?"

She didn't realize how much she'd expected her mom to reject the invitation until her mom nodded, and Carol nearly laughed with surprise. "Really? You'll go?"

"You're right," Judith said. "I should be there for Katie."

"And for you," Ellen was quick to add.

Carol glanced at her aunt, who was obviously, albeit subtly, urging Judith to say more.

"And for you," Judith conceded. She took Carol's hand and squeezed. "This will be difficult for you, and I should be there to help you through it."

Though she hadn't expected her mom to agree, now that she had, Carol felt a surge of sentiment rush through her. She didn't hug her mom often, but she couldn't stop herself from bending down and embracing her. "Thank you, Mom," she said softly. "Thank you."

Taking her seat, Carol clasped her hands together. Now that her mom had agreed to join her in Ohio, she had to discuss how they were getting there. This was going to be the hard part.

"You're about to push your luck, aren't you?" Judith asked flatly.

Another smile pulled at Carol's lips. "I have a list of places I plan to stop between here and Dayton. If you would like to come with me, both of you," she said, including Ellen, "I have room in the RV. We have plenty of time to make it to Ohio for the ceremony."

Judith stared. Silently.

Carol fought the urge to laugh at the apathy on her mother's face. "Have you ever been to Biltmore Estate?"

"Oh," Ellen said excitedly, "we've talked about visiting there."

"What about Washington D.C.?" Carol asked. "Katie loved looking at pictures of all the monuments."

"Oh, that would be fun," Ellen said. "Judith, wouldn't that be lovely? We could finally take a nice vacation."

"That's not a vacation," Judith said flatly.

Carol's hope started to abate. "But it could be, Mom, if you let it. We can stop other places, too. We can visit museums or historical spots. We have time. We don't have to rush. We can see things and enjoy the trip." Her excitement dimmed when her mother's interest didn't pique. "If you'd rather, I can buy you and Ellen plane tickets. I'll meet you at the airport and take you to a nice hotel. It's okay if that's what you want, but I'm going to drive so I can make some stops along the way."

Judith gazed into her glass, swirled the lemonade until

the ice clinked on the sides, and then frowned. "What does one pack for living on the road like a nomad?"

Ellen gasped, and Carol nearly jumped to her feet. Two wins in one day? She'd have to remember this as the day Hell had frozen over.

"Comfortable clothes," Carol said around her smile. "And books."

Judith sat back and shook her head. "You're exactly like your aunt, you know that?"

Carol chuckled, more than happy with the comparison. "I have a map of all the RV parks. Let's take a look so we can start planning our trip." She winked at her aunt as she pushed herself up.

Carol was digging through her bag, searching for the journal that held her notes and the map she'd grabbed from her RV the day before, when a familiar sense of dread kicked her in the stomach.

How many times had she been excited like this, just to have her mother ruin everything with her sour attitude? She'd committed them to several weeks of living in extremely close quarters. There was no way this could end other than in disaster. All the strides she'd made toward having a good relationship with her mom would be obliterated by the time this little trip Carol had suggested came to an end.

Sitting on her bed, Carol closed her eyes and took herself to Tobias's garden.

Part of getting out of this rut she'd been in all her life was recognizing that she was as guilty of ruining things as her mother. Focusing on the flowers in her memory, she acknowledged there would be stress over the next few weeks. She accepted short tempers and irritability were inevitable. Then she vowed to do her best to diffuse the situations rather than play into them.

This was an opportunity she never thought she'd have. She and her mother could take this time to heal or to further destroy each other. Carol wanted to heal, and she had come to believe her mother did as well.

Yes, there would be bumps along the road—literally and figuratively—but they could overcome them. They had to overcome them. Carol refused to accept the alternative.

Pulling her journal from her bag, she headed back to the living room, allowing her excitement to return.

EIGHT

RATHER THAN SPENDING their first night in the RV, Carol had selected a hotel two hours south of Biltmore Estate. That had been a shorter drive than she would usually do, but to accommodate her passengers, she planned to keep their driving time under eight hours a day, allotting for several breaks.

There was no need to rush. She was well aware of the time elapsing until the ceremony in Dayton—and not only because she was eager to see what the construction crew had done with the house. Dread lingered in the back of her mind. Every day was one day closer to her being a year without Tobias. Every mile was one mile closer to being with his family to remember the anniversary together. Every heartbeat was one more she'd survived without him.

She tried to blame her restlessness the night before on the unfamiliar surroundings, but the reality was, the anniversary of Tobias's death was getting closer and her grief was becoming harder to ignore. She'd had to force her attention to stay on her mom and aunt as they'd eaten breakfast and waited for a shuttle to take them to the estate—which Carol insisted was easier than trying to find parking for an RV.

"Will you look at that?" Ellen asked from the seat in front of Carol. "That's amazing."

Carol leaned forward enough to see over the seat of the little bus they were riding in. Built in the style of the French Renaissance, the house was a brilliant piece of architecture. Though Carol had picked this spot for Katie and John, she realized in that moment, this stop was really for Tobias. This was a place he had wanted to see, and he wouldn't have been disappointed.

"Why would anyone need such a big house?" Judith asked, earning a frown from her sister.

Carol smiled. True, her mother could dampen the brightest of days, but Ellen's interference made the negativity tolerable and sometimes amusing. Judith might make a fuss now, but Carol suspected once they walked inside, her mother would have to admit she was impressed by the estate.

And she was right. Even more than the extravagance of the architecture, Carol loved watching her mom and aunt taking in the mansion. For every, "Oh, Judith, look," she heard, "For crying out loud, Ellen, do you see that?"

Judith hid her expressions better than Ellen. Still, Carol could see her mother's excitement beneath the surface of her incredulity at the extravagance. Carol was so happy she'd brought them with her. She would have taken the tour, she would have been awed by the magnificence, but she wouldn't have enjoyed this experience nearly as much if she'd come alone.

The self-guided tour might not have been as informative as the more expensive tours, but about an hour in, Carol was convinced they'd made the right decision to go at their own pace, rather than try to keep up with a group. Ellen and Judith stopped to examine things longer than a tour guide would likely allow, and a little over an hour in, she could see her companions were starting to run low on energy.

Near the gardens, they found a table to sit and rest at for a while. The next bit of their visit would be to find a place to sprinkle ashes. Carol hoped they could find an out-of-the-way area in the garden, but if they couldn't, she'd seen plenty of spots in front of the home on the long lawn that was open to visitors.

As they were discussing the history of the house from a brochure Ellen had picked up, a breeze blew, and Carol's heart rolled in her chest. *Salvia*. The distinct scent of *Salvia dorisiana* touched her senses. She hadn't experienced that scent outside of her imagination since leaving her house in Houston. Since leaving the home she'd made with Tobias.

This was one of those unexpected gut-punch moments that took her by surprise and tore her apart inside. Putting her hand to her chest, she gasped as shock rolled through her.

Judith put her hand to Carol's arm. "What is it?"

She faked a smile as she lowered her hand. "Indigestion."

Ellen wasn't buying her story, and her mother didn't look any more fooled.

Carol let her forced grin fade away. "A memory of Tobias hit me out of nowhere."

Judith gave her arm a gentle pat. "I hate that."

"And people say ghosts aren't real," Ellen said sympathetically. "Want to tell us about it?"

Inhaling deeply, she confirmed the sweetness still filled the air. "Do you smell that?"

They both sniffed, but neither seemed to notice the scent.

"When the breeze blew...I thought I smelled Tobias's favorite flowers. They were all over our yard." Lowering her face, she let out a deep sigh as realization sank in. She'd imagined the scent. Being so close to the gardens, feeling the wind dance across her cheeks, thinking so much about Tobias, had caused her mind to play a cruel trick on her senses.

Judith squeezed Carol's hand briefly. "I suppose we have to find some of his flowers and see about leaving Katie there. I think they'd both like that, don't you?"

Carol nodded. "I think so."

They started toward the garden, and Ellen took Carol's hand in what was obviously a silent show of solidarity. Widows unite. They walked without speaking, and guilt tugged at Carol for ruining some of the magic of the visit. However, she guessed that magic would have faded as soon as they started looking at the area, not in wonder but with the task of finding a place for the ashes in Carol's pocket.

As they strolled the path, Carol searched for the telltale

heart leaves and bright-pink flowers that Tobias had loved so much. She inhaled deeply through her nose, hoping to catch the fruity scent. The *Salvia* eluded her. Not to be found.

"This is beautiful," Ellen said as they entered a walled area. The paved walkway led them around patches bursting with bright flowers.

They walked quietly, speaking in hushed voices as they passed the various plants as if they were in a church instead of a public setting. Approaching a small area filled with *Camassia* lilies, a sense of peace touched Carol's mind. This was it. This was the spot.

Katie would love the blue, star-shaped flowers. She would have wanted to pick a stem to take with her. Carol would have had to tell her why she couldn't, while John tried to explain why she could. The image played in her mind as clearly as if it had happened.

"Here," she said.

Judith and Ellen moved closer, both glancing around. The garden wasn't empty, but there was plenty of space in the area so no one was crowding around them.

With the container in her hand, Carol looked at her aunt. "You read the brochure. You tell her about it."

Clearly surprised, Ellen said, "Oh. Um. Biltmore Estate has two-hundred-fifty rooms, forty-three bathrooms, and..." She skimmed the paper in her hand. "Three kitchens. It was built in the 1890s and remains the largest private home in America. There are more than eighty thousand blooms in the spring and more than two hundred varieties of roses. Holy cow, that's a lot of flowers."

"That's a lot of flowers," Judith said. "Katie liked flowers, didn't she?"

"She did." Carol twisted the cap off the container.

"Wait," Judith said. "Is...John?" She lamely gestured at the container.

Carol nodded. "He'd like to be here with her," she said, hoping her mom didn't disagree.

"Well," she said. "Then he'd like to know the Biltmore added vineyards in 1971. They now have more than twenty handcrafted wines."

Ellen looked horrified, but Carol chuckled.

"Thanks for thinking of him, Mom," Carol said before bending down and sprinkling the ashes into the mulch. "We'll buy a bottle for you, John."

"And your ex-wife will drink most of it," Judith muttered.

Carol raised a brow as she gawked at her mother. However, the twitch of Judith's lip let her know that her mother had been teasing her. What had gotten into that woman?

Smirking, Carol said, "You're right. We should buy two bottles. One for me, one for everyone else."

Ellen laughed and gently nudged Carol, but then her face softened. "Say something for Tobias while we're here."

Carol's throat instantly tightened. She had to force herself to swallow. After taking the brochure from Ellen, she skimmed, looking for something that would fascinate Tobias more than the vast number of flowers planted on the grounds. "There are seven thousand solar panels. They offset the estate's energy consumption by about twenty percent.

That's a lot of solar panels," she added, mimicking her aunt's previous astonishment.

Ellen smiled. "That's a lot of solar panels."

Rolling her head back, Carol looked up at the cloudless sky and voiced the thought that had been echoing in her mind since they'd arrived. "He would have loved it here. He would have been like a kid at a carnival taking all this in." She imagined him pulling her along, flipping through a book he would have bought at the gift shop, telling her far more about a sculpture or a painting than she ever would have wanted to know. But she would have hung on every word because she had always found his enthusiasm so damned infectious.

Once again, her emotions caught in her chest. She had to fight to push the air out of her lungs. As she did, a miserable moan built. "Here we go," she said as tears welled up and rolled down her cheeks.

"Come on." Judith led her to a bench. The three of them sat, Ellen and Judith doing what they could to console Carol as she cried.

———

As soon as Carol started to drift from sleep, her chest felt heavy. Her eyes fought the need to open. Her mouth was dry, and her tongue seemed too large. Swallowing was difficult, but she managed somehow. When she did, she moved a little closer to consciousness and her sorrow started to return.

Tobias was gone.

Forever.

Her train of thought halted as her ears and brain connected. A familiar voice spoke nearby. Forcing her eyelids up, she noticed her mom and Mary talking in hushed tones in the chairs on the other side of the coffee table. Mary's little living room was filled with seating because her house was the gathering spot. Even though Elijah lived a few miles away and his house was larger, Mary's home was the hub for the Denmans. This house was all Mary could afford, being a single mother with two boys, but it was filled with love and happy memories that everyone could share in.

So, despite her living room being crowded, this was where they'd all come together to mourn.

Sometime while Carol had dozed off, Judith had arrived. That meant her aunt was somewhere. Perhaps in the kitchen, since Carol had been taking up precious space on the couch. When she'd fallen asleep, she and Mary had been alone in the house, but the sound of muted voices in the kitchen indicated that several people had since arrived.

Carol slowly sat. Her head spun a little. She couldn't remember taking one of the pills the doctor had prescribed for her, but she must have. Her body and mind seemed disjointed, which would have been an effect of the drug.

"There she is," Mary said softly. A moment later, she put a soft kiss on Carol's head. "I'll make you some tea, baby."

By the time Carol processed the words, Mary was gone. Sitting back, she looked across the room, and another layer of stress settled over her. She didn't have the energy to deal with her mother right now. "Hi, Mom."

Judith frowned, and Carol lowered her face. Undoubtedly,

she looked like a mess. She'd been crying for two days straight. Only sleeping when the drugs overcame her ability to stay awake. Not eating enough, according to Mary.

"How many pills did you take?" Judith asked.

"I don't know," she answered honestly. "Too many, I guess."

A loud sigh came across the coffee table at her. If her mind hadn't been so clouded, she would have snapped at her mother. "I don't need your judgment right now," Carol managed to say. She would have pushed herself up and walked away if her body had complied with her intention.

"I'm not judging you," Judith said. "I'm worrying about you."

"Well, don't do that either."

"Because you're fine?"

She was about to suggest her mother leave, when Judith sat next to her. "Please don't fight with me right now," Carol whispered. "I can't fight right now."

"I'm not," Judith answered with her own whisper. She put her arm around Carol's shoulders, not quite a hug but more than she was prone to giving. "I don't want to see you using pills to shut down, that's all."

"Tobias..." She couldn't finish. Tears filled her eyes and choked off her words.

"I know."

Carol ground her teeth so hard that her jaw muscles ached. She hated crying in front of her mother. Her parents had always seen crying as weak. Selfish. But she couldn't hold back the sob welling in her chest. She was awake now. The clouds were clearing from her mind, and all she could think was that Tobias was dead.

A half cry, half plea left her against her will.

Judith actually pulled her closer and put her hand over Carol's. "I know."

Carol dropped her head onto her mom's shoulder. She'd never relied on her mom for emotional support. Judith wasn't good at offering emotional support. In this moment, however, Carol was in no position to rebuff anyone's comfort. Even the stiff half embrace of her mother was welcomed.

Her latest round of tears was disturbed when someone set a cup of tea on the table in front of her. Opening her eyes, she noticed her aunt looking at her with sympathy and concern. That added to the emotional outburst, and she started sobbing harder.

"Oh, honey," Ellen cooed as she sat on the other side of Carol. Leaning in, she hugged her with much more compassion than her mother. Ellen's hugs had always been warm and inviting. She pulled Carol's head close and planted several kisses to her temple. "I'm so, so sorry."

Carol grasped her hand and clung to her as she gulped for air to try to calm herself.

After a few minutes, Ellen reached for the hot tea. "I added a little kick to help you relax."

"Not alcohol, I hope," Judith said, sounding a bit panicked. "She's been taking some kind of pills."

"It's fine," Carol said, taking the mug.

"Just a little whiskey," Ellen confessed. "Not enough to—"

"She's been taking pills," Judith stated.

"Mom," Carol soothed. "It's fine." She sipped the drink, and seconds later a wave of tingles rolled through her. By "a little" her

aunt must have meant a shot or two. Carol didn't mind. In fact, she appreciated the gesture.

She handed the mug back to Ellen. "I'm a widow." Her strained voice cracked, sounding as broken as she felt.

Ellen patted her knee. "But you're not alone. Remember that you're never alone. We're here. Tobias's family is here. We're all going to look after you."

"We'll stay as long as you need us," Judith said; however, she didn't sound sincere.

She sounded the same way people do when they say, "Let me know if I can do anything." Those were fake offers of support. Those people were really saying, "I'll be here if you need me, but please don't." Or maybe that's what Carol heard because there wasn't anything anyone could do. Everything sounded hollow. Everything seemed empty.

The front door opened, and dread knotted in her stomach. She wasn't up for more visitors, but relief settled over her when Tobias's brother and uncle walked in. They'd been at the funeral home because Carol couldn't bring herself to go. She thought she should have gone, but she couldn't.

Uncle Jerry blew her a kiss before heading right to the kitchen. He was Mary's older brother and the closest thing to a father figure Tobias and Elijah had had most of their lives. He was one of Carol's favorite people. He'd become like a father figure to her too.

Elijah eased into the chair where her mother had been sitting. He looked as shattered as Carol felt. If she could have stood, she would have given him a big hug, but she feared she'd stumble and cause them all more concern.

"We went ahead and ordered the wreath," Elijah said. "You can change it—"

"No," Carol stated. "It's... Whatever you chose is fine."

"White roses. And a pink one."

Instantly, she was a weepy mess again. She put her hand to her face as her lips quivered and more tears fell. "Thank you," she managed to say around the knot of emotion in her chest.

He nodded. "Need anything else? Want some lunch? I could go get something."

Carol shook her head. "I'm okay. Thanks."

"I'll go check on Mom, then."

He left the room about the time the soft sound of Mary's crying came from the other room. Jerry must have told her about the funeral arrangements they'd made.

"We always..." Carol started and then sniffed. "Whenever anyone orders flowers for family gatherings, we add one pink rose for Katie," she explained.

"That's lovely." Ellen put her hand to her chest, and the first sign of tears reflected in her eyes.

"I saw her picture on the wall," Judith said. "With the rest of Tobias's family."

Carol's defenses spiked. Her mother's tone was the one she used to share her disapproval without actually stating she disapproved. Tobias and his family had never met Katie, but they loved her. They loved hearing Carol's stories about her. Mary never forgot Katie's birthday. She'd call Carol every June fifth to check on her. They had embraced Katie's memory as much as they would have embraced the girl had she lived.

How could Judith be offended by that?

Carol didn't want to know. She didn't care. She had bigger problems than dancing around her mother right now. The image of a large wreath of white roses and one pink rose filled Carol's mind and broke her all over again.

Her grief compounded in that moment. Katie. Tobias. The unborn children Carol and Tobias had lost. "This is too much," she choked out. *"I can't do this."*

"You can," Ellen said. "We're going to be right here, helping you."

Carol looked to her mother, as if she would reinforce Ellen's offer. She was staring at the wall, at the picture of Katie mixed in with photos of a family who never knew her. Carol tried to see the wall through her mother's eyes. The Denman family was a mixed bunch. African-American, Caucasian, Hispanic. In the sea of various-colored faces, Katie's pale skin and freckles stuck out to those who were looking at the skin tones.

To Carol, to her in-laws, Katie fit. Katie belonged.

Carol was happy she had found this family who accepted her, flaws and all. She had no doubt her mother was seeing things through her black-and-white views, as she tended to do, but seeing Katie's picture hanging next to images of Elijah's daughters filled Carol's heart. Katie was loved, though she wasn't known.

That was special. That was important.

Carol wasn't the least bit surprised Judith didn't understand. In that moment, Carol felt sorry for her mother. Had Judith ever truly felt the sense of family Carol had found with Tobias, she too would have been moved to tears that Elijah had added a pink rose to the wreath.

Squeezing her mom's hand, Carol released the frustration she'd felt earlier and reminded herself that her mom couldn't possibly understand because she'd never had a family like the Denmans. She'd never allowed herself to feel that deeply or to love so openly.

"If I'd known about that," Judith said, "we would have had a pink rose at your father's funeral."

Ah. She wasn't confused that Katie was being included. Her mother was upset that she hadn't been included in the tradition.

"Sorry," Carol muttered.

"There was a lot going on," Ellen defended. "It's hard to remember everything when we're grieving."

Carol nodded, silently thanking her aunt for intervening as Judith continued staring at the picture on the wall. She was likely adding to the list of ways her daughter had wronged her.

"I think I'll get myself some tea." Judith pushed herself up.

"I can't worry about Mom's feelings right now," Carol blurted out once her mom left the room.

"No one is asking you to, honey." Ellen rubbed her hand over Carol's back.

Carol frowned as she looked at her aunt. She didn't believe that. Her mother clearly felt slighted, and when her mother felt slighted, funeral be damned, she was going to let Carol know.

Carol couldn't be concerned about that now. Her world had fallen down around her. Her mother's bruised ego was the least of her problems.

Carol tried to resist the need to look at the clock next to her bed, but the urge was too great. She glanced over and moaned as the time neared midnight. Her body was beyond tired, but her mind wouldn't stop and, she knew, wouldn't stop for hours. If she didn't get up and distract herself, she was going to stare at the ceiling half the night.

Easing the covers off, she rolled out of the top bed that she'd slept in when she and John were traveling. The main bed, the one she'd shared with Tobias during their adventures, was occupied by her mother and aunt since they couldn't possibly climb to the bunk above the driver's cabin.

Slipping quietly down the ladder, she turned on a dim light to see, even though she knew her way around the RV in the dark. She'd always been prone to restless nights like this, but the frequency was increasing. The ability to ignore the storm brewing inside her became impossible when the world grew quiet and there were no distractions. Memories became far too vivid when the lights were out.

Tonight's flashback was her wedding reception. Tobias held her close as they danced and whispered in her ear how happy he was. She would give anything to go back in time and live that day again. Her tired eyes burned as they filled with tears.

Her options at this point were to read or sit there and relive the past until she was so lonely and depressed, she wouldn't snap out of it for days. This was another one of those cycles she had to work on breaking.

As she poured water into the electric kettle to make a cup of chamomile tea, she made a deal with herself. She could think about Tobias and their wedding until the water boiled. Once the little machine kicked off and her water was ready, she would be done feeling sorry for herself.

She pressed the button and watched, waiting for bubbles to form over the heating element. By the time the water began to show signs of warming, her heart was heavy and her eyes had filled with tears again. The smile on Tobias's face when her father handed her over... The way he'd tenderly kissed her when they were pronounced husband and wife... How he'd hugged her so tight she thought he might crush her...

"Are you okay?" Judith whispered as she put her hand on Carol's shoulder.

Carol jumped and gasped as she turned. "Jesus, Mom," she hissed so she didn't wake Ellen. "You scared me."

"I called out to you. I thought you must have had earphones in or something, but..."

Carol wiped her cheeks. "I was thinking."

"About?"

Focusing on the kettle, she realized the water was done boiling and the machine had turned itself off. She had no idea how long she'd stood there without noticing. "I couldn't sleep."

"Seems to be a running theme for you. Would you like to talk about whatever is keeping you up?"

Carol poured water into a mug and nabbed a teabag from a canister. "The gardens today..."

"Today was...emotional. Tobias would have loved the flowers." Judith sat at the little table. She smiled at her daughter as Carol eased down across from her. "I remember how proud he was of his garden. He had quite the green thumb, didn't he?"

Carol nodded as she lost herself in the cup. The hot liquid was starting to burn her palms through the cobalt blue ceramic, but she didn't ease her hold. The heat kept her grounded in a strange way. "He spent so much time out there. I loved watching him."

"I used to sit on the couch and watch your father do the crossword puzzle," Judith said. "I swear I could see his brain working. Whenever something would trip him up, he'd furrow his brow"—she creased her forehead, imitating what she meant—"and scowl."

Carol remembered that exact scene playing out as she'd grown up. "And then he'd click his tongue when he figured it out."

They both laughed quietly.

"I miss him," Judith said.

"Me too," Carol said. "I never thought I'd feel like that, but I..." She frowned as her eyes filled again. "Damn it." Grabbing a napkin from the holder on the table, she dabbed her tears. "I get weepy when I can't sleep. Everything feels so overwhelming. I'm tired, but I can't sleep. It's frustrating and amplifies things."

"Have you talked to a doctor?"

She nodded. "She put me on a prescription, but I didn't like the side effects. I felt doped up for hours every morning. Don't start," she warned when her mom simply stared at her.

"I didn't say anything."

"You don't have to, Mother. I can read your face. You're worried. Aunt Ellen's worried. Everybody's worried."

"Because we have cause to worry. You've been through a lot, and you aren't coping nearly as well as you'd like us to believe. You would benefit from some help, Carol. Whether you want to admit it or not."

"Is therapy going to bring Tobias back? Will talking about how I feel resurrect my daughter?" She shook her head as she realized she'd snapped unnecessarily. "Don't talk to me about this right now, Mom. I'm tired and I'm going say something mean, so please don't. Let's sit here and enjoy each other's company. Silently," she added with a sly grin.

Judith sat quietly. For about ten wonderful seconds. "I...I had a hard time after your father died. Ellen convinced me to go to a doctor, and we talked about a lot of things. Not just my grief, but...other things. My parents were... I guess they were a lot like your father and me, too strict, too harsh. I wasn't comfortable with her suggestion, but I agreed to try something. I had to go through several different medications before the doctor found one that worked for me. It's not easy, I know, but the alternative is... You don't have to suffer like this."

Carol watched, waited for more, but her mother sat with her lips pressed tight as she stared at her hands. "What are you saying, Mom? What kind of medication?"

Judith seemed to consider her words before saying, "I've struggled with feeling like this for years, Carol. Before you were even born. I never told your dad because... Well, you know how he was, but after his funeral and you left as soon as you could, I...I started to see that I..."

Leaning forward, Carol put her hand over her mom's, silently encouraging her to keep going.

"I don't blame you for running as far as you could after Katie died. You knew I couldn't support you the way you needed because I never had. I never realized how much that must have hurt you until you left the day after your father's funeral without even trying to be there for me."

"I feel terrible about that, Mom," Carol said. "I didn't think."

"That's not your fault. I'd never been there for you either. Sometimes simply getting through the day took all my energy. I didn't have anything left to give to you. That wasn't your fault."

"Mom, I'm—"

"I didn't give you the coping skills to deal with all the things you've had to face in this life, but that's because I didn't have them, either." She shrugged. "I still don't most days, but I'm better now. I want you to be better too. Seeing you like this..." Her lips turned down as she shook her head. "You're breaking my heart. Life doesn't have to be this dark, Carol."

"Mom," she said on a whisper. "I'm still mourning my husband."

"It's more than that. This has been going on for your entire life. That's my fault. I wasn't there for you like I could have been. I should have intervened when your father was too hard on you. I didn't know how. I'm sorry, Carol. I'm sorry we hurt you." She finished quietly, as if she wasn't sure she wanted Carol to hear her.

Carol had heard, however. She'd heard something she had been waiting to hear most of her life. Her mother had acknowledged that Carol's childhood had been broken and her parents had been responsible. Judith would likely never say those words again, but this one time was enough. This one time was all Carol needed.

She gripped her mom's hand and nodded because she couldn't find words to respond.

"I don't want you to hurt anymore," Judith said. "You've been through enough. I know losing Tobias has been hard, but I really think there's something deeper than grief going on with you. I have suffered from depression most of my life," Judith said. "I know what that darkness can do, how it eats away at you. I see it in you too, and I'm scared for you because I don't think you're handling it well."

"Mom, I'm still trying to find my footing."

"All the more reason to get some support. *Please*."

"Okay," Carol managed to say. "I'll call someone."

"Thank you. Now, what do we have to do to help you sleep?"

The abrupt change in topic jolted her, but she went with it. This conversation was too intense. "Um, I'm going to read. I need an hour or so, and then I'll drift off."

Judith hesitated before standing. Instead of going to her bed, she moved around the table and put her hand to Carol's cheek. The move was so unexpected, Carol didn't know how to respond.

Leaning down, Judith kissed her head. When was the last time she'd done that? Had she ever? When she stood upright, she offered Carol a smile. "I love you. I'm proud of you and everything that you've overcome. I want you to have some peace."

Carol had to take a deep breath before finding her voice. "I'll get there, Mom."

"I know. You're strong. You'll find a way to be happy again. That's my biggest hope. Good night."

"Good night."

Once she was alone, she let the impact of the conversation hit her. Her mom was being treated for depression? How had she never seen the signs? Oh. She had. The self-isolation. The quick temper. The constant switches in her mood.

She'd seen the signs. She'd attributed them to her mother's cool personality. One more instance of Carol being too caught up in her own issues to see what was happening around her.

Carol looked at her tea and frowned. She was going to need something stronger than chamomile to sleep.

NINE

CAROL FROZE when her mother picked up the last slice of tomato to add to her sandwich. Unlike her mom, she actually *ate* the tomato on her sandwich. "You're just going to take that off after two bites."

Judith frowned across the picnic table at her. They'd stopped at a nice rest area on their way to Washington D.C. and decided to have lunch under a tall tree. A light breeze kept the temperature tolerable, but Carol was irritable from being up too late. She knew that and tried to talk her blood pressure down, but they were supposed to be at the Shenandoah Caverns right now.

Katie and John would have been mesmerized by the intricate formations made millions of years ago as an underground river swept away soil and minerals. Judith, however, had complained about the hike and the weather and everything else until Carol snapped that she'd visit the caverns another time. They were heading straight to the nation's capital instead.

After lunch, she was going to have to revisit the planned route she'd made before leaving Florida and call every place they had reservations along the way to change when they'd be arriving. The task wasn't insurmountable, but she wished, just once, her mother didn't make everything more complicated.

And now she was eating the last tomato slice.

"I like tomatoes," Judith said pointedly, "but too much upsets my stomach. I'll eat what I can and then take off the rest. If that's okay with you."

Before Carol could suggest her mother at least cut the tomato in half to share it, Ellen roughly ripped open a bag of chips.

"We are less than a week into this adventure," she said with a tone as light as if she were commenting on the weather and in complete contradiction to the frustration she'd shown the bag in her hands. "Starting ridiculous fights with each other isn't on the agenda until next week. So stop. Both of you."

Carol rolled her tense shoulders. *It's a tomato, Carol*, she told herself. *Let it go.*

She would buy more the next time they stopped. She wasn't going to fight over a tomato slice. "Sorry," she conceded. "I didn't get enough sleep."

"Because you were up until after three sitting at that table sniffling," Judith said.

Ellen's scowl deepened as she dropped a handful of chips

on Judith's plate. Right on top of her open sandwich...and the last tomato slice. "I heard you up as well."

Judith brushed the chips aside. "I was checking on my daughter."

"Would you please tell me what's eating you today?" Carol snapped. "Because we were fine when you went to bed last night, and now you are..." She censored herself. "You are *not* fine now."

Staring across the table, huffing dramatically as she liked to do, Judith asked, "Did you call a doctor yet?"

Carol almost laughed. She would have, but her mother was serious. "You want me to call and schedule an appointment with a therapist while we're on the road?"

"Yes," Judith stated.

"*No*," Carol countered. "I'm not doing that."

"Why?"

Carol wadded up her napkin and tossed it on the table. "Because I have to figure out where I'm going to be after I take you home. Then I have to find the therapists in that area covered by my insurance. I have to research those therapists and find the right one. There is a process to this."

"You're procrastinating," her mom accused.

"I'm not procrastinating," Carol said. "It's been like twelve hours—"

"This is what you do," Judith stated. "You find ways to drag things out—"

"I don't even know where I'm going to be. How am I supposed to find a therapist?"

Ellen snapped a can of soda open, sloshed the contents

between three small cups, and then slammed the empty can down. "You're both insane. Now shut up and eat your goddamn lunch."

Carol jolted and stared at her aunt. A quick glance across the table confirmed that her mother had the same shocked expression on her face. A chuckle erupted from Carol. "Jeez. And *we're* insane?"

"You both need help," Ellen muttered.

Carol put her arm around Ellen's shoulders and gave her a half hug. "I know. But so do you. It's genetic."

Ellen frowned at her.

"We get it from our mother," Judith said. "She was nuttier than a pecan pie."

"You're exactly like her," Ellen said.

Judith shrugged as she took the tomato off her sandwich and tossed it onto Carol's plate. "It'll give me heartburn anyway."

"Thanks."

Ellen focused on putting her sandwich together. "What made you agree to therapy?"

Carol smiled across the table. "Mom told me she is being treated for depression. You know I'll do *anything* to not be like her."

Judith used a napkin to clean up some of the mess Ellen had made when she'd poured their drinks. "I told Carol I've been seeing someone for a while and how much it's helped."

"Look," Carol said, growing more serious, "I know I'm working through some things that are concerning to you both. I don't deny that the last year has been incredibly challenging. I'm not making promises, but I will find someone to talk to. I'll listen and take the advice I feel is appropriate to me. Before I take the time to research a counselor, I need to determine if I'll be on the road or staying with you or Mary or someone else. The rest will come after that."

Judith pressed her lips together, but she didn't counter. She didn't argue. She didn't even point out that she disagreed. Carol would count that as growth.

Every time they made progress, they had a minor slip as they found their new footing. This day was no different. Last night had been a huge hurdle to overcome. Judith had admitted not only that she had a weakness but she'd been seeking help for it. She wanted help for her daughter, too, and Carol couldn't fault her for that.

In fact, she had a better understanding of why her mom and aunt were pushing her so hard to seek professional help. They'd been going through the same process with Judith and must have seen some improvements. Even Carol had noticed a change in her mom. She was still stubborn as hell but had somehow learned to give a little.

Carol smiled across the table. "Thanks for telling me about your depression, Mom. It helped me. It really did."

A hint of a smile found Judith's lips. "I don't want you to suffer if you don't have to."

"Well, I'm glad this is settled," Ellen said. "Maybe we can all get along for an hour or so."

"Probably like twenty minutes." Carol gently nudged her

aunt. "Give us a break. We've been doing this my entire life. We can't change overnight. We're trying."

"We're getting better," Judith agreed. "I gave her my tomato."

Carol giggled. "I love when you make jokes. It reminds me that you're human under that tough exoskeleton."

"Don't push your luck," Judith informed her.

Before Carol could retort, her phone rang. Looking at the screen, she didn't recognize the number, but the area code was for Dayton. Curious, she connected. "Hello?"

"Caroline?" the caller asked.

The deep timbre sent a shiver down Carol's spine, and her mouth dropped open.

She knew that voice. Decades may have gone by since she'd last heard him speak, but she'd never forgotten Simon Miller's voice. Years ago, when her marriage to John was at rock bottom, she had turned to Simon for comfort. Their affair was something she'd managed to bury in the back of her mind until John had resurfaced in her life and asked her point blank if she'd planned to leave him for someone else.

She'd never even told Tobias. He wouldn't have judged her or lost his faith in her. He knew how bad things were between her and John. However, the humiliation and shame were too much to share. Not only because she'd committed adultery but because she had come to realize that she'd used Simon. Not intentionally, but when he'd started pressing her to leave John, she had tiptoed around saying no. As much as she knew her life with Simon would be better, the codependent cycle she and John had fallen into was strong, and damned if she could walk away.

Until it was too late.

"It's Simon Miller," he said.

"I know," she managed to squeeze out around the lump that had formed in her throat. "I...I recognized your voice."

Ellen's eyes widened as she grasped Carol's hand, silently asking if she was okay.

No doubt she looked as shaken as she felt. She tried to nod at her aunt, but she didn't think she'd succeeded. Her mind was too busy trying to figure out what the hell was going on to follow orders.

"I'm sorry to call unexpectedly like this," Simon said.

Say something! Carol's brain screamed.

Ellen reached for the phone, as if she were intending to rescue Carol from whatever hell she was caught in. That was enough to snap her out of her shock.

She lifted her hand and looked away. "It's fine. I'm..."

"Surprised," Simon said.

Carol found enough connection with her brain to laugh softly. "Yeah. That's the word." The shocked gasping-fish thing she was certain she'd been doing turned into a big smile. "My God, Simon. How are you?"

"I'm doing well." The uncertainty left his voice, and she could picture his sweet smile. That smile had a way at putting anyone at ease. "How are you?" he asked.

"Good. I'm good."

He was silent for a moment too long, and her excitement started to turn to dread.

"I know you weren't expecting to hear from me," he said, "but I'm the chief of staff at the children's hospital."

Pride filled her chest. He had what it took to fill that role, and she imagined the staff loved having him lead them. He'd always gone above and beyond for his patients. She suspected he did the same for his staff. "That's amazing. Congratulations."

"Thanks. I was notified a few weeks ago that you were planning to donate your old house for parents to use. I was a little slow to make the connection, I admit, but when I saw Katie's name... I figured out it was you. I wanted to call and thank you personally, Caroline. Um, *Carol*. You signed the letter Carol."

She couldn't believe she was going to say this, but the words came from her before she could stop them. "You can call me Caroline."

"*What?*" Judith asked harshly from across the table. Carol hadn't uttered those words in over twenty-four years. She'd left Caroline in Ohio with John and had started a new life as Carol a long time ago.

Carol put a hand to her ear, drowning out her mom and aunt so she could focus on the phone call.

"Good, because I'm not sure I could stop if I wanted to," Simon said with a warmth in his voice that soothed her nerves now as much as it had so long ago. "Usually the president of the board shows up at these things, but I thought if you didn't mind, I'd swing by the dedication as well. I'd like to see you."

Her heart dropped again. Simon? At the ceremony? To

see her? The last time he'd seen her, she was a complete disaster. She'd never, not once, considered that she'd ever see him again. A strange mixture of fear and excitement exploded in her chest like a firecracker.

"If you'd rather I didn't—" Simon said.

"I'd love for you to be there," she spit out. She closed her eyes and shook her head. She'd spoken too fast. More slowly, more controlled, she said, "I'd love to catch up with you. It's been too long."

"Yes, it has," he said, his tone softer and sounding much less anxious.

"I don't think the details for the ceremony have been finalized yet, but I have family coming in from out of state, so I'm sure I'll be at the house most of the day. So...whenever you can make it... I'd love to see you." She hadn't grasped how true that was until she'd said the words.

"Good. I was afraid you wouldn't want me there."

Carol closed her eyes. As he'd always done, Simon somehow brought a calm to her mind. "I do. I'm glad you called. Thank you for reaching out to me."

He laughed quietly. "I would have as soon as I realized this was you, but I wasn't sure if I should. Once we were notified the house was almost done, I knew if I kept chickening out, I was going to miss my chance to see you."

"Well, kudos for your bravery."

"I'll see you soon, Caroline."

"See you, Simon."

She pulled the phone from her ear but didn't have time to

end the call before her aunt tugged at her arm to get her attention.

"Who is Simon?" Ellen demanded. "And don't you dare tell me no one. I saw your face when you heard his voice."

A sense of shame hit Carol hard. The only other person she'd ever confessed this to was John, and only then just because he had all but told her he suspected she'd had an affair. She looked from her aunt to her mom and then to her phone. "We, um... We worked together at the hospital in Dayton before I moved."

"So," Judith said, the word dripping with suspicion. "He was a co-worker?"

"Um, yeah. Yes." Carol sat taller and cleared her throat. "He was a pediatric pulmonologist."

"Hmm." Judith's little muttering sounded more like an accusation. Probably because she had her lips pressed tight and one eyebrow quirked.

The heat in Carol's cheeks started to burn like a scarlet letter.

"I think someone had a crush on the pediatric pulmonologist," Ellen teased. "Maybe she still does."

Carol darted her eyes to her aunt, but there was no point in denying what was bound to become obvious. If not now, then when they met the man. "I'm not... I'm not proud of this, but a long time ago..."

Ellen gasped. "You had an affair with the pediatric pulmonologist?"

Carol gawked at her. "Why do you keep saying his specialty like that?"

"Because it's fun." Ellen laughed as she bumped into Carol and looked across the table. "Your daughter was doing bad things with the pulmonologist."

Judith frowned and shook her head. "Carol. I may not have liked John, but you *were* married."

"Yes, Mother, I'm aware. Simon..." She shook her head lightly. "He was so perfect. So amazingly perfect. You would have loved him so much, you would have hired a divorce attorney *for* me," she told her mother.

"So why didn't you leave John?" Ellen asked.

Carol shrugged. "Because Katie loved her daddy. As much as I wanted to leave at times, I couldn't tear her world apart."

"Sometimes you have to put your children first," Judith said.

Carol tilted her head, and Ellen shifted beside her. Something about what Judith said was deeper than a mere observation. Carol was certain there was another layer about to be peeled away, but Judith focused on reassembling her turkey sandwich and Ellen did that redirection thing she'd mastered long ago.

"So, tell us about Simon. He sounds intriguing."

Carol debated pressing the issue with her mother but decided she'd had enough surprises in the last twelve hours. "Oh, he was."

———

The two weeks since Katie's death had left Caroline numb with shock. The prescription drugs had helped. But those were gone.

Now the shock had started to fade, and the drugs were slowly leaving her system. Something else was taking hold of her.

The moment the mailman brought a package to the door, the last bit of the daze she'd been in cleared. Katie's remains had arrived, and with them Caroline's anger revealed itself. Anger that ran so deep Caroline was shaken by what she felt.

John had opened the box, pulled back the paper that protected the contents, and lifted out the silver urn. Caroline clenched her fists so hard her nails dug into her palms as he set the small container on the coffee table. The storm inside her started raging again.

She was torn between needing to break down and mourn for her daughter and ripping her husband to shreds for what he'd done to their little girl.

The fury she felt for John grasped her, a hatred so strong, she was questioning how long she could control it. She was going to hurt him. She was going to snap. She was going to kill him. The urge to shove a knife into his chest grew with every noise he made, every time he dared to cry as if he weren't responsible for Katie's death, every time he reached out to Caroline for comfort.

Her loathing was consuming her.

John choked out a sob as he lowered his face, and Caroline imagined wrapping her hands around his throat and squeezing. After he sniffled a few times, he ran his fingers over the engravement.

Kathryn Elizabeth Bowman

Born June 5, 1989

Died June 22, 1995

Seeing her beautiful girl's name on the tiny urn broke

through the hatred, and Caroline let go of the rage as the other emotions won out. Sadness overtook her, filled her, filled every bit of her and forced its way out. She didn't want to cry in front of John, she didn't want him getting the idea he could console her, but she couldn't stop the sobs that rose in her chest and pushed their way out.

John didn't try to comfort her, however. He didn't touch her. He sat and brushed his fingers across Katie's name over and over. "We should pack now," he said. "We'll leave in the morning. I have it all mapped out."

She jerked her face to him. He was serious. All his ramblings about scattering Katie's ashes... That wasn't one of John's big talks, one of his unkept promises. He really wanted to take all they had left of Katie and toss her to the wind.

Caroline tried to argue, to tell him he wasn't going to throw Katie away, but the words stuck in her throat. He put the urn down and pushed himself up.

Once he was gone, Caroline looked at the urn, the little teddy bear carved into the surface and filled with pink dye. She wiped her face, but fresh tears replaced the old as she pictured Katie limp on a hospital bed. The horrific scene of finding her daughter lifeless played in her mind over and over until John carried two suitcases out of the bedroom and set them by the door.

"I packed your bag," he said without looking at her. "Get some sleep, Caroline."

She stared at the bags. One for him, one for her. There should have been one for Katie—a purple bag with pom-poms and glitter. That backpack was hanging on the back of Katie's door with nothing inside—no clothes, no books or toys to keep her occupied on the vacation they'd planned but would never take.

Now John wanted to take the trip and leave Katie behind along the way. Like hell he would. Caroline might have been too weak to protect Katie when she was alive, but Caroline would be damned if she'd let John take her daughter from her again. With her anger reignited, Caroline grabbed the urn off the table and carried it with her to Katie's room, where she used the purple pom-pom and glitter-covered backpack to gather a few of Katie's things and then carefully put the urn inside and zipped it shut. She grabbed her purse and the suitcase John had packed with who the hell knew what and left.

Caroline walked out of that shithole of a house, left her bastard of a husband, and didn't even consider looking back. She headed straight for the hospital. Her boss deserved to be told she was leaving, even if she had no idea where she was going. Caroline tapped into that autopilot thing she had mastered years ago as she drove the few miles to work and walked to the nurse's station. They all looked at her, shocked but sympathetic.

"Where's Eve?" Caroline asked.

"I'll page her," one of the other nurses said. As she lifted the phone from the cradle, she flicked her eyes up. Caroline was tempted to snap at her. They'd all spent so much time whispering behind her back about her failed marriage, no doubt they were all whispering now about her dead daughter. Instead of engaging, she walked away.

Caroline eased into a chair and considered that she didn't care where she ended up. She could drive and drive until the world swallowed her, and she'd still be better off than living in *that hollow house with her drunk of a husband. Or in jail because she gave in to the desire to slit his throat.*

"Caroline?"

She tried to smile as she looked up, but the kindness in Eve's dark eyes did her in. Tears resurfaced and Caroline's lip trembled. She lowered her face, unable to look at the woman who had been as kind and generous as a boss could be, given how challenging John had made Caroline's life. Several months before Katie had died, Eve's kindness had reached an end. She'd told Caroline that if she walked in late one more time, she'd be fired.

Caroline hadn't been late again. Until the day Katie died.

"I'm leaving," Caroline said to her clutched hands.

Eve put her hand on the side of Caroline's head. "I'm not surprised, honey."

"I should have..."

"Should haves don't change anything. Don't do that to yourself. You've been through enough without thinking about should haves." Eve stroked Caroline's head with a tenderness that reminded her of her mother-in-law.

Frannie. She should tell Frannie she was leaving. But Frannie would try to stop her, and Caroline would let her. No. She had to run while she had the strength. Once her weakness took hold of her again, she'd never be able to leave.

"You go," Eve said, "and start a new life for yourself. Call me next week. Let me know where to have your last paycheck sent, okay? You'll need it."

Caroline simply nodded.

Eve kneeled in front of her, grasped her hands, and waited until Caroline managed to meet her eyes. "Why don't you stay with me tonight, honey? Leave in the morning with a full stomach and a clearer head."

"That's nice, but..." Caroline shook her head. *"I don't sleep anyway, so I'd rather... I need to go before... He'll pull me back in. I can't let him do that. Not after..."*

"Okay." Eve didn't argue because she knew Caroline was right. If John talked her into staying, she'd never leave. The cycle would continue until Caroline never found a way out. *"Wait here."*

Eve disappeared from Caroline's line of sight. She took the opportunity to wipe her cheeks. She didn't dare look up, though she was certain people were looking at her. Co-workers who undoubtedly had spent more than their share of time over the last two weeks commenting how they weren't surprised that Caroline's daughter had died. Co-workers who had loved to gossip about her broken marriage and troubled life. People filled with I-told-you-sos instead of compassion for a woman who'd lost her child. People like her parents. Caroline kept her face down. Not wanting to see their judgement.

Within a few minutes, Eve returned and held out some folded-over cash. Caroline started to object. She hadn't come for a handout. She'd simply wanted to quit in person.

"Take it," Eve insisted. *"It's not much, but it will get you a tank of gas and something to eat."*

"Thank you," Caroline said, accepting the offer.

As soon as Caroline had stood and stuffed the cash into her pocket, Eve pulled her into a big hug.

"Thank you for always being so kind to me," Caroline whispered.

"You go find yourself a better life. You deserve it." Eve, more than any of the know-it-all gossipmongers at the hospital, knew the hell John had been putting Caroline through. The drinking, the arguing, the manipulations. Eve had called it emotional abuse, but Caroline had never allowed herself to believe that. That made her sound like a victim, and she didn't want that. Foolish. Irresponsible. Those were better than victim.

But she supposed none of those labels mattered now. Now that Katie was gone, Caroline had lost the one label she cared about—Mama.

Nobody was going to call her Mama now.

"Please let me know where you end up," Eve said, pulling back. "I don't want to worry about you."

"I will," Caroline said. "Thank you for everything you've done."

Eve smiled sweetly, and Caroline turned away. She was headed for the elevator when someone grabbed her hand and stopped her. She turned, and her already broken heart shattered even more as she met Simon's sad brown eyes. He didn't say a word before pulling her into a vacant room.

Another time, a lifetime ago, Caroline had slipped into a room to cry alone after a confrontation with Eve about her tardiness, and Simon had followed her. He'd comforted her, and they'd started an affair that led to Simon asking Caroline to leave her husband. Caroline hadn't. She'd left Simon instead. A decision she had certainly come to regret. She half expected him to point out her mistake, but Simon was better than that.

He put his hands to her face, as he'd done so many times

before, and searched her eyes. "What can I do?" he asked, almost desperately. "How can I help you through this?"

She fell into his chest. His arms tightened around her, giving her the security she needed to let her pain pour out. She sobbed into his chest until her lungs hurt. His hold on her was unrelenting. His arms had become the safest place in her world, and she'd walked away from him. Instead of throwing that in her face, he was offering the most comfort she'd found since losing her daughter.

She didn't know how long they stood like that, but he eventually eased his embrace.

"I'm leaving," she whispered.

"Where?"

"I don't know, but I can't stay."

"You can stay with me," he said.

She shook her head. "I can't. Simon, I'm sorry, but... I have to get out of here. Out of Dayton. Away from him."

"Okay," he said when her voice cracked.

He kissed her head, pulled her close. "I haven't sold my house in St. Louis yet. I can call the real estate agent and let them know I'm pulling the listing. Stay there as long as you need. I can put in a good word for you at the hospital where I worked. I'm sure they can find a spot for you."

The guilt Caroline felt for ending their affair returned. He was such an extraordinary man, the kind of man she should have held out for instead of getting tangled in the web of John Bowman. She would have had the life Simon had offered her—a beautiful house and a life with him and Katie. All her dreams would have come true instead of the nightmare she was living.

But she'd walked out on him, and instead of letting her fall, he was offering her the first hope she'd felt in weeks.

"Please say yes, Caroline," Simon begged. "Please let me help you."

She nodded, unable to speak. He hugged her to him again.

"I love you so much," he whispered. "And I'm so, so sorry. I'm so sorry."

Once again, she clung to him, sobbing uncontrollably and wishing she'd accepted his help months ago.

The late summer sun burned bright orange as it sank into the west. Carol sat, staring at the rapidly changing colors painting the sky, but her mind was elsewhere. Simon Miller. She was going to see Simon Miller again.

She'd never expected that to happen. Now that the reunion was inevitable, excitement was building in her. A search of the children's hospital website on her phone confirmed there was a page for the staff. She hadn't clicked on the link that would take her to Simon's biography and, likely, a recent photo of her former lover. She hadn't seen his face in years and wasn't sure she was ready to again, even if it was simply a digital image.

She'd spent the last twenty years happily married, yet part of her was hesitant to learn if he'd done the same. Of course he'd married. He'd been very clear to her that he wanted a family. He would have found someone who could commit to him and give him the life he'd wanted with her.

She hoped he had, anyway. He deserved to be happy. He deserved all the happiness Caroline hadn't been able to give him.

Though she hadn't had a single picture of him, she could see his face clearly in her mind. His soft brown eyes, the same color as his hair, lit whenever he and Caroline talked about the future they'd never have. His smile was wide, exposing slightly crooked teeth, as he leaned toward to his patients to ease their anxieties by telling silly jokes before he started an exam. The attention he had shown sick kids was one of the many things she'd found attractive about him.

When they'd met, he had never been married and had no children, but when he talked about being a family with her, he meant her *and* Katie. Katie was always in his thoughts when he talked about how happy they could be.

If she'd had the courage to leave John, she and Simon would have built a good life together. As always, though, when she thought of how things could have been, she reminded herself that if she changed the past, she wouldn't have had Tobias. And she'd loved that man.

"Just do it," Judith said as she sat next to Carol.

Carol looked over. "What?"

"You think we don't know what's been distracting you since lunch?" She gestured toward the phone in Carol's hand. "Do it. Cyberstalk the man."

She giggled. "Cyberstalk?"

"Isn't that the term?"

She nodded. "Yeah, Mom, that's the term." She bit her lip.

"I don't know why I'm so nervous to find out what he's been up to, but I am."

"Well, you're going to find out one way or another. Might as well do it now instead of stressing about it until you see him."

Her mother had a point. Carol clicked the link and waited while Simon's biography loaded. The moment the page displayed his photo, she smiled. His hair was more gray than brown now and the creases around his eyes and between his brows had grown deeper, but his eyes were still as kind and his smile as infectious. He was still gorgeous as hell, and her heart still skipped a beat when she saw him.

Judith peered at the phone. "Oh, he's handsome."

"Yeah," Carol said. "He always was."

"Charming?" Judith asked, as if that would explain how Carol had ended up having an affair with him.

"He was charming but sincere." She looked at her mom. "His charms were natural. Not...manipulative. He took care of me. I was in a bad place even before Katie died. I was struggling to keep myself together. He saw that and helped me."

"I'm glad," Judith said.

"The reason I ended up in St. Louis was because Simon had a house there. He got me a job. He gave me the ability to move on. If it hadn't been for him..." She let her words fade because she didn't know what would have happened to her if it weren't for Simon. A strange sense of fear settled in her heart. If it hadn't been for him, she likely never would have recovered. "He saved me," she said, knowing it was true.

"Well, thank God for him, then."

Carol nodded as she skimmed his biography, to be left with the same unanswered questions. There was no mention of a wife or children. She suspected if she called her sister-in-law, Lara would have all the information she could find on the man in a matter of minutes. Lara was an ace at *cyberstalking*, as Judith had called it.

"When I was—" Judith stopped abruptly.

Thankful for the distraction, Carol dropped her phone into her lap and focused on her mother. Judith had the same look on her face she'd had before she'd confessed to getting treatment for depression. An internal debate was waging. Did she want to say what had almost slipped out? Carol had to wonder if she wanted to hear it.

"When I was seventeen," Judith said, looking up at the sunset, "I met a boy. His name was Glen. He'd dropped out of school in eighth grade and become a mechanic. That was common back then. Men had to work to support their families even before they were grown. He was the most handsome boy I'd ever seen. We became inseparable." Judith's smile spread. "I was so in love with him."

Carol smiled too. Seeing her mom so serene warmed her heart. Rare were the times when Judith didn't seem to be on edge. As she spoke now, the aura around her softened.

"What was he like?" Carol asked.

"Wild," Judith stated and laughed softly. "He made me feel..."

"Alive," Carol said.

Judith nodded. "He wasn't afraid of living, and he had this

way of making me want to live too. He wasn't concerned with being proper and doing what society told him. He was free from all that, and I wanted to be free like him. He was the one person who made me feel good about myself. I wanted more of that."

Carol chuckled. "He was your John."

Judith lowered her eyes for several moments before shrugging. "I suppose he was. I wasn't as strong as you, Carol. I wasn't as brave." Sadness filled her eyes as she eyed her daughter. "I let my friends convince me I could do better. I ended things with Glen and..."

"And married Dad."

Judith returned her focus to the sky. "Dennis wasn't... He didn't have the spark Glen had, but he was steady and sensible. He was able to provide for us, Carol. And sometimes that's more important."

A slight jolt rolled through Carol. "Wait a minute. You said you met Glen when you were seventeen." Carol's mouth fell open as a smirk twitched at her mother's lips. "*Mom*! You started dating Dad when you were fifteen."

A mischievous little giggle left Judith. "I told you you're more like me than you want to admit."

Rolling her head back, Carol laughed. "Oh, my God! Did Dad know?"

Judith's amusement shifted to something sadder in an instant. "Glen and I had a meeting spot outside of town. I thought I was very clever, but your dad had grown suspicious. He followed me one night."

Carol gasped. "Uh-oh."

"I'd never seen your father angry before. He was always so calm. So...boring. His anger was terrifying. Like a hurricane that came out of nowhere."

"He always had a storm brewing inside him," Carol observed. She'd seen it every day of her life growing up.

"He...he punched Glen, and they rolled around hitting each other while I screamed for them to stop."

Carol couldn't imagine her father on the ground in a fist fight. Her father was always so stiff, so stern. So...proper. "Who won?"

"Nobody," Judith said flatly. "We all lost."

Once again, Carol felt a shock down to her core. For the first time in her life, she considered that her mom had never been happy because she'd lived a life of regret. "You chose the wrong one?"

Judith seemed to consider how to answer. "I loved your father. He was a good man."

"But he wasn't Glen," Carol said with complete understanding.

"Nobody was Glen," Judith said with a wistful smile. "Nobody could ever match him. But if I'd chosen him..."

"What?"

Judith blinked a few times before looking at Carol. "Well, I wouldn't have you, would I? What have you told me a hundred times about John? He might not have been the right choice, but he gave us Katie. And we wouldn't change that for anything. I loved your father. He was a good man."

Carol didn't miss how Judith repeated herself, as if she were trying to convince the universe she had made the right choice after all. Thinking back, she could remember her mom saying that repeatedly whenever the topic of her father came up. Judith had loved him. He was a good man.

"What happened to Glen?" she asked. "Do you know?"

Judith lowered her face as if her hands held the answer. "He went off to the war."

"Vietnam?"

Judith's sadness returned but changed somehow. This ran deeper than the usual melancholy that hung over her. Carol understood why, even before Judith softly said, "He didn't come home."

Carol took her hand and squeezed. Her heart ached for her mother's loss. How tragic that must have been for her. "I'm sorry, Mom."

"When I found out, I cried so hard. I thought I was over him, but..." She blinked several times. "I tried not to think about him. I did okay for a long time. Then you brought John home and your dad started comparing him to Glen and saying how you were exactly like me."

Carol opened her mouth, remembering how much her parents disapproved of John from the start, without even giving him a chance. "Is that why Dad hated him so much?"

Judith shrugged one shoulder. "He wasn't wrong, Carol. John and Glen were cut from the same cloth. They could both charm their way out of a wet bag. They both found good girls and tried to drag them down."

Carol laughed at that. "John didn't try to drag me down, Mom. He just did."

"And Glen would have dragged me down. I loved him and

he loved me, but he wasn't the responsible choice. John wasn't either."

Carol couldn't argue with that, but she wasn't focused on her choice. Another piece of her life that she'd never understood seemed to be falling into place. "Dad's issue with me was because I reminded him of you when you were younger."

"Your dad…"

"Was angry at me for as long as I can remember. Stop trying to sugarcoat it, Mom. He was mean for no reason, and his attitude escalated once John came into the picture. But he wasn't really angry at me, was he? I reminded him of things he couldn't forget. He never forgave me for falling for John because he never forgave you for Glen."

Judith shifted in the way she always did when Carol was calling her parents out for something. "I think you're reading an awful lot into this."

"I don't think so. The one thing I have never been able to figure out about Dad is what I could have done to create so much resentment from him."

"I told you. You were too stubborn. He thought that was disrespectful."

"Or he thought having my own mind was a threat because you used to have your own mind and it led you astray."

Judith darted her eyes to Carol. "Your father loved you."

"But he didn't like me very much. Even you can't deny that."

Judith didn't argue. She sighed one of her discontented sighs. "I don't know why he was…"

"Angry."

Once again, she didn't counter Carol's observation. "I'm sorry. I didn't know how much he hurt you. I should have protected you more. I was...I was inside my own mind by then. I didn't always see what I should have."

Carol didn't have to think too hard to know she was right. Her mom always seemed to be living in her own world. "It's okay, Mom," she said softly. "We can't change the past."

"No. We can't."

Carol took a deep breath. The air was starting to fill with the scents of the dinner Ellen was busy cooking inside the RV. Pasta sauce and garlic bread drifted on the air. Dinner would be ready soon, but she wasn't ready for the interruption. She was enjoying this time with her mom, finally getting to know her. Though, she didn't like the sadness that had settled over Judith's features again. That frown had been on her mother's face most of Carol's life. She rarely had seen the smile that had lit Judith's eyes a few minutes before.

Her mother looked as if the weight of the world had found her yet again.

Squeezing Judith's hand, Carol tugged lightly as she grinned. "So. How did you meet Glen?"

TEN

THE FIRST TWO days of their visit to Washington D.C. had been filled with museums and sightseeing. Not until the third day did Carol gather Katie's ashes and put the vial into her pocket. They were going to leave her in the grass outside of the Washington Monument, but Carol had convinced the women to make one more stop first.

She was reading the content displayed on the screen of her phone when her mom distracted her.

"We'll never find it," Judith said.

"We'll find it," Carol reassured her. "I'm looking at a website with a search engine for the names."

"There are so many." Ellen's soft voice was a mix of awe and sadness. "How can there be so many?"

Lifting her face, focusing on the wall before them, Carol did her best to detach from her emotions. She was really good at that, but still, she felt the weight of what they were seeing. Almost sixty-thousand names etched into granite—each one an American soldier lost to the Vietnam War.

The reality was overwhelming. The atmosphere surrounding the monument was solemn. Though the sun shone brightly in a nearly cloudless sky, the air was heavy with sorrow. Voices were quieter here, as if speaking too loudly would dishonor the fallen.

Judith stared at the wall, Ellen dabbed her eyes, and Carol returned her attention to the phone in her hands to continue the search for Glen Parsons.

"This way." Carol turned away from the center of the monument where they'd stopped. Rather than the seemingly never-ending list of names, she focused on the year etched into the panels. If she looked at the names, her heart would shatter in her chest. So many people. So many lives cut short.

When she found 1969, she glanced at her phone again, looking for the location of Glen's name. She counted down fourteen rows and three names in. She never knew the man, had never even known he'd existed until a few nights before, but an ache tightened her chest and tears pricked at her eyes as she found his name forever cut in stone.

She read the words several times before looking over her shoulder. Ellen was holding Judith's hand. The sisters stood motionless. Carol couldn't imagine how this must be impacting them. Having lived during the height of the war, they were certainly haunted by the horrors of never knowing who might be called to die next.

Carol touched Glen's name with her fingertips. "He's here."

Judith lowered her face as Ellen hugged her. Carol hesitated before leaving the etching to embrace her mom. Her mom wasn't a hugger, but she clearly needed comfort at the moment. Carol enfolded her tightly, her mom's tears soaking through the thin material covering Carol's shoulder. She'd never seen her mother cry. Not really cry. Not even at her father's funeral. Judith had held herself together like the pillar of strength she'd always told Carol a woman should be.

The moment didn't last long. Judith took a deep breath through her nose, straightened her shoulders, and dabbed her eyes.

"Give me a moment, please," she said weakly.

Ellen frowned. "Judy?"

"I need a minute," Judith said.

Carol held her hand out to Ellen, who seemed hesitant to leave her sister. "We won't be far, Mom."

They stepped away, leaving Judith to do what she needed to do.

"I'm glad she told you about Glen," Ellen said. "She was crazy about that boy."

Carol smiled. "I wish she'd told me sooner."

"She was ashamed. Not only of cheating on Dennis, even though she was young, but because she felt like she let Glen down by not choosing him."

"If she loved him so much, why didn't she?"

"She didn't have the courage, kiddo. Times were vastly different by the time you fell for John. Disobeying your parents didn't carry the same stigma for you as it did in our era. The Vietnam War changed a lot of things, including society. If she'd stayed with Glen, our parents would have disowned her. She would have been shamed. That would have broken her. She's not strong like you."

"She said that the other night. I don't believe it. I'm sure she was scared, but she would have survived."

"Of course she would have, darling, but things like that were more complicated back then. The movies make it sound nice, don't they? Good girl and bad boy fall in love and triumph over social norms to live happily ever after. How did that work out for you?"

A shocked laugh rolled from Carol. "*Ouch.*"

"Well, it's true, isn't it?"

"Yeah, it's true. Being with John was exciting and romantic until reality set in. Then everything was a disaster."

"It would have been a disaster for your mother too. But in those days, if you got yourself in a mess, you stayed in that mess."

Carol processed Ellen's assessment for a minute. "Did she stay with Dad all those years because she didn't believe in divorce?" Tugging her aunt's arm to stop their stroll, Carol stared her down. "Aunt Ellen. Did Mom want to leave him?"

"I think she regretted that she married your father. I think she regretted not making her own life. But if you ever tell her I said that, I'll convince her you're insane and have you committed."

Carol looked back to where her mother stood, staring at the wall. "I didn't know she was so unhappy. Well...I knew. I guess I never considered why." She frowned. "I always thought it was because I was such a disappointment to them."

Ellen put her hand to Carol's chin and turned her face back. "I don't know how many times you have to hear this before it sinks in, but you were never a disappointment to your mother, Carol. Some choices you made were disappointing, yes, but that is worlds away from *you* being a disappointment. She is, and always has been, proud of you."

She smiled at her aunt. "I'm starting to figure that out."

"Good. Then I would say you have come a long way from where you were when you arrived in Florida."

"We've both come a long way," Carol said. "Thank you for convincing her to take this trip."

"You're welcome." Ellen hugged her close and kissed her cheek. "Come on. I don't want her standing there reliving the past too long. She'll get lost in it. Like someone else tends to do," she added, giving Carol a gentle nudge.

Rejoining Judith, Carol took the paper and pencil from her bag and offered them to her mother. She and Ellen stood back as Judith held the paper to the wall and rubbed the lead over Glen's name until the etching was clearly visible on the paper.

Once she was done, Carol opened the journal she'd brought, and Judith placed the page inside. Carol closed the leather cover and put the book back into her bag, ensuring the paper wouldn't be crinkled or torn as they continued their journey toward healing.

"Next stop," she said, "that big *towner*. The one for *dat* president."

Judith laughed as she wiped her nose. "Oh, Katie was so funny."

"I'm guessing that means the big tower for George Washington?" Ellen asked.

"The very one," Carol said.

———

Caroline winced when her father slammed the driver's door of the car. She couldn't see his face from where she sat in the back seat, but she didn't have to. The anger on his face was something so familiar, she saw his pressed lips and narrowed eyes in her sleep.

"Third place," he said as he started the car. "She got third place."

"She worked hard," her mom said, buckling her seat belt.

"Clearly not hard enough."

Her father turned in his seat, but Caroline didn't look up. "How do you explain this?"

Hot tears filled her eyes as shame settled over her. If her father had let her do her project on photosynthesis, she would have gotten first. He'd made her change her topic halfway through because he didn't think the process was interesting enough. With less than two weeks left, he made her start over with a project about antibodies and blood types. If he'd left her alone...

"Caroline!"

She jumped and had no choice but to look at him now. He was as angry as she'd imagined.

"How do you explain this?" he demanded.

"I don't know," she said quietly.

"I know," he said, turning around. "You spent all weekend playing with that Carter kid."

One afternoon. She'd spent one afternoon following Maryanne Carter around, pretending they were friends. Maryanne had ignored her, as always, but Caroline acted like that was part of the game. Because being ignored by a kid her age was better than having her father hover over her, telling her how she was doing her science project all wrong.

Caroline bit her lip. She wasn't going to cry. Not in front of him. The big jerk would tell her that was wrong too.

"It's just a science fair," Judith said. "A sixth-grade science fair, Dennis. She's not being graded on how she placed."

"That doesn't change the fact that she could have done better if she hadn't goofed around all weekend."

Caroline bit down harder. And harder. Not stopping until she tasted blood. The pain and the metallic taste gave her something to focus on so she didn't hear her father complaining in the front seat. He wasn't talking to her anyway. He was telling her mom how it was her fault that Caroline had failed yet again. She wasn't doing her job as a mother. She wasn't being attentive enough. Great. Now her mom was going to be the one hovering. That was almost worse than when her dad stood over her.

At least she knew what to anticipate from him. He was angry all the time. He was never happy, no matter what Caroline did. Her mom was like an emotionless robot. She seemed empty inside most of the time, which was creepy, but then she'd snap and be mad or sad. Caroline never knew what to expect from her.

Her mom tried to explain that kids can't work all the time,

but her dad started lecturing her about how he had a full-time job by the time he was in high school. He understood what it meant to be responsible when he was young. Caroline was spoiled. That was the problem. She was spoiled and didn't think she had to work for anything.

Caroline tuned them out. An argument was going to start soon. Not an argument, really, because her worthless mom never fought back. It was more like her dad telling them how they weren't living up to his standards and her mom never standing up for herself or her kid.

He said something about how his daughter was going to live up to her potential, but Caroline was already slipping deep into her own world. She was already pulling her mind inside herself so she hadn't clearly heard him. His ranting continued all the way home.

Once they were inside, Caroline tried to rush to her room, but he caught her by the arm and pulled her with him. His fingertips dug painfully into her bicep as he all but dragged her to the table. He shoved her into a chair and leaned close.

"Third place gets you three pages. Before bed."

"Dad!" She looked at her mom but, as always, didn't get any support.

Her mom simply lowered her face and turned away. She focused on unbuttoning her jacket instead of the unreasonable punishment being put on her daughter.

"You will write three pages. Do you understand?" He didn't wait for a reply because he wasn't really asking. He slammed the encyclopedia onto the table with the notebook that Caroline had filled halfway already.

This was her punishment for getting anything less than A. Or getting a word wrong on her spelling test. Or answering wrong on her math homework. Or placing third in the science fair. She would sit there and copy the encyclopedia, word for word, into the notebook. If she wrote too big or tried to skip words, he would make her do the pages over.

"You will *live up to your potential," he said before turning away.*

Caroline looked to her mother. Three pages before bed?

Her mom gave her a soft smile and went into the kitchen.

"I hate you," Caroline muttered. "I hate both *of you." She didn't dare say the words loud enough to be heard, but she felt them. She felt them down to her bones. And she would never stop hating them. They were the worst parents ever.*

She flipped to the bookmarked page that started with Cresson, Elliott. *Sniffing back her tears, she found the last page in the notebook she'd filled and started copying the words as her mother placed a cookie and a glass of milk on the table. Caroline wasn't allowed to have anything but water after dinner, which they'd eaten before going to the fair. Her mom was breaking the rules. Caroline wasn't impressed. If Mom wanted to break the rules, she could tell Dad that his demands were stupid. She could tell Caroline she didn't have to copy three pages of the encyclopedia. She could tell Dad that he was a jerk.*

But her mom didn't do any of that. She broke the rules by sneaking Caroline a cookie that she *would get in trouble for eating if Dad found out.*

Caroline looked from the treat up to the woman who had

once again betrayed her and narrowed her eyes. "I don't want that."

Her mom's soft smile fell into that familiar scowl. "Fine." She snatched the cookie and drink away from her. A few drops of milk sloshed over the rim of the cup and landed on the notebook. As she headed back to the kitchen, she said, "Three pages before bed. You'd better get started."

Caroline glared until her mom was no longer visible and then she turned back to the encyclopedia. Using her sleeve, because her father would hate that, she wiped the milk off the notebook, smudging the ink from the last entry she'd copied.

She couldn't defy her parents by not doing the writing, but she didn't have to learn, which was why they were making her do this. She didn't have to do that. So, as she wrote, she let her mind drift. Her eyes could see the words, her hand wrote them out, but in her mind, she was thinking of where she was going to live when she was a grown-up. The dream changed every time. She'd imagined herself as a movie star in California or a scientist at NASA. She'd even pictured herself as one of the first people to live in a colony on the moon.

The one thing that never changed, not once, was that she was going to move as far away from her parents as she could get, and then she would never speak to them again.

———

Carol hadn't planned a stop in Philadelphia, but she was so glad she'd taken the detour. They were on their way to New York City, more specifically the Statue of Liberty, when they started seeing signs. Ellen had gasped and leaned forward in the passenger seat as she announced she'd always wanted to go to Philadelphia, which was all Carol needed to make an unexpected stop. Judith protested, of course, but Carol pointed out that one of the perks of living like drifters was that they could *drift* whenever they chose to. Ellen had laughed. Judith hadn't. She was worried about getting to Ohio on time.

Carol reminded her mom they had plenty of time. She found a place to park the RV, and they took a bus to Independence Hall. As much as Judith had protested, her eyes were filled with as much excitement as Ellen's when they walked into the building where the country's forefathers had gathered.

They couldn't do a self-guided tour this time, but the pace the guide was keeping was perfect for Carol's companions. She was glad they weren't relying on brochures and Carol's memory to guide them. This gave her a chance to relax and enjoy the visit rather than feeling obligated to keep her mom and aunt entertained.

Judith leaned close to Carol as they were led toward the room where the Constitution was signed. "You don't have... the container with you, do you?"

Carol smiled at the underlying panic in her mom's voice. "I do," she answered back, "but I'm not doing that here."

"Thank you."

Carol's smile widened. She wasn't sure what the fine for leaving human remains inside a national historical site would be, but she imagined doing so wouldn't be worth the risk.

She'd find a nice grassy area, as she tended to do, to leave John and Katie.

"Isn't this amazing?" Ellen kept her voice soft, like the words could disturb something precious, as they walked with their group into the Assembly Room. "Think of all the things that happened in this room." As she'd done at the war memorial, Ellen put her hand to her heart and blinked several times before looking at Carol. "I remember you used to recite the Constitution on command. You knew every word."

Carol laughed softly. "Dad took all my books away until I could repeat it." She lowered her voice to mimic her father. "There are more important authors in this world than Madeleine L'Engle, Caroline, and certainly more important things to read than *A Wrinkle in Time*."

"You might not have liked it," Judith said, "but you're the smartest person I know, and you can thank your father for that."

Resisting the urge to roll her eyes, she said, "Thanks for making me smart, Dad. And for giving me a writer's callus by the time I was ten."

Judith sighed. Ellen returned her attention to the tour guide. Carol debated if she should apologize. She didn't. She wasn't going to apologize for resenting her father's unreasonable approach to teaching his daughter.

They were back outside, strolling in the sunshine, when Ellen pointed to a sign. "This way to the Liberty Bell." She headed that direction like a woman on a mission, once again making Carol smile. Her aunt was determined to see everything she could while on this trip, and Carol was happy to oblige.

"If you can find some good in John Bowman," Judith said, once Ellen was far enough ahead to not overhear, "you certainly can find some good in your father."

Carol let the words sink in. "John was far from perfect, Mom, but we had good times. He was a good man when he wasn't drinking."

Judith snorted. "When was that?"

"Not often, in the end," Carol conceded. "But he was a good father to Katie. He made her happy."

Judith shook her head, as if she could debate, but chose not to. "We've been over this. Yes, your dad was stern, but he pushed you hard because he believed in you. If it'd been up to me, you...you would have ended up...like me."

Carol furrowed her brow with confusion. "What does that mean? Like you?"

"Do you think I wanted my life to revolve around that house? I had dreams too, you know."

Carol searched the depths of her mind, trying to recall the slightest hint of what those might have been. "You loved cooking. I remember how it seemed like the only time you were happy was when you were in the kitchen."

"When I was young, my chore was fixing supper every day. I thought working in a kitchen would be wonderful. Cooking and baking all day. I told my mother that one day. That was in the early 1950s, so you can imagine her reaction. Still, times were changing quickly. Your aunt was able to break free from social demands, but it was too late for me.

However, when you were born, I knew you would have a different future. Women were entering the workforce all the time by then. That wasn't going to change. Though your father wasn't necessarily supportive of women working, he understood you could have a career, and he wanted you to have a good one. What did I know about instilling work ethic? I left that to your father. I know he was hard on you, but he did make you what you are today."

Carol took her mom's hand. "I wish he could have seen that I needed kindness too."

"He didn't know, Carol. Can't you understand that he simply didn't know?"

"How does someone not know to be nice to his kid?"

Judith scowled. "Because no one had ever been nice to him as a child, yet he grew to be successful. He did what he knew. He never hit you; you weren't abused."

"Mom," she said with a scoff.

"He was harsh," Judith insisted.

"He was *cruel*." Pulling her mom to a stop, she held her gaze. "You may not see my scars, but trust me, he left plenty."

Judith tightened her lips in the way she did when she felt attacked, but after a few tense seconds, her eyes turned sad. "I see them," she confessed softly. "So did he. After you left, I found him sitting at the table, staring at your empty chair. He was a million miles away. When I asked him what was wrong, he said he'd pushed you away. The reason you'd disappeared instead of coming home to us was because he'd pushed you away. He knew he was wrong. He didn't know how to make it right, Carol."

The knot in Carol's chest tightened with the image her mother had painted. "He could have apologized."

Judith laughed flatly. "Oh, honey. The moon would have crashed to earth first. He was sorry, but he could never say so. Holding you accountable for leaving was easier than admitting to you that he was wrong. But he knew. He knew. And that's going to have to be enough for you."

"Well, he's gone," Carol pointed out. "I can't really ask for more, can I?"

"Forgive him," Judith said. "Forgive both of us. We did our best."

Carol filled her lungs with a cleansing breath before replying. "I'm trying, Mom. I really am. It's not easy. He didn't have to be like that. He didn't have to make me feel like I was a burden he had to bear."

"I know," Judith said. "But you have to find a way to see that you weren't. The burden he bore was his own past—his own scars. He wanted better for you. He wanted better for Katie too."

Carol bit her lip. "We all wanted better for Katie than what she got."

Judith touched Carol's cheek. "I meant the life John was giving you. He was breaking you, and Katie was starting to see that. A child should never see how broken her mother is."

The words were like an arrow to Carol's heart. "I saw how broken you were, Mom," she whispered. "And I thought it was my fault."

Tears filled Judith's eyes, but she blinked them back. "I'm sorry."

"I know. I understand now. We're going to be better now. I promise."

A smile tugged at her mom's lips. "Well, we will be as soon as you start seeing a counselor."

Carol rolled her head back and chuckled. "*Mom*."

A quiet laugh left Judith. "Come on. We need to catch up to Ellen before she gets herself into some kind of trouble."

Carol slipped her arm through her mom's. "She spent some time in jail when she was younger, didn't she?"

Judith snickered. "Oh, you have no idea."

ELEVEN

AS THE FERRY neared Liberty Island the following afternoon, Carol admired the massive statue waiting to greet them. She stood out against the clear blue sky like the beacon of hope she was meant to be. The crowd on the boat *oohed* and *ahhed*, but Carol barely heard them as she thought of the last time she was here. For twenty-two years, she and Tobias had played "Did you know..." practically everywhere they went. He knew so much about science and nature, while Carol retained historical facts.

They'd visited the Statue of Liberty years ago. The entire afternoon was spent with Tobias telling her all about the flora and fauna on the island, while she explained the statue's official name was Liberty Enlightening the World and gave him the meaning behind the seven spikes on the crown. They discussed the meaning of the statue's broken shackles and how racism continued to be an ongoing issue. Though times were changing, they still received the occasional disapproving look when people realized they were a couple.

The more unique tidbits she wanted to share with Katie, like the shoe size of the statue, were things Carol had to research. Useless facts like that hadn't been in the encyclopedias she'd been forced to memorize growing up.

Holding her right hand out, Carol examined her fingers. She no longer had the knot on her middle finger from years of holding a pencil tight, squeezing hard with pent-up frustration. Though the callus had long ago been buffed away, the years of silently loathing her parents as she copied page after page had lingered.

She hadn't blamed her mother for punishments doled out by her father. She'd blamed her mother for being too weak to stand up to him. Now that Carol was letting go of her bitterness and seeing her mother as a flawed human rather than the pitiless robot she'd always imagined her to be, Carol was starting to feel the anger at her father slip away as well.

Although she would never know her father as she was beginning to know her mother, she understood there was more to him than she'd always seen. He was a boy who'd been left on his own far too early in his life. A young man who found out the girl he loved, loved someone else. He was a husband who was so determined to hang on to his wife, he didn't know how to stop fighting. A father who didn't want his daughter to face the same struggles he'd faced so he pushed her harder than he'd ever been pushed. And he was a grandfather who lost his only grandchild and didn't know how to mourn.

He was a man who lived with regrets but never knew how to make amends for them.

That saddened her. If he'd found the courage to reach out, she'd like to think they could have made the strides she was now making with her mom. She wouldn't have felt like an outsider in her own parents' home her entire life, and she certainly wouldn't have felt like a stranger at his funeral.

The flip side of that particular coin was if she'd been able to turn to her parents when Katie died, she wouldn't have ended up in St. Louis. She wouldn't have met Tobias. Carol may have never known the family she had now had her father extended an olive branch. As challenging as starting her life over had been, she'd landed where she needed to be. She'd found the place where she'd belonged.

"Thinking about Tobias again?" Ellen asked.

Carol smiled. "Yeah, I guess I am. I was so lucky to have him. He calmed my storms."

"He was good for you. The happiest I've ever seen you was when you were with him."

Dragging her attention from the statue, Carol focused on her aunt. "Do you ever catch yourself playing 'What If' with the past? What if you had made this choice instead of that one?"

"Everyone plays that game, honey," Ellen said. "Be careful you don't get lost in it, though. *What if* doesn't change anything."

"I know." She looked out at the island again, forcing away thoughts that could have stopped her from finding Tobias. "Is this your first time here?"

Ellen held her hand above her eyes to block out some of the bright sunlight. "No, but she gets more magnificent each time. Don't you think?"

"She does."

"I've never been here," Judith said. "I've never been anywhere."

Carol couldn't help but notice the underlying anger in her mom's voice. The way Ellen leaned around her to get a look at Judith implied she'd heard the animosity as well. Carol's father had thought vacations were frivolous. They'd never taken one, and other than an occasional visit after she'd moved away or to see Ellen when she'd lived in Boulder, Carol couldn't recall them taking one after she was grown.

Carol and Tobias were married several years before they'd gotten to the point financially where they could travel. She'd loved telling her parents about all the places she had been. However, she had stopped sharing her excitement after a year or so. Her mom had always seemed dismissive when Carol would tell her where she and Tobias had been and what they'd seen, and her father had thought they were wasting money.

She had taken that as a lack of interest from her mother, but seeing through Judith's defenses now, Carol realized she'd been inadvertently rubbing her mom's nose into her misery.

"You're seeing things now," Carol told her. "We can go wherever you want, Mom."

Judith didn't respond.

"Tobias couldn't sit still," Carol continued, pretending she hadn't noticed. The ferry neared the pier where the passengers would shuffle off like cattle. "As soon as we were home from one vacation, he was thinking of where to go next. We had talked about going to Greece for our anniversary. It would have been twenty years in July."

Her mom and aunt knew that, but for some reason Carol felt the need to explain.

Ellen put her hand on Carol's. "I'll go to Greece anytime you want. Our trip won't be as romantic, but I'll do what I can to make it fun."

Carol laughed. "I believe you would. What do you think, Mom? Should we plan a trip to Greece?"

As people started moving toward the exit, Judith shrugged. They didn't rush toward the exit, though. Being in the back of the crowd was easier for the two older women. "I don't know. I've never thought about traveling. This is the closest thing to a family vacation we've ever taken, isn't it?"

"It is," Carol agreed. "But it doesn't have to be the only family vacation we'll ever take. Greece is beautiful, Mom. You'd love it."

She shook her head slightly. "That seems so extravagant. We can find someplace more affordable to visit."

"It's not as expensive as you'd think," Carol said. "We'll talk about it more later."

They were on steady ground at the moment. She wasn't going to knock them off balance over a possible vacation down the road. Instead, she followed her companions off the ferry.

"I don't want to go up to the crown." Judith tilted her head back and peered up. "That's... No, that's too high."

"No, we're not climbing all those stairs," Carol agreed, not wanting to tell her mother that she'd likely never be able to make it to the crown if she wanted to. There were far too many steps for the older women to take. "Let's find a quiet spot in the grass for Katie and John, and then we can walk around the museum."

As she tended to do when they were preparing to spread the ashes, Carol wrapped her fingers around the container inside her pocket and grew quiet. Her mind pictured Katie there with her, imagining her daughter's reaction to the world around them.

She's so big, Mama, Katie would have said. *How'd they make her so big? Why's she holding that light? What's her book say?*

This time, however, her mind didn't stay on imagining Katie's excitement. Had Katie lived, she'd be thirty now. When Carol was thirty, she was starting a new life with Tobias, and she and her mother couldn't have been further apart. She liked to think her relationship with Katie would have been better. She and Katie would have been close. They would have talked all the time, about everything.

Ellen had said *what if* didn't change anything. Carol agreed. Still, her mind fell into that trap anyway and part of her wondered, what if she and Katie hadn't been close? What if Katie had grown to resent her the way Carol had resented Judith? What if Katie had grown as angry and bitter over her childhood as Carol had?

Judith had been right when she said Katie was starting to

realize how broken her home was. No matter how much Carol had tried to hide her misery, Katie was starting to see through the façade. No matter how many excuses or lies Carol told, John's drinking was tearing them apart and Katie was beginning to see the truth. Maybe she didn't understand, but she knew her parents weren't happy.

Are you and Daddy fighting again?

Katie had asked that more than once, and every time Carol faked a smile and reassured her daughter. But Katie saw. Had she lived to be old enough to understand, she might have blamed Carol for not protecting her. She might have resented Carol for not forcing John to get sober. She might have held the same anger in her heart that Carol had carried all these years. Tears filled Carol's eyes, and she had to force the air from her lungs. The thought of Katie seeing her through those eyes made her chest ache.

Unlike Judith, however, Carol thought she would have had the courage to reach out to Katie. She would have worked endlessly to build a bridge between them. She wouldn't have let her daughter's life pass by without knowing her, without being a part of Katie's ups and downs, as her parents had done with Carol.

Then again...

She hadn't done a damn thing to try to fix things with her father. She'd let the seed of resentment he'd planted in her as a child expand into a forest. The trees had grown so thick and strong she hadn't even been able to uproot them when he'd died. His funeral hadn't been a time to forgive him and put those bad memories to rest as she should have done. His funeral had highlighted the rift between them.

She'd felt as unwanted and unwelcomed when he was in a casket as she'd felt when he'd loomed over her, demanding she strive to do better, work harder, be more serious about life. He was gone, but she'd continued to sense him looking down his nose at her—disapproving of her very existence.

Almost four years after his passing, and she was finally beginning to see him as human. She was starting to allow herself to feel something beyond blinding anger. He'd robbed her of the opportunity to have a secure and carefree childhood. He'd embedded such a deep sense of unworthiness in her that she'd carried that feeling into adulthood. Though she'd managed to push those feelings into the shadows, they still haunted her, and she'd hated him for that.

No matter how hard she'd tried to give her daughter a better life, Carol had started to fail. She'd started to crack under the pressure of balancing motherhood, work, and John's drinking. She *had been* failing. Katie was beginning to see through her to the pain beneath her forced smiles, and there was no way for Carol to know how that would have impacted her child or their long-term relationship.

Despite all her efforts, she hadn't been the perfect mother. She hadn't protected Katie. In fact, her efforts to protect the innocence of Katie's childhood had inadvertently laid the foundations for the accident that took Katie's life.

Just as her father's determination to give his daughter a better life had inadvertently caused emotional damage Carol still hadn't finished sorting through. Carol had always seen him as heartless. Maybe he was scared. Like Carol had been scared that Katie would grow up loathing her the way Carol had loathed her parents. Scared that Katie wouldn't love her or forgive her for not helping John before his addiction consumed him.

Maybe her father was so terrified of being left by his daughter, like his parents had left him, that he was too scared to let himself love her as much as he should have. Maybe if she'd been stronger, braver, and had reached out to him, he would have reached back. Maybe they could have fixed things and she would have known what it was like to have a more caring father.

She would never know. Her father was dead. They would never have a chance to mend and heal because she'd been too angry and, yes, too scared to try when he was alive.

Regret grabbed hold of her heart and squeezed hard enough that an unexpected sob rolled from her. Carol stopped in her tracks and put her hand to her mouth as tears fell down her cheeks.

"What is it?" Ellen asked, panic evident in her voice as she put her hand to Carol's arm.

She couldn't answer. Even if she could find the words to express how much remorse had suddenly filled her, she couldn't talk around the lump of emotion in her throat.

Judith put her hand around Carol's lower back and pushed her toward a bench. "Sit."

Carol didn't sit as much as fall onto the seat. Leaning forward, she buried her hands in her face. She couldn't stop the tears. Her father had been dead for almost four years, and this was the first time she felt the grief of his loss touch her heart. She'd kept the feelings at bay all that time because she'd never really felt like she'd lost him. How could she lose him when she'd never had him?

Except now, she could see that her mom and aunt were right. He had never been the kind of father any child would wish for, but he'd been her father. He was flawed and broken, but he had been there, pushing and hoping she'd find a better life than he'd had.

She'd always known he'd been disappointed when her life jumped the tracks he'd carefully set before her, but she'd never really understood that his disappointment hadn't necessarily been directed at her. He was disappointed in himself. He'd felt like he'd let her down somehow. Even when she got her life together, her father had never stopped feeling like he'd failed her. He hadn't blamed her; he'd blamed himself. Why hadn't she seen that sooner?

"This is getting to be too much," Judith said. "We need to stop this foolishness and get her home."

Carol shook her head as she wiped her cheeks. "No."

"I think she's right this time," Ellen agreed.

"I was thinking about Dad," Carol said. "All these years, I thought he hated me because I wasn't good enough. But he didn't hate me."

"Of course he didn't," Judith stated. "How many times—" She stopped short when Ellen lifted her hand.

"He didn't express his feelings well," Ellen said gently.

"Because he was scared of how much he loved us." Carol's

voice was thick. "Because he remembered how much it hurt to lose his parents. He didn't want to hurt like that again. He thought it was safer to not let anyone know how he felt."

She looked at her mom, gauging her response. The sympathy she saw there made her eyes fill again. "I'm sorry, Mom. I'm sorry I didn't get that sooner."

"He was a complicated man, Carol."

"But he loved me," Carol said, as her mother had said many times before. "I see that now."

"You do?"

Carol nodded and accepted the tissue her aunt held out to her. "I started thinking about how Katie might have seen me if she'd lived. How she might have judged my mistakes, and all of a sudden, I realized how harshly I've been judging his. I'm still mad," she said. "He didn't have to be so mean, but I...I understand now. I get where he was coming from."

Ellen patted her knee. "Understanding is a big step toward forgiveness."

Judith pulled her closer and kissed her head in one of those rare shows of affection. "Have you been drinking again?"

Carol laughed through her tears. "Not yet." She wiped her eyes and nose as she looked out at the water and the skyline in the distance. Serenity settled over her as she took in the scenery, and the grief that had knocked the wind out of her eased.

She liked to think moments like these were signs from Katie or Tobias, but in that moment, she felt like her dad was there, thanking her for realizing that he'd been human and had made mistakes. Warmth spread through her as if his soul was embracing hers. The bitterness and anger eased the stronghold that had kept her from forgiving him. She wasn't there yet, but she'd get there. Someday.

"This is the spot," she said. Leaning over enough to take the container from her pocket, she clutched it in her hand. "This is where we should leave them."

Judith managed a sad smile while Ellen held out another tissue. Carol managed a light laugh. After wiping her eyes again, she told Katie and John how big the statue was, how long it took to assemble after arriving in three-hundred-fifty separate pieces from France, and, of course, that she wore a size eight-hundred-seventy-nine shoe. Judith explained that the arm and torch were damaged in 1916 after German spies planted explosives on a nearby island, and Ellen said that the statue's skin was only as thick as two pennies pressed together.

Carol pushed herself from the bench and sprinkled the ashes into the grass. Looking up at the statue as she closed the container, something she hadn't felt in a long time filled her. Courage.

Lady Liberty meant so many things to so many people— freedom from tyranny or a new start—but in that moment, for Carol, the statue seemed to be telling her that she was strong enough to keep going. She had faced a lot in the last few months—she could face the next step in her journey too.

———

The sky was overcast as Carol walked with her mom and aunt toward the gravesite. She'd been numb since getting the call that her father had died. As she tended to do where her parents were concerned, she pushed the emotions down and didn't let them show.

She didn't know what she was feeling anyway. She'd been celebrating Thanksgiving in Missouri with Tobias and their family when she'd gotten the call from her mom. She had tried to call her mom before they sat down to eat but hadn't gotten an answer. When her phone rang right as they were passing the food around, she almost hadn't answered.

If she didn't, she decided, her mom would give her that cold shoulder she was so good at. Carol decided she could take a few minutes to answer the phone and excused herself from the table. What she hadn't expected was her faux-happy hello to be answered with her mother's flat voice informing her that her father had died.

Carol heard the words but couldn't make sense of them. Her stomach knotted while her brain tried to dissect her mother's meaning.

"He...collapsed and died," her mother continued. "Right after dinner. He had a heart attack."

Tobias had instantly sensed something was wrong and jumped up to join her. She grabbed his hand. Usually that would ground her, but everything from that moment to this one that found her standing at her father's grave was a blur.

Tobias hadn't joined her for the funeral since her parents had never cared for him.

Luckily her aunt was there. Carol thought she should be the first line of support for her mother but was thankful that her mom seemed to be leaning on her sister more. Carol didn't know how to be that way with her mom. They'd never been close enough for her to feel like she would be her mother's first choice for that role anyway. So she held back and let Aunt Ellen take care of Judith.

That was best anyway. She and her mom tended to butt heads more than not, and now wasn't the time for that. Carol heard the priest speaking but didn't really hear the words. She was in robot mode. Long ago, she'd learned how to fake her way through being present. Years of sitting at a table, tuning out her father's tirades, of shutting out judgement, had taught her how to fake being present.

She thought it odd, though, that she couldn't seem to connect now, in this moment, when she should be feeling something. Her father was gone. He was dead.

How was that not bringing her to her knees?

Was she even human?

Maybe her dad was right about her. Maybe she didn't deserve all he'd done for her. Maybe she was too ungrateful and spoiled.

She blinked when someone nudged her. She looked at her aunt, who nodded for her to do something. Carol looked at the grave and realized it was her turn to toss a rose onto the casket. She looked at the red rose in her hand before putting it onto his casket. "I'm sorry, Dad. I wish I'd been better."

Stepping back, she took her spot beside her aunt again. The sting of tears started in the back of her eyes, but Carol blinked them back. Her father would have hated if she'd cried. He'd never been one for displays of emotion.

Besides, the urge to cry wasn't for him. Standing over his grave, knowing he was gone forever, the tears she felt weren't for him. They were for the little girl who had never been enough, no matter how hard she had tried.

As the service ended and people started to leave, Ellen put her hand on Carol's arm. "How are you, honey?"

"I'm fine." She looked at her mom, who was talking to someone Carol didn't know. "How's she?"

"She'll be okay. How long are you staying?"

"My flight's early tomorrow, so—"

"Tomorrow?" Ellen asked, clearly shocked.

Carol had done the wrong thing. She hadn't considered it wrong when she'd made travel arrangements, but clearly her aunt had expected her to stick around longer. "Uh. I could...stay, I guess."

Ellen frowned. "Does your mom know you're leaving so soon?"

Glancing at her mother again. Carol shook her head. "We've barely spoken since I arrived. She's busy. I'll come back soon. Once all this quiets down. You know how these things go. Everyone hovers for the first few weeks, and then they forget. I'll come back when they stop hovering."

Her aunt didn't point out that she knew better. That Carol knew better. She'd leave and go about her life, and she'd forget too. Because that's what she and her parents did. They came into each other's orbits only when necessary, and then they moved on. *Now her father was gone, and she could hardly wait to get out of her mother's orbit.*

She'd feel bad about that if she hadn't received the same treatment when Katie had died. They hadn't spoken to her at the memorial for her daughter. They'd shown up, accepted condolences from others, but had avoided John and Carol. Not that Carol had cared. She'd been so doped up at the service, she'd barely been aware of anything.

She was aware now. She was aware that her mother had barely looked at her. They'd only talked briefly. Her attempt at consoling her mother had been awkward for both of them. Maybe other families mourned together, but the Stewarts tended to keep those things to themselves.

"It's best for me to go, Aunt Ellen. She doesn't need me here. She needs you."

"Carol," Ellen said.

Leaning in, Carol gave her aunt a hug. "She's having a hard time. My being here will make it worse. She doesn't need that. None of us do."

She walked away before her aunt could argue. There was no point. They both knew she was right. She and her mother would never be close. Losing her father wasn't going to change that.

———

After leaving Liberty Island, the women settled in for a night at an RV park a few miles outside of the city. The contradiction in the scenery had distracted Carol more than she would have liked. She related in some strange sense. The hurried and hectic city loomed just a short distance from this peaceful place, like the chaos inside Carol was always boiling beneath the calm.

Carol had to blink several times to refocus her attention on the woman who was sitting across the picnic table. Her mother had said something, but she'd been lost in her own thoughts and hadn't heard her. "I'm sorry?"

"The cemetery," Judith said. "I want to go to the cemetery. We should leave some of Katie's remains with your father."

Carol nodded. "Yes, we should." The thought triggered another in her mind. "Do you happen to know where Frannie and Mark are buried?"

"I don't."

A sense of shame clouded her heart as she once again thought how they'd never even seen Katie's urn. "I'm sure I can find out with an Internet search. I'd like to take some ashes there too."

"They'd like that," Judith said.

Carol wiped her hands on her napkin and looked around the RV park, but she wasn't seeing their surroundings. She was reliving the past again.

"I saw Frannie at the mall once," Judith said. "Did I ever tell you that?"

"No, you didn't," Carol said as her heart twisted inside her chest.

"She asked about you."

"She was such a sweet woman."

Judith didn't agree, but she didn't remind Carol how Frannie and Mark gave in to John too much, as she used to do. "She was happy when I told her you'd finished school and remarried. She wanted me to tell you that she loved and missed you."

Creasing her brow, Carol asked, "Why didn't you?"

"Because I thought it was best not to bring up the past to you," Judith said.

Frustration lit in Carol, something she hadn't felt directed toward her mom in a few days. She was filtering her response when Judith shook her head.

"No. That's not true. I didn't tell you because I always hated how close you two were," her mom confessed. "It was enough I had to compete with Mary. I didn't want to add Frannie back into the mix."

Carol glanced at Ellen, who looked like she was waiting for a duel to begin. Instead of giving in to her frustrations, she forced her anger away. "You don't have to compete with anyone, Mom. Look at us. We're only fighting once a day now."

She let the words linger before smirking. Judith smiled too.

"You'd left everything and everyone behind," Judith said. "I thought it best to leave it alone. But she did worry about you, and she didn't seem angry that you'd left. I think she understood."

"I hope she did." She still wished her mother had told her, but she wasn't upset about it enough to point that out. "I loved Frannie. I love Mary. And I love you."

Since Judith seemed embarrassed about her comment, Carol didn't press harder, but she'd felt she had to point out that she could love them all. A few weeks ago, she wouldn't have thought her mom was concerned about that. After the improvements they'd both been making in their relationship, she could see why she needed to reassure her mom that she did love her.

Putting her hand on Judith's arm, she offered her a soft smile. "How are you feeling about getting back to Dayton tomorrow?"

"Good. I guess I didn't realize how much I missed it. I thought, if you don't mind, I'd invite a few people from church to the ceremony. I wish I'd thought of that sooner. I'm not sure if they can make it on such short notice."

"I think that would be lovely, Mom." She tilted her head at Ellen. "And you?"

She blew a raspberry. "It never did feel like home there. Take me to Colorado, though, and I'll introduce you to the craziest bunch of old biddies you'll ever meet."

Carol laughed. "Deal. What do you think, Mom?"

Judith sighed and shook her head. "I think I've had enough of life on the road for now. Maybe next summer."

"Next summer it is." Carol wasn't surprised. She hadn't expected Judith to last this long on the road. By the time she got them back to Florida, her mom would probably never want to step foot inside her RV again. "I reserved a hotel for us while we're in Dayton. I thought we could all use a break."

"From each other or from such tiny living quarters?" Ellen asked.

"Both." Carol grinned and winked at her. "I reserved one room, but if you'd like your own space—"

"I was kidding," Ellen said.

"Even so," Carol pressed, "I'm happy to get each of us a room if needed."

Judith shook her head. "We should stick together. Women traveling alone are vulnerable."

Carol saw her mother's lecture coming before she even started, so she quickly redirected the conversation. "I'm excited to see Katie's House. I'm glad we're going to arrive a day early. It's going to be emotional enough without me being overwhelmed by the changes."

Ellen smiled. "I was thinking that I'd like to donate some art. Do you think that would be okay?"

"I think that would be great. Thank you," Carol said.

Her brow creased. "I'm not sure how I'd get it there, though."

"We'll work that out when it's ready," she assured her aunt. "I'll talk to someone at the hospital to see if they would be willing to handle the package."

"By someone, she means Simon," Judith said to her sister, but she was eyeing Carol with a twinkle in her eyes.

Seconds passed before Carol realized her mom had teased her. She was too shocked to respond.

However, Ellen nudged Judith. "Sounds like he's already handled her package."

Carol widened her eyes. "Did you just... *Aunt Ellen*! In front of my mother?"

Ellen laughed heartily. Even Judith giggled.

"It's not like I don't know what you two were up to," Judith said. "Your father and I—"

"No." Carol practically jumped from the table. "No. *No.*"

The laughs from the other side of the table increased.

"It's not as if a stork brought you," Ellen added.

"Stop," Carol warned. "This conversation is over. Dead. Done. Never to be brought up again."

She grabbed her plate and walked into the RV as they continued laughing. If this had happened any other time, Carol would probably have regretted confessing her true relationship with the man, but this odd moment of bonding was worth the embarrassment. She waited until she was inside to laugh as well.

TWELVE

THE ATMOSPHERE in the RV changed when the trio arrived in Dayton. The weight of what would be coming the next few days seemed to become more than they could bear. Not just the ceremony and the anniversary of Tobias's passing, but also the planned visit to Dennis's grave. A place Carol hadn't been since his funeral. And two graves she'd never visited. Frannie and Mark Bowman had been gone for years.

The stress of what they would be facing in the coming days had gone unspoken but not unnoticed. They had all grown more pensive as they carried overnight bags to the hotel room at the same hotel where she and John had stayed the last night of their trip. Instead of cooking another meal in the RV kitchen, they'd sat at the restaurant off the hotel lobby, but even then, the conversation was quieter, more serious.

Once they returned to their room, they rotated through the shower and getting ready for bed. Her mom and aunt had turned off the lights above their bed almost immediately, but

Carol knew she wouldn't sleep. Her mind was racing, replaying the last night of John's life over in her mind.

Looking back now, she should have known how things were going to end. He'd been calm that night. He'd been aware. She'd known his time was running low, but she hadn't realized he'd be gone the next day.

She hadn't let herself think about that night in weeks, but being in the same hotel made the last bit of time she'd spent looking after him come rushing back. When he'd first shown up at her office, she was reminded how much she hated him. By the time he'd died a few weeks later, she'd realized that despite everything they'd been through, part of her had still loved him. He was the father of her child, the man who had helped her break the cycle of people pleasing, the first person who had ever made her feel like she was worth something.

Despite all she'd come to despise about him, those things had remained and she'd still had love for him because of them. She was glad that he'd found her. That she'd had a chance to meet the man he'd become—a recovering alcoholic willing to admit he'd been flawed, instead of a selfish drunk who blamed the world for his problems. She'd always known he could be more.

Thinking about John was a distraction, however. The real reason she couldn't sleep was because the anniversary of losing Tobias, the light in her life, was getting closer minute by minute, and she suspected it was going to hit her like a wrecking ball. She'd been hoping having the ceremony, being surrounded by family, would help, but now she was beginning to think she would have been better off hiding in her RV alone somewhere so no one else had to see her fall apart.

And then there was Simon. She should have told him not to come to the house dedication. She should have told him she couldn't see him.

On the anniversary of losing Tobias? What had she been thinking? She was going to be a mess, thinking about how she'd lost her husband. About the last time she'd heard his voice. The last time he'd kissed her head. The last opportunity she'd had to tell him she'd loved him but she'd rolled away from him and gone back to sleep.

Carol rubbed her hands over her tired eyes and silently cursed herself. What the hell had she been thinking?

"Stop it," a soft voice came from the other bed.

Carol dropped her hands. "Stop what?"

"Obsessing about whatever you're obsessing about," her mom said.

She smiled, but her lip trembled and tears filled her eyes. "You were right, Mom. This is too much. I shouldn't have... Why did I..." A wry laugh left her. "It's too much."

"Which part?"

"All of it." She snagged a tissue from the box between their beds and wiped her eyes.

As she did, Judith slipped from her bed and walked around Carol's. She got under the covers on the other side of the queen bed and leaned against the headboard. "Let's work our way down the list. Start with John so we can get that out of the way and move on to more important things."

Carol chuckled, but her smile faded quickly. "He killed himself."

Her words hung in the air before Judith said, "I thought he had cancer."

"He did, and it was winning. He was in a lot of pain and was losing control of his body. He waited until we got to the house and then he took a bunch of pills when I was in Katie's room. I found him outside. In the grass. Right where..." She sniffed and clutched the tissue in her hand.

Judith pressed her lips together for several seconds before saying, "He shouldn't have done that to you."

"He didn't want to continue declining."

"He *shouldn't* have done that to you," Judith stated again.

"Looking back, I think I knew he was going to," Carol said. "I knew he wouldn't let the cancer win. He wasn't that kind of man, you know. He was going to go out on his terms."

"Going on his terms would be admirable if he hadn't left you holding the bag like he always did."

Carol smiled. "Who else was going to hold the bag for him, Mom? He didn't have anyone else." She put her hand on her mom's, stopping her before they could spiral into an argument over John. "I owed it to Katie to help him say goodbye to her. I don't regret it. I'm just sad about it."

"Sad over John Bowman," Judith muttered. "The man was..."

"Complicated," Carol said. "Like Dad."

Judith pressed her lips together for a few seconds. "Okay. We've discussed John. What's next on the list?"

"Katie's gone."

Judith nodded. "We miss her."

"Very much. But I've made my peace with her loss. I can think of her now and smile and know that she's okay. Wherever she is, she's okay."

"Tomorrow will still be difficult. Going to the house, remembering how things used to be," Judith reflected.

Carol swallowed hard. "At least now it won't look like the museum John had kept. He still had her red rain boots," she whispered.

A gasping sound left Judith. "Oh. She loved those boots."

Glancing at her mother, Carol said, "I packed up some things before I left the house to the contractor. Her boots, some old photos, things that I'd wished I'd taken. I left them at Mary's."

"I think I'd like to see them again someday."

"We can make that happen," Carol said.

Judith was quiet for a moment. "Okay, we've hit John and Katie. Shall we discuss Tobias?"

Carol's tears returned. "A year ago..." She wiped her eyes and sniffed. "We thought we had time. We thought we had years to spend together. We didn't know." She bit her lip, but even that old trick wasn't enough to stop her from crying. "I didn't know."

Judith squeezed Carol's hand. "And what would you have done differently if you had known?"

"I would have said goodbye to him. I would have looked at him. I would have..." Her voice trailed as she considered all the things she would have done.

"I was with your father, you know," her mom said. "I was

with him, and I said goodbye to him. I was holding his hand as he let go. Guess what, darling. That didn't make grieving for him any easier."

"I just... I didn't know how precious that last morning was."

Patting her hand, Judith asked, "Do you remember the night before?"

Carol nodded.

"Tell me about it. What did you do the night before he died? And keep it PG, please."

Carol laughed slightly. "He picked up Chinese food on his way home. We both had late meetings. We ate outside, and I cleaned up while he checked his plants. Then..." She closed her eyes and remembered. "Then we had a glass of wine and talked about our days and the weather, and I complained about not being ready for my presentation. When we went to bed, I sat up and worked while he slept beside me. It was perfect. Boring but perfect."

"Instead of regretting that you didn't wake up to enjoy your last morning, you should embrace how perfectly boring your last evening was."

Carol looked at her mom. "I never considered that. I mean, of course I remember that night, but..."

"But sometimes it's easier to get pulled into the things we wish we could change instead of the things we wouldn't."

"That's incredibly insightful of you, Mom."

Judith grinned. "I have an incredibly insightful therapist. I could introduce you."

"Oh my God," Carol muttered.

Judith laughed lightly as she squeezed Carol's hand. "Listen, Tobias knew you loved him. Like he loved you. The losses you'd faced together brought you closer. Made you value each other more. He knew you loved him, Carol. Don't ever doubt that."

"I don't. I just miss him. I miss him so much."

"You're always going to miss him. You're always going to wish you'd had more time. Like you'll always wish that with Katie. And it will get easier, as it has with Katie. Life goes on. As hard as it may be sometimes, those of us left behind have to go on too. The next few days are going to be difficult, but you'll get through them. And then you'll get through the next few days, and the days after that, and then you'll realize that you've started to heal."

"I know," she whispered. "I know I'll heal. I'll be okay someday. It's the time before then that sucks."

"Oh, I know."

Looking over, Carol took a few moments to write this moment in her memory, something she'd come to realize was important. "How are you doing, Mom? Really?"

"I'm better. I'm very happy we took this trip. I know I was hesitant, but we needed this time together. To do our own healing."

"We're getting there, don't you think?"

Judith smiled. "I do."

"So let's take another trip next summer. Take Ellen to see her crazy old biddie friends?"

Despite the smile that spread on her face, Judith rolled

her eyes. "Oh, I don't think that's a good idea. I don't think that's a good idea at all."

———

Caroline slowed her car as she approached her parents' driveway. She didn't like asking them for help watching Katie, but sometimes she ran out of options. Every time she had to leave her daughter unsupervised with her parents, she'd first casually remind Katie of how much she was loved.

"You're the best girl, kitty cat," Caroline would say. "Don't forget that."

Before she'd leave, she'd kneel down and look her baby in the eyes and whisper, "I love you bigger than the world. You know that, right?"

Katie would always smile. "I love you bigger than the world, Mama."

She suspected her parents were aware they weren't her first choice for looking after Katie. She wasn't great at hiding that fact.

"If you'd rather she didn't stay the night—" she'd start.

Her mom always cut her off. "We don't mind, Caroline."

Still she hesitated.

But this morning, her hesitation had nothing to do with worrying about how her parents were treating Katie. She was shocked by what she was seeing.

Parked on the street, she sat for several long minutes watching her father trotting behind a bright-pink bike with white streamers dangling from the handlebars. Underneath the purple bike helmet, Katie had that laser-like focus she got when she was trying something new as she pedaled hard.

Caroline had never learned to ride a bike. Her parents had told her bikes were dangerous. She could walk if she had somewhere to go, which she rarely did because she wasn't allowed to do that either. Seeing her father steadying the bike for Katie was something so foreign, Caroline didn't quite know if she should trust her eyes.

She stood on the sidewalk, feeling like she'd been caught in some kind of dream, until Katie noticed her.

"Lookit, Mama! Lookit!"

The bike wobbled, causing Caroline to gasp, but her dad reacted before Katie could topple over. He grabbed the handlebar and steadied her.

"Ready?" he asked.

"Ready!" Katie yelled.

He released the handlebar, keeping his hand close in case, but Katie had regained her balance. Caroline bit her lip when he released his hold on the seat and let Katie go. Katie kept pedaling and her smile kept growing. She rode, without any help, right to where Caroline was standing. She'd made it about ten feet without her grandpa's support, but that was ten feet more than Caroline had ever traveled on a bicycle.

At five years old, Katie had surpassed her mom. Caroline's heart filled with pride.

"What is going on?" she asked her daughter.

"Grandma and Grandpa bought me a bike."

"I see that. Where are your training wheels?"

Her dad approached them. "She didn't want them."

Since when did her dad care what anybody else wanted? Since when did he teach kids how to ride bikes?

She kept her observations to herself. "Nice job, kitty cat." She held her hand up, and Katie gave her a high-five.

"You look tired," her dad said.

Caroline lifted her eyes to him, gauging if he was making an innocent observation or a subtle cut. "We lost a patient last night. That's always hard."

"Well," he said, "that's the job."

Again, she tested his words. Was he trying to be supportive or remind her that she could have been a pediatrician if she hadn't screwed up her life? She couldn't tell. Returning her attention to Katie, Caroline smiled. "So, I guess I don't have to ask if you had a good time with Grandma and Grandpa."

Katie beamed. "I can't wait to show Daddy."

Caroline's dad huffed out a sigh.

"He'll be excited," Caroline said, ignoring the sound of disapproval that always followed mentions of her husband. "Let's put your bike away now and get your things."

"No," Katie whined. "Mama."

"Katie," she warned. The last thing she needed was her father commenting on Katie's newfound tendency to argue.

"I wanna stay."

"She can stay," Dennis said.

Caroline darted her eyes to him.

"We'll practice bike riding more. She'll be a pro by the end of the day."

Caroline was tempted to ask what the hell had gotten into

him. *When he looked at her, though, he smiled. Not a big smile, but more than she was used to seeing.*

"Go home and get some sleep," he said. "We'll bring her home after lunch."

"Please, Mama," Katie begged, distracting Caroline from her confusion.

"Dad—"

"It's okay," he said again. "Go get some rest, Caroline. You had a long night."

Leaning down, she puckered her lips and waited for a kiss from her daughter. As soon as Katie realized that meant she got to stay, she giggled and gave her mom a kiss.

"Love you, kitty cat."

"Love you, Mama."

"Thanks, Dad." With that, she left the surreal world she'd stumbled into.

Her sense of wonder didn't leave until she got home and found the table littered with beer cans. She was tempted to charge into the bedroom and get John out of bed, demand he clean up his mess, but the fight wasn't worth it. The longer he slept, the more quiet she would have.

She gathered the cans and tossed them into the trash before slipping into the bedroom to gather clean clothes. As she showered, she let the water rinse away the stress of the night, and her mind drifted back to her father and the strange scene she'd found. The image of him steadying Katie on her bike was far from the man she knew.

Caroline still had a hard time believing what she'd seen, but she had to hope her father teaching Katie how to ride a bike was the first step toward reconciliation. Katie's sixth birthday was coming up soon. The time had come for her and her father to let go of old grudges. It was time to be a family.

For Katie.

———

Carol handed the car driver cash as her mom and Ellen slid out of the back seat. "Sorry about that," she said to the man.

He chuckled. "Don't worry about it."

"If it's any consolation, she nags about my driving too."

He laughed as she climbed out of his car. She closed the door and turned her focus to the house. The contractor and his team had done an amazing job updating the siding and landscaping, but it was the colorful sign that caught her attention. Her mom and Ellen were staring at that as well.

Katie's House spelled out in stacking blocks looked even more amazing in person. That familiar lump of emotion rose to Carol's throat.

"Wow," she whispered. "It's perfect."

"She'd love it," Judith agreed.

A little sound left Ellen before she pressed her hand to her lips. "Carol, this is amazing."

She nodded her agreement because she couldn't make the words form. They stared for a long time before Carol started for the house. Ellen and Judith walked behind her and waited for her to enter the code on the box on the door. Inside, the contractor had left the keys for the lock. Carol's fingers trembled as she pulled them out, reminding her of the first time she'd come back. John had reminded her to breathe.

"We had good times here too," he'd added, because the past was coming at her like a hurricane.

Remembering that, she turned to her mom. As she expected, she saw the same panic in Judith's eyes that she was certain had been in hers.

"We had good times here too," Carol said, repeating John's words to her mother. "Remember her birthday party. How much she loved her presents. How she danced around as we sang to her."

Tears trickled down Judith's cheeks. "I don't know if..."

"You can," Carol said. "You can do this. Remember the good times." She unlocked the door and eased it open. Unlike the last time she was here, peering into the house didn't leave her with an emotional gut punch, but she remembered how that had felt. Stepping in, she held the door and monitored her mother's reaction.

Judith clung to Ellen's hand as they took their time walking in. Judith pressed her lips tight as she looked around.

"Oh, look what they've done," she said with a quivering voice. "It's beautiful. It's so beautiful."

Carol had already stared at the photos long enough to know what to expect—cream-colored walls, stained pine floors, and light-gray furniture to fill the living room. As they walked into the living area, the kitchen came into view. The old chipped linoleum countertops had been replaced by butcher block, and gone were the scratched cabinets. New appliances filled the space. Though the kitchen was small,

Carol thought any chef would be happy with the updates made.

She didn't intentionally forget about her companions, but as it always had, Katie's room called to her. When Katie was a baby, sleeping soundly, Carol had never been able to walk by the room without peeking in to check on her daughter. Something about that room pulled at her. Even now. She stopped at the door, and a smile spread across her face.

The space was even better than in the photos. A little twin-sized bed sat along one wall, the same spot Katie's bed had been. Buckets filled with toys sat on either side of a shelf filled with books and games. The pale-yellow paint was calming and neutral. No matter the gender of the child who slept in this room, they were bound to feel like this space fit them. Though the room looked different from how it had when Katie was there, the spirit of the room remained. This still felt like her space.

"Oh, kitty cat," Carol said softly. "You'd love this."

She took another minute to soak up every inch of the room before crossing the hall to look at the bathroom. Again, the space was small, but the updates made the room much more appealing than it had been before. The master bedroom had a wrought-iron frame holding a queen-size mattress. A television was mounted above a long dresser. Carol didn't know who Daryl had hired to decorate the house, but he'd made a brilliant choice.

Everything, from the little statue on the dresser to the tissue holder on the nightstand, was perfect. Carol's heart felt close to bursting. She had to put her hand over her chest. Perfect. Everything was absolutely perfect.

"This is amazing," Ellen said, coming into the room.

Carol spun and wiped her cheeks. "How's Mom?"

"She probably could use you," Ellen said.

She had to take a breath, brace herself to be the strong one, and then left her aunt in the bedroom. She found her mom sitting on the edge of the little twin-size bed. Hearing the woman quietly sob made her chest ache.

"Mom?" she said, her voice barely louder than a whisper.

Judith sniffed as she focused on Carol. A weak smile tugged at her lips. "I was thinking about how she always wanted one more bedtime story."

Carol grinned. "Just one more."

"No matter how many you read, she wanted one more until she dozed off." Judith pressed her lips together, but she couldn't seem to stop them from trembling. "She reminded me of you so much."

"Me?" Carol stepped into the bedroom and scanned the contents, but she wasn't seeing the new shelf or the tubs of toys. She could see Katie's pile of stuffed animals and shoes tossed carelessly aside. "I always thought she was more like John."

"You were the same way when you were younger. Your thirst for knowledge was unquenchable. She was just like you." Judith put her hand to her mouth as she sobbed again. "I...I'm so sorry I didn't know how to be there for you when you lost her."

Carol tilted her head and sighed. "Oh, Mom, we're past this. None of us were in a good place back then."

Judith sniffled. "You should have been able to turn to your parents, Carol. I regret that. If I could change one thing in my life," Judith stated firmly, "I would change that. I would have been there for you. I don't know why I failed you, but I know that I did, and I am sorry. I'm deeply sorry."

Crossing the room in three long strides, Carol dropped to her knees in front of her mom and grasped her hands. "Mom, it's okay."

Judith shook her head again as she put her hand to Carol's cheek. "I don't know how much time I have left in this world, but I will spend every last breath I have in this old body reminding myself to be better to you."

Leaning forward, Carol wrapped her arms around Judith and hugged her tight. In what was becoming the new normal, Judith hugged her back and kissed the top of her head. Carol couldn't pinpoint the emotion that surged through her, but it was overwhelming. She felt like this was the final breakthrough they'd needed.

"I love you, Carol," Judith said.

"I love you, Mom." Leaning back, Carol smiled up at her. "Let's stop revisiting this now. Let's move forward, okay?"

"Okay."

"Are you ready to see the backyard?" She didn't expand that to include spreading the ashes, but they both knew what she meant.

Judith nodded, and Carol stood and helped her to her feet. She called out to her aunt as they left Katie's old room.

Walking through the living room toward the sliding glass door that would lead them to the backyard, Carol's heart rate increased and her mom tightened her hold on her hand.

"It's okay," she said to reassure herself and her mom.

"I haven't been out there since her sixth birthday party."

Turning, Carol looked her in the eyes. "You don't have to go out there."

"Yes," Judith whispered, "I do. We need to bring her home together."

Carol looked at her aunt. "Are you ready?"

"Ready."

Carol led them outside, and her smile returned. The lawn John had given little care over the years she'd been gone was completely redesigned. Flower beds outlined the fence, and a wooden playset monopolized the lawn. This was the perfect place for a family to relax after spending hours at the hospital with their sick child. This space would bring peace to a lot of people.

A tree had been planted with a plaque in honor of John. But Carol was drawn to what was beyond that. A garden filled with a variety of flowers, including *Salvia dorisiana*, Tobias's favorites. Sitting inside the rock barrier was a plaque. She ran her fingers over the raised text.

In honor of Tobias Denman
Beloved stepfather to Katie Bowman

Before the ceremony to give the keys to the hospital, there would be a family gathering to honor Tobias. She hadn't told them about this garden, but she knew they would love it. There was no better way to remember Tobias than by planting flowers for him. He would have loved that.

However, it was in front of John's tree that Carol pulled the ashes from her pocket. She waited for her mom and aunt to join her. There were no useless bits of information to be shared this time. There were no rare or unique things to tell Katie.

Carol simply bent down, sprinkled the mix of Katie and her daddy into the grass at the base of John's tree, and whispered, "Welcome home, baby."

THIRTEEN

A CLOUD HAD HUNG over Carol's head from the moment she'd woken up. Her mom and aunt had done everything they could to distract her. They'd brought her breakfast, hovered, chatted, and made jokes. Carol had tried to participate. She'd tried to let them steer her mind from the inevitable destination.

One year ago, she'd pulled the covers over her head and gone back to sleep while her husband went for a morning jog without her. He never came home.

Her mom had told her to focus instead on the perfect time they'd shared the night before. She tried. But in her mind, she heard the phone ring. Heard the stranger's voice on the other end telling her she needed to get to the hospital because her husband had been in an accident. She pictured herself rushing to pull on clothes and driving faster than the legal limit.

She could see the doctor's face as she told Carol that

Tobias had been hit by a truck. She was reliving that horrible moment when she'd walked into his hospital room and knew, without a doubt, that he was never going to wake up. His soul was already gone. His body was there, being kept alive by tubes, but he was gone.

As soon as she'd sat up in bed, her mom had handed her a cup of coffee and looked at her with obvious concern. Tears had formed in Carol's eyes and had been there since. She hadn't broken down though. She had to give herself credit for that.

She'd gotten up, eaten, showered, and dressed without completely coming unglued. The urge was there, but she held herself together. Right up until they arrived at Katie's House and she recognized the SUV in the driveway. Tobias's family had gotten there before them.

She paid the driver who'd brought them to the house and then rushed toward the three girls bouncing with excitement as they called out, "Aunt Carol." Her three nieces embraced her as they rambled about how they had missed her and how cool the house was. Carol hugged them tight, kissing each one's head until they backed off. The tears she'd managed to control fell as soon as Tobias's brother, Elijah, wrapped her into a big hug. They'd always been close. From the time she and Tobias had started dating, Elijah had treated her like his sister. Feeling him hug her now made her crack.

Elijah had been the first call she'd made from the hospital. She didn't know how to tell Mary that her son was in critical condition and she had to get there as fast as she could. Instead, Carol had taken the easier way and called his brother. That was the moment Elijah had become more than a brother and turned into the pillar of strength Carol had leaned on more than once over the last year.

"I gotcha, sis," he said in her ear.

"I know," she muttered.

"Let me have my girl," Mary ordered.

Carol laughed lightly as she pulled from Elijah and hugged her mother-in-law. Mary kissed her cheek several times before leaning back and searching her eyes.

"I'm okay," Carol said. "How are you?"

"Happy to see you." She subtly nodded her head toward the two women Elijah had gone to greet. "How's that going?"

"Good," Carol said honestly. "We've found some common ground."

"I'm glad." Putting a hand to Carol's face, Mary smiled softly. "Been a tough year, but we made it."

Carol's eyes filled again. "We made it. Thank you for coming."

"I wouldn't miss this," Mary said. She looked at the sign in the front yard. "She'd like this. I know she would."

"Yeah, she'd love it." She pulled from Mary enough to hug Elijah's wife, Lara. "Good to see you."

"How you doing?" Lara asked.

Carol let out a slow breath. "It's going to be a tough day, but I'm okay."

Lara nodded. "I brought tequila, so whenever you need a shot, you let me know."

"She's not allowed to drink that anymore, you know that," Mary chastised.

"There's a story there," Ellen said, coming up behind them. "And I want to hear it."

"Oh, I'm sure you will," Carol grumbled as she grasped Mary's hand. "Come on. I don't need to be reminded of that."

As they walked away, Lara started telling Ellen about that *one* time Carol had too many margaritas on a family vacation in Mexico and passed out face first into her fish tacos.

Carol gave Mary a tour of the house before leading her to the backyard and to Tobias's garden. Mary ran her fingers over the plaque several times before tears fell from her eyes.

"He'd be happy that you brought part of him here to be with Katie," Mary said.

Carol nodded because she couldn't speak. Her lungs were tight from holding in her own tears.

"Girls," Lara called, "be careful."

Carol turned in time to see the kids taking over the swing set. She smiled. That's what the playset was there for. To keep kids distracted from the sadness around them. "Did you tell my aunt that I got sour cream up my nose?" she asked, draping her arm around Lara's shoulder as she joined them.

Lara smiled. "You know I did."

"I'm never going to live that down now," Carol said.

"You never were anyway," Mary chimed in.

They all laughed through the air of sadness.

"Want me to get everyone so we can say a few words? I think we should leave plenty of time to pull ourselves together before the ceremony for Katie starts," Lara suggested.

Carol nodded and focused on Mary as Lara walked away. "Ready for this?"

"Nope," Mary stated definitively. "But we're going to do it anyway. One foot in front of the other, baby. Like I've been telling you."

Mary *had* been telling her that. She couldn't remember how many times. Tobias's birthday, their wedding anniversary, or simply a bad day. Mary had been there, talking Carol through her pain, making sure she made it through to the other side.

"I wouldn't have gotten through this if it weren't for you all."

"We're family," Mary said. "That's what we do."

Once the others joined them at the edge of the garden, the knot in Carol's stomach grew. "I, um, I guess I should have made a plan for this. I'm not sure what we're supposed to do." Her voice cracked as emotion hit her.

Elijah put his arm around her shoulders. "When we were kids, Tobias used to boss me around. He thought he was the man of the house or something. I'd get mad, but when I got older, whenever I got in trouble—"

"Which was often," Mary offered, causing a few quiet laughs from the group.

"Which was often," Elijah admitted, "he was there. He never let me down. He was a good brother."

Lara said, "He was always there for us. We knew we could count on you two," she said to Carol. "That's what makes us family. He was a good uncle, too, wasn't he?"

The girls nodded in unison, but the eldest spoke for them all, as she tended to do. "He was the best uncle."

"He was a good son," Mary said, her voice emotional but filled with pride. "He worked hard to get where he was. He had a good job, a loving wife, and family who loved him more than the sun in the sky. He looked out for everybody without ever asking for anything in return." Her lips trembled as she put her hand to her chest. "He's still looking out for us. I feel him with me all the time. I know he's with us. I know he's looking down right now, happy we're all here together."

Ellen spoke next. "I remember when Carol called to tell me they were getting married. She was happy. Happier than I'd heard her in a long time. He did that for her. He gave her back some of the happiness we feared she'd never find again. That's really special," she said, smiling at her niece.

"I knew he'd take care of you," Judith said to Carol. "I could worry a little less because I knew he'd take care of you. He was a good man, and I was proud of the life you built together."

Carol smiled at her mom. Up until a few weeks ago, she'd thought her mom hadn't liked Tobias. She'd thought her mom was ashamed of her interracial marriage. Hearing her say differently warmed Carol's heart. She hadn't ever expected to hear those words.

Now it was her turn to speak, and she was at a loss. The tension in her lungs reminded her to breathe. "I was already head over heels in love with him when I told him about Katie. I don't know why I was scared, but I thought he might think less of me for losing her." She shook her head slightly. "Of course he didn't. He asked about her because he wanted to know her. From that day on, he talked about Katie as if she was a part of us, as if she was our child. He really did love her as if she was his daughter. You all accepted her and kept her with me all these years, and I could never thank you enough for that." She gestured toward the plaque. "Tobias may have never met his stepdaughter, but he loved her, and that made me love him even more. I miss them both, but they're together now, and that brings me some peace. They're taking care of each other, and Mary's right, they're looking down and they are happy their family is together."

"Let's have a little moment of silence," Elijah said.

They joined hands, and while everyone else lowered their faces, Carol looked at each one and thanked her lucky stars for them. For Elijah's strength, Lara's humor, her nieces' innocence and hugs, Mary's love, her aunt's support, and most of all, her mother's willingness to let go of the past and move forward.

She loved every single one of them. Each one of them had played a role in helping her survive losing Tobias. Each one had boosted her up enough to keep going. She couldn't have done this without them. She wouldn't be standing there if they hadn't each pushed her in their own way to keep going.

A light breeze blew, lifting Carol's hair off her shoulder as a tickle brushed her cheek. The scent of *Salvia dorisiana* enveloped her. Looking up at the sun shining down on them, she felt a wave of warmth roll through her.

"I love you too," she whispered as she smiled.

_____

Guilt tugged at Carol as she skimmed the letter she'd written to Simon Miller. Since leaving Ohio, she'd lived in his house rent free, but as soon as Tobias suggested they move in together, she knew she had to give up this last tie to the past.

She'd considered calling Simon several times, but she stopped before ever dialing the phone. Every time she thought of him, she remembered the last time she saw him. The night she left John with nothing but a suitcase of her clothes and a backpack of mementos from Katie's room.

And an urn.

As much as she had wanted to reconnect with Simon, memories stopped her each time. The urge eased once she and Tobias had started dating, but Carol never lost sight of the fact she owed Simon for the life she had now.

He'd given her a safety net when she was freefalling. He'd provided a soft landing rather than one that certainly would have killed her had she been left to find the bottom on her own. The depression would have won. It nearly had many times in the last years anyway, but Carol had found her footing. She'd found a place to stand and start again.

She owed that to Simon. He deserved more than a thank-you note, but she didn't know what else to do. She considered calling him, but what would she say? How could she explain what she'd been through? How could she tell him that she still loved him but could never be with him because simply thinking of him reminded her that if she'd left John, Katie might still be alive.

That wasn't a burden she was going to place on him.

He didn't deserve to know that her screwed-up brain had tied him to the worst time in her life and no matter how good he was to her, she couldn't untangle him from that web.

No, he didn't deserve to have that placed on his shoulders, and she didn't trust herself not to blurt the words out if she was to talk to him.

A letter was best. A letter was easy.

Or so it should have been. She'd stared at the blank page for a long time, wondering how to thank someone for rescuing her during her darkest hours.

Looking over her words now, she debated tearing up the page and simply sending him his keys without a note. But she owed him more than that.

Simon, *she'd written, because Dear Simon seemed too* intimate.

Thank you for allowing me to stay in your home. As always, you provided me a safe haven when I needed it most. However, it's time for me to stand on my own, which I never would have been able to do without your kindness and generosity.

I recently graduated with my master's degree in medical science. Unfortunately, I've realized I'm no longer in a place to become a pediatrician like I'd hoped. I will continue my education and get my doctorate, though. I haven't yet decided where that will take me, but I am moving forward. I couldn't have done that without you.

I hope you are well.
Caroline

She had intentionally left out any mention of Tobias. Somehow she felt that would be a betrayal to the man who had helped her without asking for a damn thing in return. Simon didn't need to know that she'd fallen head over heels in love with someone else. Simon didn't need to know that he'd provided her a new life that she now planned to share with someone else.

"Hey," Tobias called from the other room. "Carol?"

She folded the letter and tucked it into an envelope with the key to the house she'd moved out of. "In here," she called before licking the tab and sealing her goodbye to Simon inside.

Looking up when Tobias walked into the room, she smiled. She always smiled when Tobias walked into a room. Setting the letter aside, she met him with open arms and a willing kiss. "What took you so long?" she asked.

He winked. "I had to make a stop on my way over."

She tilted her head and eyed him suspiciously. "What did you do?"

He simply smiled and hugged her again. Within an hour, she'd know what he'd been up to, because she'd be crying as he slipped an engagement ring on her finger.

Carol's attention was drawn like a magnet until she focused on a man across the lawn. He'd had that same effect on her twenty-five years ago. The moment Simon Miller had entered her world, he'd had a gravitational pull she couldn't deny. Even now, after all these years, her soul somehow sensed his. She looked over, and there he was, staring at her as she'd caught him doing over and over before they'd given in to their desires.

"Excuse me," she said to her mom and aunt as she stepped away from them.

Simon smiled as he headed for her too. She moved into his arms as easily now as she had then, and he hugged her as tight as he had the last time she'd seen him. This time, however, she wasn't falling apart. This time she was stronger than he'd ever seen her.

"I can't believe you're here," he said softly.

She pulled back and skimmed over his face. He was even more handsome than she remembered. His eyes were more serene, his smile even more soothing. She couldn't stop herself from putting her hand to his cheek and stroking over the short-trimmed beard he was sporting. The thought that touching him intimately might be inappropriate didn't even cross her mind. He didn't seem to mind. In fact, he stroked his hand over her hair as he'd always done before putting his forehead to hers.

"I am *so* glad to see you," she said.

"Me too. It's been too long."

"Thank you for coming." Stepping back, she put

respectable distance between them but clasped his hand so he couldn't leave her side.

He didn't seem interested in walking away anyway. He put his other hand over hers and smiled down at her. "I know I'm early, but I was hoping I could get a few minutes alone with you."

"Carol?" came Judith's voice, full of curiosity.

"Hold that thought," Carol whispered to Simon before turning to find her mother and aunt smirking knowingly. "Simon, this is my mother, Judith, and her sister Ellen. This is my friend Simon."

"Simon, we've heard *so* much about you," Ellen said as she extended her hand.

Carol lifted her brows in warning, but Ellen ignored her.

"Nice to meet you, Ellen." Simon gave Judith the same welcome, but before they could drag him into a volley of questions, Carol grabbed his arm and gently pulled him closer.

"I need to give Simon a tour," she said, guiding him away. "Don't worry," she muttered as they walked toward the house, "they'll corner you later."

He laughed, and a million memories hit her at once. "I have no doubts about that." He followed her into the newly remodeled house. "This is really great of you, Caroline. As you know, families fare better when they aren't cooped up in hotels for long periods of time. Not to mention the financial burden placed on them when they have to pay to stay close to the hospital."

"Katie would have wanted it this way." She led him to the

living room and stopped in front of the framed photo of her daughter. Beneath was a plaque with her dates of birth and death. Like Tobias, Simon had never met Katie, but Carol had spoken of her often when they were together. So much so that when he'd made big plans for their future, he'd included Katie without hesitation.

"She looked like you," Simon said gently as he wrapped his arm around Carol's shoulders.

Carol slid her arm around his back and rested her head on his shoulder. Though they'd been lovers long ago, they'd also been friends, and that friendship seemed to have instantly been rekindled. She didn't feel the least bit awkward standing with him like this. She wished then that she'd reached out to him sooner. They could have been friends. Thinking they couldn't have was foolish on her part, but he was part of the mess she'd had to leave behind, and she'd had to let those mistakes go for her own sanity.

"She might have looked like me," Carol said, "but she sure did act like her daddy. Always getting into something. They kept me on my toes, that's for sure." Pulling from him, she stepped back enough to look up at his face. "How much do you know about what led to the dedication?"

"Not much." He laughed lightly. "I pretty much got caught up in the fact that you were going to be here to hand over the keys. Nothing else seemed important after that. But I do know John died."

Sitting on the sofa, she waited for him to take the space next to her. "He had cancer. I was living in Houston, and instead of seeking treatment, he found me and begged me to help him put Katie's memory to rest. I was resistant, as I'm sure you can imagine. But I did, and I took care of him in the end so we could make peace with the past. He had never remarried and left the house and his life insurance policy to me."

"And this is what you're doing with it."

"Yeah. We agreed to this before he died."

Simon ran his hand over her back. "I'm glad you were able to make peace with him."

"Me too. I hadn't realized how much I needed to do that until he showed up in my life after so long. We wanted to do this so she wouldn't be forgotten."

"We won't let that happen," Simon assured her.

"Making amends with John made me realize how much I needed to forgive myself for some things I'd done." Taking his hand, she held it between hers and searched his brown eyes. "I want you to know that you saved me, Simon. I don't think I would have found the strength to go on with my life if you hadn't helped me. I wish I'd treated you better. I'm sorry."

He furrowed his brow at her. "Treated me better? Caroline—"

"I used you, Simon," she said before he could come up with some reason to excuse her behavior. "I was in a miserable marriage, and instead of leaving, I...I used you to get through it."

"You didn't use me," he stated. "We were there for each other. There's a difference."

"That's kind of you to say, but I was incredibly selfish to get involved with you when I was married."

He shook his head. "I knew you were married, and I fell for you anyway. In case you've forgotten, I was the one who pushed things to go to the next level. I can't blame you for not leaving your husband. You had a daughter to consider. You had a family. It was wrong of me to try to convince you to leave him."

"Fair enough, but I'm not only talking about our affair, Simon. You gave me a new life, and I... I returned your key with a thank-you note through the mail. You deserved more than that. I don't know what would have happened to me if you hadn't sent me to St. Louis. I'm scared to think what would have happened to me. I'm not sure I would have ever recovered."

He brushed his thumb over the wedding ring on her finger. "Did you find a good life?"

"I found an amazing life."

"Then you gave me exactly what I wanted." Meeting her gaze again, he smiled softly. "All I ever wanted for you was to find a way to be happy again. Now that I know you did, consider any debt you felt you owed me repaid."

Carol placed a soft kiss on his cheek. "Thank you. I know you wanted me to stay. I just couldn't. Everything about this place, including you, reminded me of what I'd lost. If I'd stayed, I would have sabotaged what we had between us."

"Is he here? Your husband. I'd like to meet him."

Her heart grew heavy, as it did every time she had to explain where her husband was. "He passed away. A year ago today, actually."

Simon's lips fell opened and his eyes widened. "Oh, no, Caroline."

"It was an accident. He went quickly. There's some solace in that."

"I'm sorry."

She smiled softly. "His name was Tobias. He was a good man. To be honest, he reminded me of you in a lot of ways, always so kind and considerate. You would have liked him. His family is here. I'll introduce you. What about you? Married?"

"Divorced. I don't have to tell you how hard doctor hours can be on a relationship."

She nodded. "Kids?"

"Two daughters. Emily and Christine. Both in college now. Did you have kids with Tobias?"

Carol shook her head. "We tried, but..." Instead of going down that depressing tale, she tilted her head and smiled at him. "Did you have a good life?"

"I did."

"Good. I'm happy for you." She leaned to see around him when the front door opened. Ellen seemed hesitant to enter, and Carol nearly laughed. Knowing her aunt, she was expecting to walk in on some sordid scene.

"Sorry to interrupt," Ellen said. "There's a reporter here to cover the ceremony."

"We'll be right out," Carol said. As soon as they were alone, she tightened her hold on Simon's hands. "Thank you for being here. For always being there when I needed you."

"Caroline," he said, holding on to her hand before she

could stand. "I want you to know how much it's eased my mind knowing you're okay. I've always worried that you'd never recovered from your loss. I'm glad you were able to have a good life."

"Me too. We'll talk more before you leave, okay?"

"Definitely."

When she started to stand, he stood too. He followed her out of the house and into the role of hospital chief of staff. Carol hadn't had to put on her executive persona for some time, but like Simon, she slipped into the role naturally. She detached herself from the emotion of the house and gave the reporter and Simon an official tour before introducing them to her family.

As the afternoon progressed, she explained over and over that while her ex-husband was dying, they agreed this was the best way to honor their fun-loving, precious, slightly mischievous little girl. She had anticipated feeling drained after speaking about Katie all afternoon while simultaneously grieving the year anniversary of Tobias's death, but by the time she ceremoniously handed over the keys to Simon, she felt like she was walking on air.

Katie would never be forgotten. So long as the hospital stood and families needed the comfort of a home while caring for an ill child, someone would be here keeping Katie's memory alive. Carol couldn't have possibly anticipated how much that would fill her heart.

She would never completely heal from the pain of losing her daughter, but Carol could go on knowing Katie would go on too.

Having Simon there as the person she was giving this responsibility to was more than she could have asked. The fact that he was the one accepting this gift was fitting because his gift of a home to Carol so long ago was what had saved her.

So, yes, she was exhausted by the time the gathering started to thin, but her heart was full. Even more so when Simon approached her with that bright smile of his on his face.

"I should go," he said, though he sounded as if he didn't want to.

She would have asked him to stay, but there was no logical reason for him to. The ceremony was done. The house now belonged to the hospital. Her family had started cleaning up the food and trash from the celebration. The party was over, but she didn't want him to go.

"When are you leaving?" he asked.

"In the morning," she said.

"Dinner?"

She gestured toward her in-laws. "Busy."

"Breakfast?"

She gestured toward them again. "Busy."

Simon nodded, as if accepting that he was being blown off.

"But I can walk you to your car." She put her arm through his, and they strolled down the sidewalk. "Thank you for being here."

"Thank you for letting me."

"I'd like to stay in touch if that's okay."

Simon put his hand over hers. "That's more than okay. Did you say you're in Houston now?"

She bit her lip. "Well. Not anymore. I, um. I did something kind of crazy. I retired, sold everything, and am now living in my RV. So, technically, I live with my mother-in-law in St. Louis. But in reality, I'm a homeless drifter."

Simon laughed. "That's great, Caroline."

"It is for now. I'm sure in another year or so I'll find a place and replant some roots. For now, being on the move is keeping me going."

He stopped in front of a silver sedan and pulled a card from his pocket. He scribbled on the back and held it out to her. "My cell. Call me."

She looked at his scribbled handwriting and thought of another time he'd written his information on a scrap of paper for her. That time, it'd been his address when he'd invited her over to initiate their affair. This time, she didn't have to hide the note. She had no one to hide it from. Taking her phone from her pocket, she texted her name to his cell phone, which dinged a moment later.

"Now you have mine," she said. "It was really good to see you." She slid into his embrace again, and he hugged her close. When she leaned back, she touched his cheek as she'd done when he'd first arrived. "Take care of my girl's house, okay?"

"As if it was my own." He planted a soft kiss on her cheek before climbing into his car. She stepped back, watching until he drove away. When she turned back to the house, she realized she had an audience. Her mom, aunt, and mother-

and sister-in-law stood in the driveway without even bothering to act like they weren't being nosey.

"Mind your business," she warned them all as she approached.

"He's cute," Lara said.

"Cuter than the picture you showed us online," Ellen said.

Carol rolled her eyes, knowing The Inquisition was about to begin. She looked to Mary for help, but Mary crossed her arms over her chest and lifted her brow.

The stern look lasted a moment before Mary chuckled. "Your aunt already told us all about him. I guess he's okay since he's the reason you ended up in St. Louis."

Carol gawked at Ellen, who simply shrugged. "Hey, Lara, I'm going to need that tequila now."

FOURTEEN

AFTER SEEING the Denmans off the next morning, Carol ushered her mom and aunt into another car. This one didn't take them to Katie's House, though. This time, they went to the cemetery where Frannie and Mark Bowman were buried. While her mom and aunt sat in the back seat of the car, Carol walked to where the map directed her until she found the wide headstone she was looking for.

The granite had their names and dates of birth and death, and her heart ached for them. They had been good to her. They had been the loving parents she'd never had. The moment John had introduced her to them, they'd made her feel wanted. That was so much more than she could have said for her parents back then.

Though she hadn't seen them since she'd left Dayton, standing at their graves made her heart break for their losses. The world had been a better place with them in it.

"Frannie," she whispered as she kneeled down. She pulled a few weeds from the base of the headstone and tossed them aside. "I'm sorry for leaving the way I did. I'm sorry for taking Katie and never giving you a chance to say goodbye to her. I know I must have hurt you. I never wanted that. I hope you understand I was broken and leaving was the only way out for me."

She put her hand on the monument, looking at her former father-in-law's name. "Mark, you saw through the façade. I know you did. You knew how bad John's drinking was, but you never made us feel ashamed about it. I don't know if that was the right thing or not, but I know confronting him was never easy. Thank you for trying to step up for Katie and me when John couldn't. If you could see the house now, you'd be amazed. All those little repairs you'd always had to make were enough to keep the house going, but it's absolutely stunning now. You'd be proud."

She pulled a container from her pocket and opened the top. "You'd both be proud of John. He got sober. He's the one who grew up enough to try to make things right." She scoffed. "I know that's hard to believe, isn't it? But it's true. He's the one who made things right. I love him for that. If he hadn't, I would still be running from the past."

She sprinkled Katie's and John's ashes onto the ground and set the flowers she'd brought on top. "I know it's been a long time, Katie, but you're with Grandma and Grandpa Bowman now. They missed you, baby, but you're here now. And so is Daddy." She put her hands to her thighs as she stood. "Rest well."

Another bit of the guilt she'd been carrying for far too long slipped away. She may not have given Frannie and Mark an opportunity to see Katie's urn, but that was just a container. Katie was with them, wherever they were.

Seeing her mom and aunt in the back seat as she approached the car was a good reminder to Carol why she'd been so determined to reconcile with her mother. Her mom was still healthy, still of sound mind, but that wouldn't always be the case. Carol had already lost too many people—she was going to cling to the ones she had left.

The craziest thing about all of that was, she had John to thank for making her realize the importance of holding on to loved ones. If he hadn't snapped her out of her depression, she'd likely be lost in it. She wouldn't have spent the anniversary of Tobias's death celebrating Katie's life or honoring his memory. She would have been in a dark room with blankets pulled over her head, wondering what she had to live for.

John had reminded her that she had a lot to live for, and she was going to embrace it.

But before she could, she had one more stop to make. Sliding into the front seat, she glanced back at her mom. "Ready?"

Judith nodded. "Ready."

Carol told the driver the address to their next stop. The cemetery where her father had been put to rest. The drive was quiet. Heavy emotion hung in the car. Carol hadn't visited his gravesite the last time she'd been in Dayton, when she'd brought John home.

Visiting her father's grave hadn't even been on her list of things to do. She couldn't avoid his grave forever though. Today would be the day she returned to the cemetery, and she had no doubt it was going to be emotional.

She'd accepted that he'd been a flawed man rather than the monster she'd always made him out to be in her mind. This was the first time she'd be facing him and not seeing through the scratched lenses of her bitter childhood.

Her heart sank as their driver turned into the cemetery. Though she hadn't been there in three years, she knew where her father was buried and was able to give directions. Once the car stopped, she looked at the man beside her. "This one might take a bit longer. Are you okay waiting?"

"Take your time," he said.

She joined her mom and aunt outside of the car and her stomach knotted. Taking her mom's hand, Carol walked with them to the gravesite. As soon as they stopped in front of the headstone with her family name inscribed, emotion formed a lump in her throat. She'd never grieved for this man, not really. She'd never allowed herself to feel his loss.

She felt it now. Like a lightning bolt to the heart.

Holding her mom's hand a little tighter, she read her father's name and the etching, *Beloved Husband, Father, and Grandfather.*

Once again, she imagined her father broken and crying over the loss of Katie. Something she never would have thought possible if her mom hadn't shared that intimate moment with her. She recalled how hard her father had been, how angry he'd been over Katie's death, but she never thought about him being broken.

He had loved Katie. She knew that. Now she could see that he'd loved her too. In his own way. A way that was not always easy to see or understand.

Carol took another container from her pocket. This one was for her father. This one was for him and Katie. "Should we say something?" she asked her mom.

Judith looked at the little bottle and hesitantly held out her hand. "May I?"

"Of course," Carol said, handing Katie's ashes to her mom.

Her hand trembled as Judith accepted the container. Looking out over the cemetery, she seemed to be gathering her thoughts before focusing on the headstone. "I told Carol how sorry you were for being too hard on her, Dennis. It's been a difficult few weeks, but we're doing better, and she's working on understanding how much we have always loved her. I know you couldn't find a way to tell her, so I told her for you. I told her that you loved her very much. And that you loved Katie very much. We're here to bring her to you."

Carol put her hands out to catch her mother should she start to fall as Judith kneeled down. Judith emptied the container and put flowers down before standing. She wiped her eyes and sniffled.

"Say goodbye to your father," she said softly as she put her hand on Carol's arm.

She waited for her mom and aunt to head back to the car

before sighing. "I'm sorry I didn't see through your tough act sooner, Dad. I'm sorry I didn't try harder to understand why you thought you needed it. Mom's right. I am trying to understand and move beyond it. I know you loved me." She bit her lip to hold her emotions in before she laughed at herself. Even when she was standing over his grave, the old habit of not letting him see her cry lingered. "I loved you too," she said as she let her tears fall. "I'm sorry I hurt you when I left. I'm sorry I didn't see that you were hurting too." She put her hand on the stone. "I'm going to look after Mom now. I know it's a little late to start, but I'm going to be here for her now."

Standing upright, she scanned the cemetery to find her companions. They were standing a few rows back, and Carol knew they'd found their parents' resting spots. Carol had never known either set of her grandparents, but from the sounds of it, she hadn't missed out on much.

Katie had been lucky. She had four loving grandparents who had doted on her as she'd grown. It had taken a long time, but Carol was happy she'd been able to reunite her little girl with so many of the people who had loved her.

Her father's grave was the last stop they'd intended to make in Dayton. When they got back to the RV, they'd get on the road back to Florida. Carol couldn't believe she felt this way, but she was going to miss traveling with her mom and aunt.

She hoped, as she watched them holding hands, they would be able to take the trip the next summer they'd planned. She hoped they'd have many more vacations together. She had years of memories to make with her mother in a short time.

She was looking forward to that.

———

Caroline clutched the steering wheel of the family car so hard her knuckles ached. She didn't know why she had tried so hard to convince her parents to let her get a driving permit. She was scared of everything, and driving was even worse than she'd imagined.

"Breathe," her mother said from the passenger seat.

A rushed exhale left her as she stared at the light above her. Any second it was going to turn green and she was going to have to move the car. On the road! Why was she driving on the road? Where there were other cars. She wasn't ready for this.

"Go, Caroline," her mom said calmly.

Easing her foot off the brake, Caroline pressed on the accelerator and the entire car lurched forward.

"Sorry," she said.

"You're doing fine."

Caroline looked in the mirror at the line of cars behind her when one honked.

"Ignore them," her mom advised.

"Should I pull over?"

"No. You should focus on the road ahead of you. You're too close to the curb."

Caroline drifted closer to the center lane.

"Not that far! Not that..."

Swerving back, she held her breath. "Sorry."

Her mom pointed ahead to a road on the right. "Turn there."

Caroline turned on her blinker. The click-click-click sounded so loud she was tempted to turn it off, but she didn't. She was too focused on slowing down and making the turn.

"That was good," her mom said.

The brief moment of praise ended when her mom leaned over and looked at the dashboard.

"What?" Caroline asked. "What'd I do?"

"I was checking your speed."

She eased off the accelerator until she was practically crawling down the road.

Judith chuckled. "You can go a little faster."

She sped up and, after a few minutes, started to feel more comfortable as they navigated the residential streets. This wasn't too bad. She could probably do this. She could...

"No," she squealed when a dog darted in front of the car. She jerked the steering wheel to the right and stomped her foot down...without removing it from the accelerator to the brake. The car lurched forward and up over the curb, causing a loud scraping sound to fill her ears.

"Brake!" her mom yelled as she reached across the car. "Brake!"

Caroline snapped to and hit the brake pedal hard. They jerked to a stop. "Did I hit the dog?"

Judith looked back. "No," she said flatly. "But you did hit the curb. Shit."

She'd never heard her mom curse before. She swallowed hard so she wouldn't start crying.

"Put the car in park while I check the damage." Judith climbed out as a man rushed from the house, likely to also survey what Caroline had done. They both leaned down to look, and Caroline's stomach rolled as bile burned her throat.

Holy crap. She'd wrecked her dad's car. He was going to kill her. Absolutely kill her. She wasn't supposed to be driving unless he was in the car, but she'd begged her mom to give her a lesson without her dad intimidating her from the passenger seat.

Now she'd wrecked his car!

Her mom and the man chatted for a minute, and when her mom gestured toward her in the driver's seat, Caroline wished the world would open and swallow her. She'd never seen her mom so animated before, but as she talked to the man, the tension on his face eased and he started nodding, and then...he laughed. Her mom made someone laugh?

The man smiled at Caroline and waved his hand as if to tell her to not even worry that she was half parked in his yard. He looked as if he was sorry his curb had gotten in her way...even though she'd had to leave the road to hit it.

Her mom smiled at him before heading for the passenger door. No, no, no. Her mom needed to drive now. Caroline started to open the driver's door to get out, but her mom peered through the window, pinning her in place.

"Hey," the man said as soon as her mom opened the door, "It's okay, kiddo. We all have accidents sometimes."

She wanted to thank him for his kindness, but if she opened her mouth, she was going to start crying. She thought she'd managed a smile but wasn't sure. Once her mom was in the passenger seat, Caroline finally found her voice. "I-I-I don't want... I don't want to drive anymore."

Her mom nodded once. "I know. I understand, but you need to understand that if you stop driving now, you might never ever start again. Put the car in reverse, Caroline."

Tears pricked her eyes. "Mom—"

"Put the car in reverse, Caroline."

"I can't," she whispered.

Her mom stared at her for several seconds. "You can drive us to the store, or we can sit here until dark."

"Mom."

"If you don't drive now, you may never again," her mom said sternly.

"Dad's gonna—"

"We're not going to tell him you were driving," Judith said. "We're telling him I got distracted."

"You're going to lie to Dad?"

Judith was quiet for a moment. "It's not a lie, Caroline. It's... Do you want him to take your permit away?"

"No."

"So, we're going to tell him I got distracted and hit the curb. Okay?"

"Okay," she said quietly.

"Reverse off the curb. Slowly."

Caroline held her breath and backed the car off the curb with two big thumps as the tires left the curb and found the road again. Though her hands were trembling, she shifted to drive and started down the road again.

Three days after the ceremony in Dayton, Carol sat on the soft red sofa in Ellen's art studio thinking about how much had changed in the weeks since she'd last been here. She was in a good place. Not just with her mom but with Tobias's loss. A year had gone by, and she was starting to feel stronger. She had the support of her family. *All* of her family.

She wasn't alone.

She was no longer angry and resentful of the past.

She could think of her father without dread and remember her mother without anger. Even John and Katie could wander through her thoughts without making her feel the shame of having let them down. And Tobias. Losing him still hurt, but the pain was no longer crippling.

Her heart was lighter than she could ever remember.

In the morning, she'd get back on the road. She'd make that stop at Shenandoah Caverns and go on to Niagara Falls —two stops for John and Katie she hadn't made for the sake of her companions. She'd be on her own now, though. At least for a while.

That wouldn't last. She wouldn't let it. She'd swing by somewhere and grab someone to join her on her trips. Whether it was Mary or her mom and Ellen. Maybe even she and Lara could take a trip and do some fun things now that the girls were older.

Carol had to laugh as she considered how Elijah would react to the idea of being alone with his three girls for days. No doubt he'd warn them about tequila consumption.

A soft knock on the door disturbed her thoughts as she finished packing her bag. She shoved a shirt into her bag as Ellen poked her head in.

"You're not going to believe this," her aunt said with that familiar hint of mischief.

"What?"

"I convinced your mom to have a margarita. To see you off."

Carol widened her eyes. "What?"

"Come on. Before she changes her mind."

She followed Ellen from the room. "But Mom doesn't like margaritas."

"Oh, yes, she does."

"*What*?"

Ellen simply giggled in response.

Carol walked into the kitchen, where her mom was slicing limes. "What is happening right now?"

"Your aunt is a troublemaker. That's what's happening."

Ellen laughed. "Oh, phooey. Tell her the real reason you don't drink margaritas."

"You mean there's more to the story than her not liking them?" Carol sat at the table and watched the sisters add ingredients to the pitcher. She started to warn her aunt about how much tequila she was pouring into the mixture, but her mom's dramatic sigh distracted her.

"I had margaritas *one* time. I didn't like how they made me feel."

Ellen chuckled as she winked at Carol. "I think she liked it a little too much."

Carol cringed. "If this is going to turn into a story about my mom's sex life, I'm out."

Ellen laughed, and Judith tossed a towel at her sister.

"I didn't..." Judith started and then frowned. "One time when I was visiting this misfit in Boulder, after you moved to St. Louis," she clarified, "I went out to dinner with your aunt, and she ordered us margaritas."

"Your mom went *wild*," Ellen said as she raised her arms and waved her hands.

"Wild how?" Carol sank back in her chair when Judith glared at her sister. "*Mom*?"

"I...I may have..." Judith stuttered.

"She got arrested," Ellen spit out. "For disorderly conduct."

Carol gasped and held her mouth open wide as she processed that information. "What did she do?"

"I didn't *do* anything," Judith stated. "I was intoxicated in public."

"Oh, there's more to this story," Carol said. "I want details." She creased her brow. "Or maybe I don't. I'm not sure."

Ellen started to talk, but Judith turned on the blender to drown her out. Carol watched her mom smirk as her aunt threw her head back and hooted out a laugh. In that moment, Carol didn't care why her mom had gotten arrested. She didn't care about anything. This moment was perfect. This was the best, and most surprising, way to end her visit.

They were happy in that moment. All of them. Even her mom, who Carol had spent most of her life believing didn't know how to be happy. She didn't have to know what her mom had done. She laughed anyway.

As the blender stopped, she confessed. "I got arrested too. Last year."

Her mom and aunt stopped moving as they stared at her.

"I, um..." She giggled. "I took a tire iron to the road where Tobias got hit. Apparently that's illegal in the state of Texas." She smiled, despite the concern on their faces. "Come on. Picture this. Me waking up alone in the morning and getting so angry that I drove five blocks, in silk, leopard-print pajamas, and stood in the road hitting the asphalt. In heels, no less, because I couldn't find my slippers."

Ellen glanced at Judith, clearly gauging her response, before filling a glass. "Sounds like something that would happen on a soap opera."

Carol chuckled, but her mom didn't. She hadn't meant to ruin the mood, but in that moment, she realized she had. A cloud suddenly seemed to be hovering over the room, and Carol hated that. They'd been in a good place. "Mom," she said firmly but with a smile on her face. "Relax. That was a year ago. I'm fine now and completely capable of laughing at the situation. You should too."

Judith shook her head and grabbed two margarita glasses. "Well," she said, walking across the kitchen with the drinks, "you still haven't outdone your aunt, even with the leopard-print pajamas and heels. Go ahead, Ellen... Tell her all about your criminal record. Or at least part of it. We don't have all night."

Carol widened her eyes and let her mouth drop open. "*Aunt Ellen*! How many times have you been arrested?"

Ellen grinned as she joined them at the table. "Well. The first time..."

EPILOGUE

THE TRANQUILITY CAROL felt standing at the banister while mist from Niagara Falls washed over her was something she'd never felt before. She was healing. Really healing. Her hurt wasn't gone, but she had learned she could live without bottling the pain up and pretending like it didn't exist. She'd probably struggle the rest of her life with some of the choices she'd made, but she had accepted that she'd done her best.

She'd been the best wife to John she could be at the time. She'd been the best daughter she could be given the circumstances. She'd been a wonderful mother to Katie. Not perfect, but she'd done her best. Age had given her the courage to face her faults, and she was doing better now. That was something to be proud of. She *was* proud.

This was the last stop on the list she had plotted out for John and Katie. She'd done what she had promised him.

She'd done what she could to honor him and what he'd meant to their daughter.

The next leg of her journey would be for Tobias. Taking a deep breath, she imagined the scent of the *Salvia dorisiana* he'd so loved. The sweet smell would forever and always remind her of their life together.

Another wave of peace came over her. She felt the calm that thinking of his garden brought to her, as if he were there, reading her thoughts, telling her the time had come for her to say her goodbye to him. She was ready. Hard as it had been, she was getting better at saying goodbye. She looked up at the rushing water one more time before walking away.

As soon as she returned to her RV, she shook out her raincoat and hung it in the small shower so it could properly dry. Snagging a towel off the hook, she wiped away the lingering moisture from her face and hair.

Sitting at the little table where she'd left her laptop and phone, she tossed the towel on the surface. The last thing she'd wanted was for her phone to get damaged by the ever-present mist in the air. Rather than risk taking the device, she'd left it behind.

Tapping the screen to bring it to life, she noticed she'd missed a call. She would have expected it to be from her mother, who called and checked on her almost every day now. The call wasn't from her mom though. The missed call was from Simon Miller.

Though they'd texted a few times, staying in touch as they'd agreed, they hadn't spoken since she'd seen him in Dayton. Curious, she dialed into her voice mail.

"Caroline." He laughed awkwardly. "Um, it's Simon, and um..."

She smiled as she sat back. He used to fumble like this around her all the time. He'd be the world's most confident doctor when dealing with the parents of his patients, but he could barely ask her to pass him the ketchup in the cafeteria. She'd loved that about him then, and apparently she still did, considering the size of her smile.

"I know it's not my place to worry about you," he continued rambling, "but every time I think about you out on the road alone, I get a knot in my stomach. Would you please call me and let me know you're okay? I'm sorry if I'm overstepping. I guess I always did where you were concerned."

Carol sat a bit taller. She hadn't been expecting that.

"Shit. This all sounded so much better in my head," he said. "Would you call me? Please. And wait until you're done laughing about what an ass I've made of myself. Thanks."

She wasn't laughing, but she did giggle at his last statement. When his message ended, she hung up without deleting the recording. Turning her face toward the refrigerator, her eyes immediately caught on the photo of Tobias and her. The one that had been there from the day they'd bought the RV.

A strange sensation of guilt nagged deep in her gut, but she pushed it away. She and Simon may have reconnected after all these years, but she had no reason to feel bad for that. There was no forbidden romance blooming this time. There weren't going to be any secret glances or whispered arrangements to meet somewhere. She wouldn't be stopping by his apartment for a quick rendezvous before heading home to her miserable marriage.

Simon had been a friend before he'd been a lover, and he could be a friend again. Even with that decision made, she glanced at Tobias smiling down at her and pushed her phone away. She'd call Simon later. For now, she had plans to make.

With the weather quickly changing, she intended to head south. Southwest to be more specific. She had a few places to get to on her list before the cold set in. Then she would head to St. Louis. She'd promised Mary she would be there for Thanksgiving.

She'd also told her mom and aunt she'd be in Florida for Christmas. They hadn't been together on Christmas Day since the year before Katie had died. Carol was looking forward to being with her mom for the holiday. That was new.

So she'd go from New York to the Southwest and then back east for the holidays.

"Then what?" she asked herself.

Then, she realized, she would figure out the next place. One step at a time, as Mary had told her so many times over the last year. One step at a time.

The first step was...

The first step was returning Simon's call and letting him know she was okay. Carol grabbed her phone and tapped the screen.

Closing her eyes, she took a breath and let it out slowly as the line rang.

"Hey," he answered.

Just like it had done all those years ago, the sound of his voice soothed her nerves, put her mind at ease, and brought a smile to her face. Looking at Tobias's picture, Carol could have sworn she heard his voice repeating her new mantra.

One step at a time.

Carol Denman's journey continues in
A Life Without Regrets.
Coming soon!

ALSO BY MARCI BOLDEN

A Life Without Water Series:

A Life Without Water

A Life Without Flowers

A Life Without Regrets (Coming Soon)

Stonehill Series:

The Road Leads Back

Friends Without Benefits

The Forgotten Path

Jessica's Wish

This Old Cafe

Forever Yours

The Women of Hearts Series:

Hidden Hearts

Burning Hearts

Stolen Hearts

Secret Hearts

Other Titles:

ABOUT THE AUTHOR

As a teen, Marci Bolden skipped over young adult books and jumped right into reading romance novels. She never left.

Marci lives in the Midwest with her husband, kiddos, and numerous rescue pets. If she had an ounce of willpower, Marci would embrace healthy living, but until cupcakes and wine are no longer available at the local market, she will appease her guilt by reading self-help books and promising to join a gym "soon."

Visit her here:
www.marcibolden.com

facebook.com/MarciBoldenAuthor
twitter.com/BoldenMarci
instagram.com/marciboldenauthor